Jackson, Marni, author.
Don't I know you?

10/16

Don't
I Know
You?

MARNI JACKSON

FLATIRON
BOOKS
NEW YORK

To Brian

This is a work of fiction. All of the characters, organizations, and events portrayed in this novel are either products of the author's imagination or are used fictitiously.

The Library of Congress Cataloging-in-Publication Data is available upon request.
ISBN 978-1-250-08979-3 (hardcover)
ISBN 978-1-250-08978-6 (e-book)

Our books may be purchased in bulk for promotional, educational, or business use. Please contact your local bookseller or the Macmillan Corporate and Premium Sales Department at (800) 221-7945, extension 5442, or by e-mail at MacmillanSpecial Markets@macmillan.com

First Edition: September 2016

10 9 8 7 6 5 4 3 2 1

"WE ALL LIKE PEOPLE WHO DO THINGS, EVEN IF WE
ONLY SEE THEIR FACES ON A CIGAR-BOX LID."

The Song of the Lark, by Willa Cather

AUTHOR'S NOTE

These stories are works of fiction. Despite some autobiographical elements, they are all inventions—just as celebrity itself is a kind of fiction, since stars can only exist at the point where their public roles and our imaginations meet. In a sense, we author their fame.

While a number of celebrities or artists, some living and some deceased, engage with the main character of these stories, readers should not assume that I have met them, or that the actions and words I have attributed to them represent things they have done or said in real life. But whenever artists share their creative gifts with us, when we are consoled or inspired by their words, lyrics, and performances, we come to feel we know them. Their presence in these stories is meant to represent the powerful and intimate roles that famous people sometimes play in our ordinary lives.

CONTENTS

Doon

The Doon School of Fine Arts occupied the former summer house of Horatio Walker, a modestly celebrated (there is no other kind) nineteenth-century Canadian painter. Two of his canvases, landscapes with sulfurous skies and tossing trees, hung on the walls of the dining room, where art students doubling as waitresses set the long communal tables and served the meals: shepherd's pie, weeping coleslaw, hard rolls on a side plate. Dinner always began with tomato juice in a slender glass, like the red line in a thermometer.

I had just turned seventeen. My parents, eager to encourage my precocious "way with words" and my "flair for art" (I excelled at drawing horses in profile) had signed me up for summer courses—one week of Introductory Oil Painting, followed by a week of Introductory Creative Writing. My father kept urging me to send something in to *Reader's Digest* for the "Humor in Uniform" section, overlooking the fact that I was not in active military service. I was in grade twelve. But I did have a sort of uniform—the pink smock I wore for my part-time job as a shampoo girl for Rico's House of Beauty. With the word "Rose" embroidered on one pocket. I had a sort of boyfriend too. But I was growing tired of Larry, so I agreed to go to Doon.

It was 1963, the first year the school offered a writing course, and they were pleased to welcome John Hoyer Updike as the inaugural instructor. He had published a book of poems, *The Tessellated Hen*, which I couldn't find in the Burlington library. But I didn't need to read it, or his new novel about an aging basketball player. His stories had been published in *The New Yorker* and that was godlike enough for me.

The photo in Doon's brochure showed a mild, goatish-looking young man with a long nose and bushy eyebrows, smiling. His brown hair was cut short, a thatch at war with multiple cowlicks. His gaze met the camera as if sharing a joke, and his upper lip had an appealing dip in the middle, like the waist of a violin. It was an expression of mischief, intelligence, and appetite. He was young, probably not even thirty, but to me anyone over nineteen was generically adult.

On the page opposite was a picture of the art teacher, Emilio Renzetti, looking truculent and disheveled with black hairs curling out of his open shirt. I showed his picture to my father one morning as he was reading the paper. "That guy looks like trouble," he said, snapping the business section open. I decided not to show him the slightly satyr-faced Harvard grad who would help usher me into the pages of *Reader's Digest*.

It was the summer I wore my blond hair short, in a "cap cut" with comma-shaped side curls that I Scotch-taped to my cheeks each night. This sometimes left faint shiny patches on my cheeks. My legs were long and tanned and I wore shorts most of the time, although these were always part of carefully engineered outfits. A pair of pale-yellow Bermudas with a matching halter top, both reversible to a blue plaid fabric, was my number-one outfit. I wore it the day my parents drove me to Doon to meet my fellow students—all women—for Art Week.

The seven of us shared an airy dormitory at the top of the stairs where we kept our suitcases under iron-frame beds covered with chenille spreads in pastel shades. There were two brisk and wiry older women who wore unusual eyeglasses. Real painters, they had brought along folding chairs for working outdoors. I was by far the youngest of the group, with my three stiff, never-used brushes.

Horatio Walker's house sat in a sort of dell across from a willow-shaded river. The Grand flowed through Doon with a Wordsworthian stateliness that set it apart from the stolid farmland and creeping suburbs of southern Ontario. Languid, pastoral, and somehow secretive, Doon already felt fictional to me—the perfect setting for a murder, or a love affair.

On our first morning, the dorm ladies convened downstairs for a Life Drawing session. This took place in the dining room with a naked model posed on the same draped table we would later sit around for dinner. With sticks of charcoal we worked at easels on big sheets of beige newsprint. The idea, Emilio told us, was to work fast; if a sketch wasn't getting anywhere, we should flip the sheet and start afresh.

I found I was good at it, the quick, intuitive first strokes. I liked the focused silence of the room, all of us scratching away in a circle, heads tilting up and down. For me—a virgin—it was also sexual in a perfectly manageable way. Sometimes the model was one of the waitresses who would later serve us, which was a little shocking. There was a stool in place for her to step up onto the table. I learned that the trick was to take in the fact of her nakedness and then to see through it, break it down into lines and shadows. Soon you were inside the state of nakedness with her, which almost caused it to disappear. This made the prospect of my own potential nakedness less alarming.

In the afternoon, we switched to oil painting, outside. We trailed across the lawn behind Emilio into the woods, where we were expected to find a particular stump or rock or split-rail fence that took our fancy and paint it en plein air.

"Just paint what speaks to you," said Emilio, who seemed faintly irritated by all of us.

I had no idea how to discover the contours in the mess that was Nature. One tree looked like another to me. My new wooden palette fit the curve of my thumb in an agreeable way, and I liked squeezing wet rosettes of paint onto it, then twirling them flat with my brush. But while the rest of the group got down to work, dabbing away in silence, I couldn't seem to find a subject that drew my eye.

As I wandered more deeply into the woods, I stumbled on the foundation of a ruined barn—a dark, stony tooth socket in the earth with a still-intact staircase in one corner. Stairs to nowhere. I tried to paint these red pointless steps rising out of the earth, perhaps recognizing something hopeful, aspiring, but wildly out of context, like me.

On our second day, fed up with my efforts, I filled another canvas with an agitated pine tree that at least had some turmoil and energy to it. It was every color but green. Emilio came by, frowning. He studied my tree for a moment, then pointed to a whirling ochre bit. "Very painterly," he murmured and passed on.

That was encouraging. But the next afternoon, when I tried to repeat myself, it didn't work.

So I gave up on art.

———•———

Still, the daily routines at Doon pleased me. I liked sleeping in the dorm with the gentle snoring ladies, and coming down at the end of the day to tomato juice and jellied salads on the two long tables. We'd wait for the swinging doors to open as the waitresses, some of them local girls with dancing pony-tails and other things on their minds, came in and out carrying metal water jugs. I liked playing sad, precocious bits of Erik Satie on the loose-keyed piano in the parlor, or taking solitary walks in the rain down to the stone bridge over the Grand, dressed in a man's yellow rain jacket that came to the bottom of my shortest stretch-terrycloth shorts.

One night after a downpour, the river turned the color of milky tea and rose almost to the height of the banks. A crew from a local TV show came by in a van and shot me standing pensively (needless to say) on the bridge. I saw myself on the news that night and was shocked by how normal and round-faced I looked. I thought I was working on a different sort of character, the girl with cheekbones who reads Albert Camus and plays sarabandes at dusk.

Doon was less than a hamlet—just a cemetery, a gas station, and a general store. Nothing ever happened there after dark, except Ping-Pong. In the evenings some of us would wander down the road, passing under the single moth-orbited street-light as the frogs kept up a chorus as loud and rhythmic as a polka band. When we reached the Shell station, we'd throw stones at the orange metal sign, which would silence the frogs. Then the chorus would start up again and we'd head back to the dorms.

One of my roommates, I noticed, was reading *Rabbit, Run*. Sherry was the best painter of the group and the oldest. I asked her if she liked it and did she know that John Updike himself was coming to Doon in a few days.

"He's quite good at description. But the hero is a man who sells vegetable peelers and doesn't much like his wife," she said with a dismissive flap of her hand. "It does have spicy bits though. Very spicy." She looked over the navy-blue frames of her glasses. "Not for you, my dear."

I reviewed the thin sheaf of writing I would present to John Updike. This included the grad notes I had written for our high school yearbook, many of which were shockingly inappropriate. ("Most likely to die young.") A story about a picnic, told from the point of view of an ant. Several self-deprecating essays about trying and failing to do something, such as knitting a sweater for my dog.

But the quality that most equipped me for writing, perhaps, was a chronic sense of unease. I felt outside most things, a shy and yearning observer—if not a fly on the wall, then an ant at the picnic. At seventeen I was already the omniscient narrator of my own life, both everywhere and nowhere at once. I also had the remnants of a childhood stutter, and dreaded being called upon in chemistry class in case I had to say the word "carbon" with its unforgiving hard c. My stutter did make me choose my words more carefully, though. It fed writing.

No, the most remarkable thing about me that summer at Doon was the fact that I was full of longings I couldn't name. I thought these longings had to do with art. And in a way, they did; first loves are partly works of fiction.

Day after day the weather was humid and lethargic, with pulses of sheet lightning in the evenings. All the women dressed skimpily. I had no sense of being pretty, but did feel in possession of some mysterious new power, a little. I noticed that men were willing to take their time with me, to help me out, and that I didn't seem to have to do anything to earn this attention. I believed they were interested in my "talent."

Then the week ended, the lady painters all left except for me, and the writers arrived. My heart sank. They were an ungainly group: a stooped fellow in a short-sleeved shirt who made claymation films and wished to learn how to write crime novels; a retired Ottawa Valley schoolteacher documenting her dead husband's war experiences; a poet named L'Orren who had actually published her poetry in journals with names like *Axis* and *Penumbra*. L'Orren had a stormy mass of dark hair that she kept capturing in a large saw-toothed barrette and then releasing, like a little animal. She wore black liquid eyeliner and semitransparent Indian shirts with black tights, despite the heat.

There was a playwright, Steve, hoping to improve his dialogue. Also a fellow with cloudy glasses who said that he had been working on his "picaresque sci-fi" novel, *Dark Matter*, for the past four years. I thought he'd said "picturesque." Dinner that first night was awkward and there was no Ping-Pong afterward.

The next morning, the group gathered on the deep front porch, dragging the wicker chairs into a semicircle. We exchanged names and a few words about our projects then lapsed into silence, waiting for the arrival of John Updike. He was late. "Well, I have some poems I could read," said L'Orren, but just then a tall, ruddy-faced, bony-shouldered figure dashed up the steps with a stack of books and papers in his arms. He wore khakis and a button-down oxford-cloth shirt with pale blue stripes.

"I apologize, everyone—crossing the border took longer than I expected." He took in our listless group and patted one of the white faux-colonial columns that framed the porch.

"This is all rather grand. I was expecting little cabins."

He handed out the week's assignments and a long, long reading list. I recognized a few names—Philip Roth, James Thurber, Marcel Proust. None of which I had read. One woman, Edith Wharton.

L'Orren offered him her chair but he sat on the top step of the porch with his back against a column, smoking a cigarette. He'd been going through customs at Niagara Falls, he explained, when the authorities undertook a very thorough search of his car, an "unremarkable" Ford Falcon.

"I had nothing to hide," he said, "but I was overwhelmed by a t-tidal wave of irrational g-guilt."

A stutter! I looked away. What if it triggered mine?

"Everyone feels like a criminal when they cross a border," said L'Orren. That earned a smile from John Updike.

Our first assignment was to describe one five-minute period in our day. It was to be a close description of what we observed, not our finer emotions, or, God forbid, ideas. "Ideas are easy," he said. "First, tell me what you *see*."

What I saw was L'Orren beside me, gazing at the lawn and the push mower that had been abandoned there with avid, writerly eyes, already basking in the radiance of the ordinary. "I thought Art Week was over," I whispered to her, but her frown shushed me.

He set up appointments with each of us and collected our bits of writing. Then, with a kind of relish, as if describing a good meal, he told us that writing was "mostly an ongoing experience of self-doubt and falling short of the mark." He laughed, a sharp sound, almost a bray. "But an absolute freedom exists on the blank page, and we must make use of it."

The next morning after breakfast I found him waiting for me on the steps of the porch, smoking. His way with a cigarette was languid, a little feminine. The day was already still and hot; the cicadas had begun to make the sound that marks the zenith of summer just before the downward tilt.

He fanned the pages I had given him, including my prize-winning senior essay "The Lonely Road." ("A road is only lonely when there's someone walking down it . . .")

"Anything else you want me to read?"

"No, not really," I said. It was my entire oeuvre. "Except for this." I opened my notebook to a poem and passed it to him. It was inspired by a *LIFE* magazine photograph of a homeless black man with anger burning in his eyes.

He read it with a pencil in his hand, ticked an image here and there, and put an X through the weeping part. "No tears," he said, "especially not in poems." Then he made diagonal slashes to indicate line breaks that would improve the rhythm.

I saw that he was right; a poem was more than fetching similes in a stack of arbitrarily short lines. The point, he suggested gently, was not to put my own sensibility on display but to arouse thoughts and feelings in others. He turned the page to finish the poem and came upon some sketches of the naked model.

"Are these yours?"

I nodded, praying that he wouldn't go further and find the childish cartoons that filled the back of the notebook. But he kept studying the nude.

"This line is strong." He traced one of her parabolic thighs. "Very graphic. Do you like Edward Hopper?"

"I think so," I said. I held my breath and he turned the page. There was Mickey Mouse, with his impenetrable black irises and dimpled white three-fingered gloves. There was Donald Duck, having a tantrum as he stomped on his sailor hat, releasing little puffs of dust.

Mortified, I reached for the notebook.

"Don't be embarrassed," he said. "In college I only wanted to become a cartoonist—writing was my second choice." He tapped the page. "I am jealous of your Mickey."

"My father taught me how. You start with the three circles, ears and head."

"Is he an artist?"

"No, but when he was young he was really good at drawing. The local newspaper published his cartoons."

"So you have his gift."

"He even got a job offer from Walt Disney when he was nineteen, but he couldn't afford the trip down for the interview."

"Too bad, you'd make a good California girl. What did he end up doing?"

"Engineering. He said there wasn't much call for cartoonists on the prairies, in the D-D-D-Depression."

There. It had happened. But John Updike said nothing, only asked if I had written about my father.

"No. After that he just worked, got married, had us kids, and things like that. Ordinary stuff." He nodded.

"But to write well about the ordinary stuff—that's the hard part, don't you think? To give the mundane its beautiful due."

He flipped back to my stories and ticked the phrase "lozenge-shaped" to describe a patch of sunlight. He approved of my yearbook's typeface. "It's Dutch, from the seventeenth century. Not often used these days." He liked my description of crows on a hydro wire looking like musical notes on a staff, "although crows are not really *round*, are they?"

I found his attention to my lines—more attention than I had devoted to them in the first place—both pleasing and unsettling. It also made me acutely aware of my outfit that day, the blue-and-white capri pants and a blue sleeveless top with white rickrack along the bottom. For the first time I questioned my fondness for things that matched.

"I like that," he said pointing toward the white trim. "Does it have a name?

"Rickrack."

"Rickrack." He smiled.

"My mother sews. She's always adding stuff to my clothes."

"You're lucky. I have an embellishing mother too."

Then L'Orren banged through the screen door behind us, impatient for her appointment. She carried a thick three-ring binder and smelled of patchouli oil. I ducked past her into the coolness of the foyer.

Before lunch I went into the gallery to play the piano as usual and found John Updike examining one of Horatio Walker's tornado-green landscapes. He beckoned me over.

"There's more than a little Constable going on here, don't you think?"

Why did he assume I understood all his references? Didn't he know any normal seventeen-year-olds?

"Especially that figure in the red hunting jacket," he said, pointing to a man on horseback, scarcely visible.

"Well, *seeing things* is not my forte," I said.

"What makes you think so?"

Then I told him about the failed red stairs in the forest.

"Are you sure about that? Why don't you show it to me?"

Reluctantly, but already excited, I went upstairs to the dorm, where I had turned the botched canvas against the wall. I brought it down to John Updike, who held it at arm's length for some time. I had to look away. I saw nothing in it but turbulent, vegetal mud, with a raw geometry of scarlet in the middle, a gash.

"I like what you chose to paint," he began carefully. "The way it juxtaposes the human and natural worlds."

"You mean the barn and the trees?"

His hand floated across the bottom of the canvas, as if painting over it.

"The foreground is a little nebulous, but the overall sense of gloom is good."

"The forest makes me nervous."

"That much is clear."

"I don't hate this part"—I pointed to a troubled triangle of sky visible through the tree branches—"even though it's that weird yellow."

"You're very adventurous. A chrome-yellow sky would never occur to me."

"Well, I only brought eight tubes of paint. Some of the others have that many different shades of red."

He gave the canvas back to me.

"I know a little something about this, you know," he said. "I spent a year at art school in England after college. If you like, I could help you. You shouldn't give up on this so easily."

Was he saying that my writing was hopeless?

"I don't know. Art Week's technically over." In the next room, the waitresses dashed the cutlery onto the long tables, setting up.

"Let's go find your stairs after lunch. I could use the walk."

"Okay. Maybe Emilio would lend me extra paints."

"I wouldn't involve Emilio if I were you. Meet me down by the mailboxes, where the lawn ends."

I raced back upstairs, where L'Orren was sprawled on her bed, writing in a notebook. She gave me a searching look but I said nothing, only changing out of my capris into something that would protect my legs in the woods.

Lunch was salmon patties, potato salad, and the fat, cushion-shaped tomatoes that Emilio grew behind the painting studio. John listened politely to the war widow beside him as she discussed the architecture of Normandy. He sent me a look, not quite a wink. Then everyone drifted away for Individual Work Period. I gathered up my paints and canvas and went down to the mailboxes. All empty.

He had changed into a polo shirt with a logo on the pocket, a little black man golfing. His forearms were golden-haired and deeply tanned; this was from walking on the beach, he said. He and his family lived near the ocean, north of Boston. His wife, Mary, stayed at home with their four children.

"Holy cow," I said, "that's a lot."

He laughed. "Yes, it is. That's partly why we left Manhattan for the suburbs. That and the fact that New York is overstocked with writers and agents and other weisenheimers."

The forest, crosshatched with deadfall and nettles, was not easily penetrated. I showed him the shy white three-petaled trilliums, the "provincial flower," illegal to pick. We struggled on.

I had a moment of panic when I couldn't find the stairs. Had I invented them? But once we had leaped over a boggy ditch, there it was, the ghost barn with its dark cavity. One slumped wall remained, like the hindquarters of a lame animal.

"I see what you mean," Updike said. "Nice."

As I set up my easel he sat nearby on a stony ledge, the remnants of some enclosure. The staircase seemed duller and less meaningful to me than before.

"If I can suggest something," he said. "When you look at it, try to banish the words 'stairs' or 'barn.' Just keep looking and let what you see flow onto the canvas."

I did as he said and it helped. I lost track of the literal thing and only received its presence in the dappled, trembling light of the forest. The stairs became shrine-like—an Incan altar or a broken letter of the alphabet, some forlorn human shape rising out of green decay.

John sat in silence as I painted. Not silence—birds darted among the treetops and sang their repetitive, ardent songs. We shared a spell, the charm of work going along. I no longer felt apart from things.

When we emerged from the forest I held the newly wet canvas away from my white pants. I stole another glance at it; yes, it was better, it was all right now. It might even be the beginning of a story, although its meaning was still obscure to me.

As we crossed the deep sward of grass I saw with a sinking heart that Emilio was in his glass-walled studio, painting. He glanced up and gave us a curt nod.

"See you at dinner," John said with a little salute as we parted.

That night, after the expedition to the Shell station to throw stones at the sign, as everyone was heading for bed, John Updike came to the foot of the stairs.

"Miss McEwan?" he called up to the dorm. I think he meant this as a joke about our teacher-student relationship.

I came halfway down the stairs.

"I brought these for you."

He handed me a short-story collection, including one by

him, and a slim anthology of Canadian poetry called *Love Where the Nights Are Long.* "I just reviewed this," he said, wagging the poetry, "and thought you might like it."

I thanked him and went back up to the dorm, where I kept my light on long after the others had fallen asleep. First I read his story, about a teenage boy who worked as a cashier at the A&P. Three girls in bathing suits come in and cause a stir. There wasn't much to it. And it had so many details, especially about the way one girl let the straps of her suit fall down her shoulder. Did he see *me* in such detail? The thought made me nervous.

I opened the poetry book. P. K. Page, Irving Layton, Milton Acorn, Al Purdy, Leonard Cohen. *"As the mist leaves no scar on the dark green hill/ So my body leaves no scar on you/ nor ever will . . ."* In school they taught us only British or American authors, and I didn't know that such writing, full of snow and longing and places that I recognized from my own life, was allowed. The love poems struck me with the force of samizdat, something clandestine and illegal.

The next day, I found a picnic table near Emilio's studio, where I set up my portable green Olivetti to do some serious work. Not the boring details of five minutes in my boring day, here in Doon where nothing happened; instead I was going to write a play about three women—but in fact, they were all aspects of one woman! The "real" woman sits on a bench at the front of the stage and does nothing. Behind her, two women talk to her, representing her hidden thoughts and everything she can't bring herself to do or be. I had read a play by Harold Pinter, and had seen a Little Theatre production of Edward Albee, so this premise felt modern and edgy to me. I wanted to write something out of the ordinary to impress John Updike.

"This is an intriguing start," he said when I showed him the three pages I had managed to type. "But don't forget that in the theatre, things *happen*. It might be a good idea to include an event."

He was right. It was a play in which absolutely nothing took place. The woman never even left her bench! But hadn't that worked for Samuel Beckett? Didn't he bury one of his characters up to the neck in sand? What about his play where one character is always saying, "Well, shall we go?" and then nobody moves? I flounced up to my dorm and pulled out my canvas with the whirling pine tree. Screw writing. I could always paint.

"Miss McEwan?" John called up the stairs after lunch, which I had skipped. I showed myself at the top of the stairs.

"How about a walk?"

I said nothing, but went and got my insect repellant, and also my red jacket with the navy patch pockets and the nylon hood rolled up inside the collar. I came down the stairs, vaguely aware that the other students might notice us slipping off during Individual Work Period. We headed across the back lawn without saying a word, complicit already, and trudged up the road, cresting the hill, where we would soon be out of sight of the others.

The cicadas shrieked. When I looked back at the house and the cottages behind it, that little world seemed somnolent and far away. I tried to restrain myself from chattering nervously. I had already alluded to Larry.

"Your boyfriend must be missing you," John said.

"He's not actually my real boyfriend," I answered, feeling it at once as the treachery it was.

"Oh?"

"I just don't want to hurt his feelings."

"That doesn't sound promising."

Two could play this game, I thought, turning toward him.

"Your wife must miss you too. With all those kids."

"Yes. But I think she's also secretly relieved to run the house as she likes when I'm away."

"Larry writes me every day," I said, rolling my eyes. My callousness knew no bounds.

We reached a cemetery and turned into it. The path faded into uncut grass and scatterings of wildflowers, yellow and white. Most of the old tombstones were drifting down into the earth. A bunchy-looking tree stood in the middle of the cemetery, laden with small green apples. We sat under it. I had on my second-favorite seersucker shorts and was careful to avoid any mushy fallen ones.

"Did you get a chance to read any of that poetry?" he asked.

"Yes, I read it all, last night."

"And?"

"I loved it."

"Good. I'll give you more."

"And I read your story about the A&P boy too. It's very well written."

At this he smiled.

"Burlington has an A&P too," I added.

In the shade of the tree, the ground was a little damp. To avoid getting a wet spot on my shorts I jumped up and went over to a tombstone and read the epitaph aloud. " 'Here Lies our Belov'd Annabelle/Who Is with the Angels Now.' Look at the dates," I said; "she was only fourteen years old when she died."

He came over to read it and we stood together, arms touching. As I brushed away some vines that were creeping over the inscription, he took my hand and inspected the back of it.

"What's this?"

"Warts," I said. I withdrew my hand. "I've had them since I was ten." There were three on my ring finger, small and white, scarcely noticeable, but I was self-conscious about them.

"In the Middle Ages, people thought warts were caused by someone putting a curse on you, and that a charm could cure you too."

"Witches, you mean."

"For instance, they thought that driving nails into an oak tree could prevent a headache, or that wearing a ring made from the hinges of a coffin could heal cramps."

He ran his fingers over the pale bumps with their mottled, brainlike surface. "What do you think—shall I try?"

"I don't know. The doctor burnt them with some frozen liquid stuff last year but they just grew back."

He brought the back of my hand to his lips. That's when I got scared. The sound of a truck laboring up over the hill, unseen, grew louder. I turned and began walking quickly toward the gate.

"But you have to believe in the spell, or nothing will happen," John said, right behind me.

"What is it with you and things *happening*?" The truck driver with his load of lumber sped past us without a glance at this ill-matched couple walking single-file in the afternoon heat.

"It's a perfectly good beginning for a play, Rose," John said. "You just need to keep working on it."

When we reached the grounds of the school, we made our separate ways into the house, him through the back door. It was understood that we had embarked on something secretive. Up in the dorm, L'Orren was sitting cross-legged on her bed writing in her notebook with a thick-nibbed fountain pen.

"Where were you?" she asked. That girl did not beat around the bush.

"I went down to the bridge for a walk. I'm having trouble with my opening scene."

"We missed you at lunch," she said unconvincingly.

It soon became evident that no one in our class was a writer of any real promise, so John busied himself organizing entertainment to fill our evenings. He found some National Film Board shorts in the parlor cabinets, and we screened them on a tacked-up bedsheet in the rec room. There were two live-animation, stop-motion films called *Neighbours* and *A Chairy Tale* by Norman McLaren—little comic parables about the childishness of human conflict. Like the love poems they made a deep impression on me about what is possible in art. I didn't think playfulness and humor were allowed.

We found some records on the basement shelves too, Louis Armstrong, Charlie Parker, and Ravel's *Bolero*. L'Orren and the novelist danced around the Ping-Pong table to the orgasmic pulse of *Bolero*, eyes closed, waving their arms like seaweed, a sight that mortified the rest of us.

Earlier that day L'Orren had spent a good two hours with John, going through her narrative cycle of poems about an Inuit woman who wants to become a hunter like the men, but is stoned to death by her relatives instead. For some reason the two of them met in the greenhouse. I could see them both from my perch on a window seat in the dorm. I was working on my assignment that day, a descriptive scene about nature using no figures of speech. This I found challenging, as I believed similes and metaphors to be the sine qua non of fine writing.

I had a good view of her facing John, braiding and unbraiding her hair. Through the streaky glass I could see him, occasionally laughing, tipping back in his chair. After a long time

L'Orren left the greenhouse and strode toward the house, hugging her binder with a hopeful, preoccupied air.

I had moved over to my bed by the time she came into the dorm.

"How was your meeting?" I asked.

"A-mazing. He wrote his thesis on Robert Herrick and I have this whole sonnet cycle about the metaphysicals."

I worked all afternoon and sat at the opposite end of the table from John at dinner. He looked tired and bored. The war widow was sitting next to him, talking steadily, sometimes tapping the back of his hand. I felt sorry for him, stuck with all these amateurs. I left the table before dessert was served and in the hall I heard his chair scrape back.

He caught up to me by the big newel post at the bottom of the stairs.

"Miss McEwan. Feel like an excursion later on?"

I shrugged. "Maybe. If I get my work done."

"Work now, then meet me at the greenhouse at ten. Wear something warm."

L'Orren came into the hallway and gave us a look.

"Prepare to lose!" said John, and he headed downstairs to play Ping-Pong with her and Axel, the claymation man. But instead of finishing my story I left the house and walked down to the bridge to watch the swollen river run. Then I came back to the house to use the communal phone in the hall to call Larry.

He was working in his dad's car dealership for the summer and he missed me tons, he said. "There's a brand-new 1961 LeSabre here with room in the back for both of us," he said.

"I miss you too," I said wanly, although it wasn't the least bit true. This is how you marry the wrong person, I told myself.

"I have to go now, Larry, I've got work to do."

"Bye, doll," he said. "Be good, and if you can't be good, be careful."

You're not going to read late again are you?" said the war widow, who slept in the bed next to me. It was almost ten p.m. She had her hair up in pink brush rollers and wore a quilted blue housecoat and sock-slippers with leather soles.

"Actually, I think I'll read downstairs for a while. I'll just take a blanket."

"You won't need insect repellant in the parlor," she observed. I had my sneakers on and a roll-up stick of 6-12 in my hand.

"The screen door has holes in it," I said, and gently closed the door. I almost flew down the stairs; I was about to write my first love poem, my first Best Canadian Short Story. The narrative of the night, rich with similes and metaphors, raced ahead of me. All I had to do was catch up to it.

The lights were still on in the painter studio, where I could see someone moving around. Emilio probably, he liked to work at night. I circled around the back of the lawn to the greenhouse, which was dark. No sign of John. I thought about Larry, and my parents, and felt a little sick. But maybe he just wants to talk, I thought. Maybe he's just missing his family.

"There you are," he said. He saw the blanket. "Good girl," he said with a laugh. I held up my little baton of 6-12. He showed me a flashlight.

"Let's go the front way. We don't want to run into Emilio."

In the shadows we crossed the lawn, wet with evening dew, to the road. There were no streetlights, no moon. But if we kept feeling the gravel under our shoes that would mean we were still on the road as it rose toward the top of the hill and the cemetery.

"I can carry that," he said softly, taking my blanket. When we were out of sight of the school, he said, "I brought some candles too."

Candles! He was so not Larry, who had to have the hockey game on the car radio when we went parking.

As we made our way into the cemetery, I felt flat bare rock underfoot. John's light found the inscription:

ESTELLE CHRISTINA BETZNER BORN 1910, DIED 1959.

I lay down on the stone and crossed my arms over my chest.

"*Here lies Estelle/she's not very well,*" I said, laughing nervously. John shone his light on my hands and then my face. His face had an odd, bright expression.

"Up you get," he finally said, giving me his hand. The night was cool; I thought I could even see my breath. The starry blackness above us seemed curved, like a cupola.

"Will we see the Northern Lights?" he said.

"No, of course not. This isn't the Arctic." Americans, I thought.

"What do they look like? I've only seen pictures."

"Sort of like curtains. Spooky green curtains that billow and move across the sky. I saw them a couple times, up at camp. Usually all we can see from Burlington at night are the lights of Buffalo."

"Mary has a great romance about the aurora. She was jealous that I might get to see them up here."

"Well, we won't."

I didn't want to know too much about him, or Mary. That

wasn't part of our story. I was proud of understanding the rules without him having to spell them out. It would be only this time for us, and only here in Doon. When the week was over, we'd never see each other again.

Looking up at the blackness was making me dizzy. I spread the blanket under the apple tree, our spot.

"Wait," he said. He cleared the grass away from a flat tombstone close to the roots of the tree, and lit a candle. He let it drip onto the stone and lit the other candle, rooting them both in the warm wax. The flames wavered but the night was still and they kept on burning. We lay down. John wrapped the edges of the blanket around my back.

"I'm a virgin," I said with my face inches from his.

"Sure, okay," he said, "I wondered."

"It's not a big deal either way, I just, I want to wait."

"In a sense that makes things easier."

"But I'm up for anything else," I said brightly.

He laughed and slipped his hand inside my rust Shetland sweater. "I can see that, Miss McEwan."

John Updike kissed me. Our teeth clicked at first; he seemed to have a lot of them. His mouth was warm and his tongue felt quick and intelligent and questing, just like the rest of him. Blue light blossomed behind my eyelids as the kiss went on, changed, settled.

"You've obviously done this before," he said.

I was so happy in the crook of his arm like that, looking into his shiny, candlelit eyes.

"Yes, I'm an old whore at kissing." I felt cocky and comfortable. He was married to someone else, anchored in a family, and I would be back home in Burlington soon.

My hand on the back of his neck came across a rough, scaly patch. He reached up and covered it with his collar.

"D-Don't worry, it's not contagious," he said, pulling out of the stutter smoothly. "Psoriasis. It tends to flare up when I'm away from home." For a moment he looked like a fourteen-year-old country boy.

Then we stopped talking. Under my sweater I had on a padded bra because my breasts weren't perfectly symmetrical, a secret that mortified me. But he didn't seem to notice or care. We were lying on our sides, pressed together. I could feel his erection but we ignored it. That happened with Larry too. John Updike seemed happy just to cover my breasts with his hands and to kiss me again and again, like someone reading a book in braille.

"Could I look at you?" he said. "Just look." He propped himself on one elbow. I pulled my sweater up in the wavering candlelight.

What a power I felt then, the power that my body, the mere sight of it, had over him. He was gazing at me as if I were a Dutch painting, something valuable and important.

"You look like moonlight, a thin sheet of moonlight."

"Show's over," I said, pulling down my sweater and settling back into his arms.

We were safe; I was in bliss. The tree above us created a dark, starless scallop in the middle of the sky, a kind of roof. The candle flames shivered but persevered, like a tiny aurora. Even the mosquitos stayed away.

The postman for Doon was a handsome boy my age who drove a cube van and left the mail in a basket on the porch, ignoring the mailboxes. I had already had six letters from Larry, written in ballpoint on his dad's dealership stationery. *Ronnie Craig Autos.* He wrote about missing me and how boring Burlington was in the summer. In the last one he had folded the letter around some cartoon stickers because we shared a thing about Yosemite Sam.

The morning after the cemetery, I got another letter from Larry but didn't open it right away. There was an envelope in the basket addressed to John. I turned it over to read the return address: Mary Updike, 26 East St., Ipswich, Mass.

Nice handwriting. A little on the prim side. I left Larry's letter on the stairs up to the dorm and took the envelope around the back of the house to John's cottage. I knocked on his door. Normally this was off limits.

"Well, good morning," he said. He looked as if he'd just woken up, although I glimpsed paper rolled into his typewriter on the desk. He pulled me into the shadow of the door and kissed me as if it were still the night before.

"I brought your mail," I said, pulling away and tossing the letter on the bed. I didn't mean it to sound the way it came out.

"Thank you. Did you talk to Roy?"

"Roy?"

"The handsome postman, who always rings twice."

"No, I did not," I said, vaguely insulted.

"Anyway, this is nice of you. Cup of tea? I have a kettle."

"No, thanks. I should really work." I sighed, like a middle-aged hack with a deadline. I turned to leave.

"Miss McEwan?"

"What." I was facing him but not looking at him.

"Come here." I moved sullenly into his arms.

"Have you been down past the stone bridge yet? I know you are famous for standing *on* the bridge. But I think we should investigate further, maybe take a picnic. We still have three more days."

"I have to finish what I'm working on first. The scene."

"Of course. I have a session with Axel too. But skip lunch. I'll meet you down by the Shell station at two p.m. Bring the blanket, and I'll bring the food."

"Okay," I said, not wanting to leave anymore. "And we'll need hats too."

I ran back across the lawn, waving to Emilio as he stood in the painter studio scowling at the canvas on his easel. How stupid it was to waste your time on art, I thought, when there was so much joy available.

Beyond the bridge the Grand forked and one branch became shallow enough to wade across. Barefoot, we felt our way upriver, over stones, against the current.

"Emilio said that Horatio Walker's grave is around here somewhere," I said to John. "A large crypt in its own field."

"Guess he didn't want to mingle with the locals."

I had worn the only dress I'd brought, a white cotton piqué sundress that had a full skirt with a pattern of green leafy vines on it. "Very fetching," John had said when he found me waiting at the Shell sign. I hoped he didn't take it as a sign of slippage on the virgin front. In fact, what made our trysts so exciting were their clear boundaries. I had the impression that his life at home was complicated, and that this restored something in him. It was infidelity of a different order.

John had rolled his khakis up above his knees. His legs were skinny and white; I felt a wifely pang of embarrassment for him. He wore a backpack with our lunch in it, plus a bottle of Orangina for me and a beer for him. I had my sandals in one hand. The Grand narrowed as it bent away from the road. After wading upstream for a while we saw something, maybe just a shed, at the top of a mowed field. We left the river and still in bare feet made our way toward it.

"I feel like we're in that Andrew Wyeth painting," I said. "The one where the woman is sort of crawling up through a field towards a house."

"She was his mistress, the model for that," he said. "Not that it makes any difference."

The shed was indeed Horatio Walker's grave, a stone crypt with steps leading down to a sunken entrance. The bronze door had a carved border featuring a stag in one corner and a ship on the high seas in the other. No epitaph. Just HORATIO WALKER, PAINTER, 1847–1908.

John put a small stone on the threshold

"He's a good painter, actually. I was surprised."

"Why? Because he's not American?"

"No, but his work tends to be quite literal."

"But so is yours. That A&P story."

"Literal? You think so?"

It was the first time we had talked about his writing.

"I mean, it's definitely not experimental, like that movie *A Chairy Tale*."

"True." He opened his beer and drank from it. I changed tack.

"What I mean is, the writing isn't show-offy. It's more like a real story, with real people."

"Right. But I do use the present tense. Which some would consider experimental."

"But . . . it's just about three girls going into a supermarket in their bathing suits. Which to me is not a big deal."

"To a nineteen-year-old boy it is, trust me."

"How about here?" I said impatiently. I only wanted to lie down with him and stop talking. We were on the far side of the grassy hill, well out of sight of the road. I spread the blanket. Our home.

John poured some Orangina into a plastic glass for me. He lay out some slices of cheese, tomatoes, and buttered bread on a tea towel and began to assemble sandwiches while I kept a nervous eye on the top of the hill.

"I hope there aren't any bulls around."

"I wish I could take a picture of you in that dress."

We both knew this wouldn't happen; photographs were taken with cameras, on film that had to be developed by other people, in drugstores.

"You could take a picture of my warts too." I enjoyed being as unseductive as possible around him—it felt connubial and relaxed.

"Okay, let's deal with those right now."

He took a piece of paper out of the backpack and began to read, holding my hand in his.

Fleurs du mal
These seeds of night
Long to eclipse
Their field of white
Soul-scouring spirit
Wield your powers—
Maledicta, hence!
Skate off, dark flowers!

I was at a loss. I thought he should at least ask permission before casting a spell on me.

"I like the 'seeds of night' part. Should I be feeling something now?"

"In two or three weeks they'll be gone, trust me."

"But by then . . ." I stopped. I didn't want to break our rule.

"When you go back home," John said, "look at them every morning, really concentrate on them, and say the word 'Begone.' Say it out loud."

"I can't, I'll just feel silly."

"It's not magic, it's scientific. Having faith triggers the body's own power to heal. Witchcraft and voodoo just tap into that."

"How romantic."

He handed me a sandwich.

"All I mean is that your hands are beautiful, you shouldn't hide them. And you must believe in yourself."

"Okay," I said. "I will do it. For you."

"Here's something more romantic."

He took a notebook out of the pack. I put my head beside his so I could look at the words while he read the poems, two short ones, out loud. They were rhyming poems with some words I didn't recognize, like "weir" and "sein." One was about a silver fish tangled in a silver net. I could sense the logic that held them together and was relieved they weren't dopey or sentimental. But I couldn't really grasp their meaning.

"Wow," I said. "Can I keep them?"

"Of course, they're for you. I have copies."

The heat made us listless but I was content to just lie there on the side of the hill with my head on his chest. His hands moved over me undemandingly. I had become one of the women, not too many I hoped, who could recognize the sound of his heart, its eager pacing. It was all new to me, these feelings. But the week was almost over. I felt almost excited about how this would be the end of us; I would then have a secret, an "affair" with an older man, a writer who had written poems for me, about me.

And nothing would be broken or harmed by this—not me or Mary or anyone. Well, maybe Larry. It would be our story, that's all. A fiction, almost.

Then we heard shouts.

"I found it!"

Axel appeared on the horizon, followed by L'Orren. They were heading toward the crypt. When they reached it they had a clear view down the grassy hill to our encampment under the young trees. I saw L'Orren shade her eyes. Axel put his hands on his hips, looked our way, then quickly looked down at his feet.

"Don't move," said John, holding my face against his chest. "They're too far away to really see us."

"But my white dress," I said. "L'Orren will know."

"It doesn't matter anyway," he said gallantly.

A breeze came up, as if the air had been stirred by their arrival. A crow in our trees gave a warning caw.

Axel and L'Orren took a few photographs of the crypt, then turned and disappeared over the hill. The crow flew away. John smoothed my hair and tried to joke about it, but his touch was distracted now. There was no recapturing our moment.

"If only I hadn't worn this stupid dress."

"What can they do? The week is almost over."

John looked solemn. I had the feeling that he was thinking about his children. I imagined my parents reading a stern letter from the director of Doon about my expulsion. The future was swirling around us now.

We gathered up our things. Instead of making our way down the river we went straight across the field to the road, but slowly, so we wouldn't overtake the others.

L'Orren didn't say a word to me when I got back to the dorm, where I changed into my shorts and the plaid side of my reversible halter top. I considered making up a story about Larry visiting, and how we'd gone on a picnic. But I wasn't sure I could pull it off. Axel blushed when he saw me in the dining room. John poured some water in my glass. Maybe nothing will come of this, I thought.

Then, after dinner, someone had the bright idea to play a game of Charades. "I'll start," said L'Orren, of course. Ever the initiator. We descended to the rec room.

L'Orren began. She made a twirling gesture beside her head.

"Movie," John said.

She held up her fingers.

"Four words."

She began striding back and forth with her hands clenched in front of her, as if pushing something. She'd push, then back up a bit, then push forward again.

"Pushing a stroller—*And Baby Makes Three!*" said the schoolteacher. L'Orren shook her head no.

"You're shoveling snow . . ." John said. "Rosebud! *Citizen Kane* . . . *It's a Wonderful Life* . . ."

L'Orren made the "rhymes-with" sign, turned around, and slapped her rear end.

"Ass," said Axel. "Gas . . . grass. You're mowing grass!" L'Orren stabbed her finger yes at him, then lay down on the floor and hugged herself, looking rapturous.

"*Splendor in the Grass*," cried the schoolteacher, leaping up, as the rest clapped. I saw the color leave John's face. L'Orren got to her feet and brushed off her clothes with a little smile on her face. She shot a look my way as she took her place on the sofa beside Axel. For a long moment no one spoke.

And that was how the week ended, really, although two

more days remained. We still had 180 pages of Axel's novel to read. The schoolteacher's memoir had veered away from her husband's experience in the war to her rage at being abandoned at home with a small baby. She was going gangbusters, she said, and wanted to finish it before we all dispersed. As for me, I was still working on my event-free play, which L'Orren had read. She urged me to read Lorca and said she thought absurdist drama was "a bit masculinist."

On my last night, I stayed away from John's cottage and wrote a long, newsy note to Larry. It was too late to mail it, but I could give it to him when I got back. I called my parents to find out when they were picking me up. Then I put on my yellow rain jacket and walked down to the bridge, alone. The Grand was milky-brown and swollen but subdued, coursing along.

I crossed the back lawn on my way to the dorm. John's cottage was dark. I wanted to retrieve my red-stairway painting, which I had left to dry in Emilio's studio. That too was dark, except for what looked like a throb of candlelight in one corner. I knocked; no answer. As I opened the door I glimpsed L'Orren's massive hair all but covering Emilio as she lay naked on top of him, on paint-splattered drop sheets. She was making a sound that didn't seem to belong to her, almost a coo. I closed the door as softly as I could. Was this sort of thing going on everywhere? Was the whole world awash in lust, and I hadn't noticed?

On the last day, from my window seat in the dorm, I saw the school director walk across the back lawn to John's cottage. He knocked on the door, John answered, and he stepped in. Maybe he's just thanking him, I thought, and saying goodbye. About twenty minutes later the door opened and the director emerged, unsmiling. I wanted to run across the lawn and throw myself in John's arms. Instead, I wrote a new scene in my play, in which the woman lies down and embraces her bench.

"John's been fired," L'Orren said when we were packing up. She was going home that afternoon. "Apparently one of the waitresses complained about him being out of line." She carefully folded her white Indian shirts. "Or something like that."

"But he's leaving tomorrow, so what's the point of firing him?"

She gave me a long-suffering look. "What it means is that he won't be back. I was going to sign up for next year. Now I'm not so sure."

"Then they should fire Emilio too," I said. "He'll screw anything that walks."

L'Orren said nothing, just slid her copy of *Bonjour Tristesse* into the side pocket of her suitcase.

Her mother was downstairs waiting to drive her home, which cast L'Orren in a slightly different light. She looked small and pale, maybe hungover.

"Don't forget what I said about Lorca," she said as she left the room. "Reading him truly changed my life."

"What if I like mine the way it is?"

At dinner that night, John didn't seem upset. He stayed on after dessert, playing Ping-Pong with the others. I went into the gallery and sat at the piano. But I didn't want to play Satie or Bach, because now I knew what I was feeling, and why. If I played that music, it would be like broadcasting our secret through the house.

Everything I wrote, or did, was now about my secret life with John Updike.

On Saturday morning my parents arrived looking heart-breakingly trim, jovial, and innocent. I showed them my pine-tree canvas and my mother was so pleased. "Emilio said it was painterly," I reported. I added that I was still working on my play about feminine identity. It wasn't done yet, but Mr. Updike had been encouraging.

"Can we meet him?" asked my mother, peering around the gallery.

"I think he's already left," I said. Then John walked in with some books under his arm. I introduced him to my parents. I could tell my mother was surprised by how young he was. She had probably imagined someone more professorial. My father beamed at John, this bright mentor for my untapped talents.

I was dying inside.

"Your daughter's very talented," John said to them. "But I want her to keep reading." He handed me several books, including Baudelaire's *Les Fleurs du Mal*, and his novel. Then he looked at me fearlessly, as if to say, Give me your gaze, it's all right, we've done nothing wrong.

"I keep telling her to send something in to *Reader's Digest*," said my dear, irrepressible father. This remark sent my mother skittering off to study one of Horatio Walker's paintings on the wall.

"Look at that sky," she said approvingly.

"Well, I think I'm on my way now," John said. He shook my hand. "Miss McEwan."

"Thank you for everything, Mr. Updike," I managed. I was wearing the green-and-white dress.

My parents drove me down the road, under the willows, past the Shell sign and the field with Walker's crypt, back home to our split-level bungalow in Burlington, to our own Ping-Pong table, to my job at Rico's House of Beauty, and Larry.

Our first night together, in the new LeSabre, Larry and I went all the way. I love you, we solemnly told each other.

A week later, I broke it off. He took it badly. I didn't tell him, or anyone, about John Updike for a long time. Until now.

Every day for the rest of that summer I stood in front of the bathroom mirror, stared at the warts on my right hand, and said, out loud, "Begone!"

By the end of August, they had vanished.

Free Love

As soon as the locals saw our backpacks they knew where we were headed, and waved us to an empty bus parked by the curb. We were in Mires, a small market town not far from the south coast. All day long on the ride across Crete the sky had been perfectly blue and empty, as if clouds were some British invention that didn't work here. A voltage problem.

The driver stood outside, smoking. "Matala?" I asked, with my grateful-to-be-a-guest-in-your-country smile. He said nothing, just cranked open the door. Nick and I took the front seats, sitting with our packs against our knees. Then we waited. The irony of traveling, of being on the road, is how much time you spend not going anywhere.

The flat white light, the strangeness of the language, and the long deck-class night on the ferry to Iraklion had put us in a stupor. The driver clacked a row of beads through his fingers, obeying some mysterious inner timetable. The roof of the bus radiated heat.

Across the street a woman in rolled-down stockings used a twig broom to sweep the patio of her house, a white cube. Through the open door the dark interior looked cool and inviting.

I dug a halter top out of my pack and went down a laneway to change out of my sweater. Nick stayed on the bus writing in his six-ring loose-leaf notebook. When it was full he didn't start a new one, he just kept adding more pages to it. After four months on the road, the pocket of his suede jacket had stretched from the weight of it.

Back on the bus, I slid open our window. What was the holdup? We were the only passengers.

Then the driver abruptly swung up into his seat and the engine started with a noise as guttural as a tractor engine. At the sound a hippie couple carrying string bags full of vegetables emerged from the market. The girl wore a black fisherman's cap, sandals made out of car tires, an Indian skirt covered in round mirrors, and a T-shirt with a telltale constellation of tiny holes from falling hash embers. Her shirtless boyfriend had dark hair to his shoulders and an army dog tag around his neck. Their skin had the grayish tinge of having passed through sunburn to something else. Not newcomers.

"Hey," he said, flashing us two fingers in a V as they got on the bus. Nick and I were right behind the driver, hugging our packs like eager tourists. They made their way to the backseat, where the girl stretched out with her head in her boyfriend's lap. He peeled a banana and the smell filled the air as the bus pulled out of town.

"We should have bought more food," I said to Nick. "Everything will probably be shut when we get there." He nodded. He could go all day on nothing but an apple, but I got shaky if I didn't eat. I rummaged in my pack. "Don't we still have those peanuts from the ferry?" He nodded again, looking out the window at fields of dun-colored sheep, like rocks on the move. We had fallen into the habit of connubial silence on the road.

After an hour the bus left the pavement and began jolting down a dirt road. A fisherman carrying a long pole walked toward us with his catch; the driver lifted his finger off the wheel as he passed. We opened the windows as wide as they would go. I thought I could smell the sea. There were no more houses and the trees dwindled as the landscape surrendered to another element.

The driver looked over at Nick.

"First time Matala?"

"Yes, first time."

"Deutschland?"

"Canada."

"Ah, Canada!"

The driver pretended to sip on a joint. "You smoke?"

"Oh no." We knew about the police in Greece.

"I find for you, very good."

"No, that's fine, but thank you."

The driver pointed to me. "Your wife?"

"Yes, my wife."

I displayed my dime-store ring.

The driver grinned.

"No wives in Matala," he said, holding up the gold band on his wedding finger. "Everybody married to everybody." He laughed at his joke.

"Huh," said Nick.

"We're just visiting for a few days," I piped up. "To swim." I swam with my arms.

"Yes, yes," said the driver, already dismissive. "Good for swimming, Matala. But Komos better."

I dug out my journal, a school exercise book that I'd bought in Portugal. I had started it with the intention of writing about our trip, and maybe selling a story to a newspaper back home. Instead, I kept lists of Spanish and French words, useful phrases for "third-class" or "does that include breakfast?" At the back I kept track of what we spent, with long wavering columns of numbers under two headings, R and N. We split the cost of everything—every cup of tea and ten-cent bun. Nick was especially frugal. Once, when I was pining for a real lunch in a restaurant he patiently waited outside, reading a book while I sat at a table eating my *salade composée*.

Nick never complained about the discomforts of life on the road—the endless walks to reach the outskirts of a city to start hitchhiking, or the hours of standing on the side of a road as cars sped by. I was less stoic. And more anxious. There was always a little current of panic in me ready to spark if we arrived someplace after dusk and couldn't find the hostel or a place to eat. At a certain point in the day, I needed to be inside and safe.

So on the bus to Matala, with my face out the window, I was determined to be okay, to not repeat our time in Morocco. That was when things had started to unravel.

I got sick in Tangiers. It was just a stomach thing but it amplified the culture shock. Fresh out of college, I was overwhelmed by Morocco—the beggars in their backward rubber boots, the rheumy-eyed expats in cafés, the street kids a hundred times savvier than us, leading us to silver teapots and carpets and hashish. At first, after the macho advances of Spanish and Italian men, I was relieved to be ignored by the men in the soukh, whose gazes slid over me and lingered on Nick instead.

But after basking in this invisibility for a few days, I began to feel myself vanishing limb by limb, like the Cheshire cat.

We lay under the ceiling fan in our cheap hotel (an incredible 31 cents a night according to my journal), with the clamor of the soukh a few lanes over drifting through the shutters. Who was I? Tangiers demands a sturdy sense of self, and I didn't have one.

After a few days of scurrying down the hall to the hotel's single bathroom, a dark, damp booth with water sluicing around the two stone footprints (a welcome arrangement when you are already doubled over), I told Nick we had to find a doctor. We went out into the streets but it was some religious holiday and everything was closed. As we searched through the streets I shat myself a little, a harmless but soul-forfeiting experience. We came to a gated compound with a doctor's name on it and knocked on the wooden door. Minutes passed. A peephole slid open and a pair of eyes regarded us.

"My wife is sick," Nick said as I stood beside him, mute, well fed, and clearly not bedridden. "We're looking for a doctor."

"Not here," the eye-person murmured, and slid the peephole shut. I began to weep. This was not "touring Europe." It was not even bohemia. I just wanted to go home.

Our plan was to make it to Fez and spend some time in the desert. But when we got to Marrakesh I got sick again. The hostel was coed, and the man in the bunk above me slept with a long knife. We were sitting in a café staring at chunks of lamb that I couldn't bring myself to eat when I told Nick that I wanted to turn back—back to the thirty-one-cent hotel in Tangiers, and back to Spain, where at least I knew how to read a menu. Morocco had shown me just how little weight this independent-modern-woman thing had in the wider, older world.

If we left now, I argued, we would have more time in Greece. We could stay on some island for a few weeks. He could get more writing done.

Nick agreed.

On the ferry to Gibraltar, we watched the immaculate blue-and-white coast recede like a sailboat. I felt bad that Morocco had unmoored me. Nick would have pushed on to the mountains and the desert if he'd been on his own.

We stood at the railing of the ferry, the wind whipping our hair. I leaned into him, trying to amuse. "We'll always not have Fez."

Nick smiled. He didn't seem to hold it against me. He just wrote a little more in his notebook each day.

So on the bus to Matala, I decided that whatever was going to happen on Crete, I would put up with it. I was in love with him. And he was the first.

Over the next hill we caught sight of the Libyan sea, cupped on the horizon like a darker distillate of the sky. The heat and the flat white light were dreamlike; only a few animals moved through the landscape. We passed a donkey with a high-pommelled wooden saddle, flicking his tail. A black-clad woman sat against a white wall with a gaping basket of fish for sale. Then the road ran out into sand and we arrived at Matala. Nick and I got off the bus with our packs and stood wondering where to go.

The village was nothing more than a small cluster of houses on a crescent of white sand facing Africa, unseen across the water. No hotels, no electricity except for one generator-run refrigerator. Bracketing the beach were two yellow-white sandstone promontories. The longer eastern arm tilted down into the sea like a gently foundering ocean liner. On that side we could see two or three tiers of cave openings, maybe twenty altogether. The caves were man-made but very old—perhaps a former Roman burial site, or leper colony. In Greek mythology, Matala was thought to be the place where Europa, future queen of Crete, was raped by the god Zeus, in the form of a white bull.

"The folksinger Joni Mitchell is staying here too," said Rick and Souki, the couple from the bus, as we walked toward the cliffs. "But she's pretty shy. You see her sometimes in Delfini's. She's hanging out with the cook there."

The other café was the Mermaid, where the owner had a battery-operated record player. There were parties, Rick said, lots of parties. "And they can get pretty wild," said Souki, her hoop earrings swinging. They'd been in Matala for three months now.

"The cops hate the hippies but they can't arrest us or throw us in jail, because the caves are an archeological site, run by some other government department," said Rick. "They're okay with weed if you don't flaunt it, but, like, painting the walls with Day-Glo is not cool."

Besides, he went on, everybody at Matala was into a drug that could be bought right over the counter—a cough syrup called Romilar. Some combination of codeine and speed.

"It's like acid," Souki said, "but more floaty and visual?" She wafted her arms. Nick perked up at this; he was a fan of acid.

"Is there an outhouse or anything?" I asked. My post-Moroccan fixation.

"There's the shit cave," she said. "Which is not as bad as it sounds. It's at sea level, and when the tide comes in it washes everything away."

Rick pointed down the beach. "Kostakis's boat is coming in. Let's go see what he's caught." They headed off.

We could see figures moving about or lounging in the door-ways of the caves. As we ground our way across the sand we came to the Mermaid café, with dark-blue tables set out on a cement patio. Someone had painted a sun-faded cartoon of a busty mermaid on one wall.

In the heat of the day the patio was deserted. Twisting up through the cement was a grape tree that offered a scrap of shade. We sat down under it and ordered Cokes from a silent boy of twelve or so.

A kid our age, long-limbed and American-looking with shoulder-length blond hair, approached us. He carried a plastic canister and a funnel.

"You two just arrive?"

"Yeah."

"Buy your kerosene here. Delfini's charges more."

"Thanks."

He shook our hands, soul brother–style, holding eye contact. He had a nice Southern drawl.

"I'm Hoot, from San Antonio. Did you come over on the midnight ferry?"

"Yeah."

"Hey, so welcome to paradise. How long you planning to stay?"

"A week or two I guess," said Nick.

"Oh yeah. When I got here I thought I'd stay a couple days, swim, catch some rays." Hoot laughed. "That was two months ago." He sat down at our table and gazed out at the ocean as if he'd never noticed it before.

"Today's Saturday, right?"

"Right."

"Come down to the Mermaid later on, that's where every-body goes on Saturday night. You'll hear the music anyway."

"Are the caves all full?" I asked. "Can we, like, reserve one?" Something close to the shit cave, preferably.

"A couple from Amsterdam just left, so maybe—although I think Joni has her eye on that one. Joni Mitchell the folksinger, you know her?"

"Yeah, we heard." This secretly thrilled me. She wasn't famous yet, this was the year before *Blue* came out. But I loved *Ladies of the Canyon.*

"Let's go check it out," said Hoot. We followed him across the sand and up a stony path to the second tier of caves.

"Here's me," Hoot said, pointing to a waist-high entrance. "It's bigger than it looks from the outside. Sort of a split-level."

We passed a guy with an Afro grilling little fish on a charcoal brazier and came to a doorway covered by a canvas tarp.

"This is maybe the third biggest one. I would have moved in myself, but my stuff is all set up the way I like."

The round, dark entrance was like a tooth socket. We stepped inside to coolness and a clean smell of earth. The cave was ten or twelve feet deep with a couple stone ledges. Against one wall was a flat gravel-covered area. The bedroom.

"Got camping mats?" We didn't.

"Doesn't matter, just put your clothes under your sleeping bags. You don't need many clothes here anyway. Although when the police are around, it's not cool to go around naked. They're more uptight about that than the drugs."

I felt something unfamiliar as we toured the cave: domestic lust. Yes, I thought, we can sleep over there, store our packs in that cranny, and I can hang my batik Indian scarves over the door. Line up our books together on the shelf. Here I could wash my hair as often as I wanted and dry it in the sun. The two of us could settle down.

"This is perfect," I said, like a client at an open house. I set my pack on the "bed" in a proprietorial way and looked at Nick, desperate for him to agree.

"Yeah, it looks okay," Nick said. "Although we'll have to buy stuff to cook with."

"Stelios can tell you where to get anything. He runs the Mermaid."

Hoot ducked out of the entrance, momentarily blocking the sunlight's blare. "So I'm down the way, if you need me. It's the one with the cowbell nailed outside. And you'll meet everybody tonight at the Mermaid."

He put his hands in a prayer position and gave a slight bow.

"Welcome to Matala."

While I unpacked Nick knelt in the entrance and looked out at the ocean. A few kids in cutoff jeans were in the water, standing in swells that raced far up onto the beach before the waves broke into a bluish-white ruffle of foam, and then shrank back into the sea. A steady soft breeze blew. The only sound was when the tide sometimes surged into the sea-level caves with a booming clap.

I unrolled my sleeping bag on the gravel bed, then took Nick's bag and smoothed it out alongside mine. They were different makes but with some patience the two could be zipped together into one cocoon. The bed side of the cave was tucked away from the door and quite private.

Nick changed into his bathing suit, opened his notebook, and uncapped his pen. I lay down in our new bedroom where the walls radiated a stony coolness. I turned to a fresh page in my journal and wrote the word "Matala." If it took living in a cave to play house, I was game.

Feb. 10th, 1970

Yesterday we took a trip into Pitsidia and bought ourselves the local version of a BBQ—a little brazier that holds charcoal—and an iron frying pan. A kerosene lamp, extra wick, and candles. Some of the coarse salt they use here, twisted up in brown paper, fresh oregano, eggs in a cloth. Plus a bottle of olive oil the color of baby snakes.

We spent seventy cents on a fish in a plastic bag with ice that melted on the 4 k. walk back to Matala. Found the old guy in the village who sells bundles of firewood. He wraps each one tenderly in grapevines. So we're all set up now.

The caves are better than a hotel in some ways. They're sound-proof, for one thing. No thunder from your neighbor's shower (I wish). And they never lose their coolness even in the heat of the day. The shit cave is not great, you have to watch your step, but it does get "flushed" twice a day. Garbage is burnt in the beach bonfires, and we don't generate much. Anything perishable the local dogs take care of.

There's only one tap for all of us and lugging cans of water up the cliff is a chore. On Sundays the tour buses arrive and people with cameras roam around the cliffs for an hour or so, apologetically poking their heads into our homes as if we were Maasai warriors living in mud huts. Well, they are caves.

Nick's writing a lot, and has finished some really good poems. I like it when we're both in the cave at dusk, waiting for the charcoal embers to get perfectly white, and he's scribbling away—it's pathetic, this playing-house thing, I know. But I'm tired of always being on the move and out of my element (whatever that is). So far everyone here is friendly and nice except for a few weirdos who live on the opposite cliff and don't hang out much. I like the way the weather rules everything here. A full moon means late parties on the beach, and on windy days with high surf, everyone holes up (literally).

In the cave next door to us are a brother and sister from South Carolina—I think he just went AWOL from the marines. She's some sort of musician, a classical pianist I think. Shy.

The other day Nick and I ventured farther down the shoreline. There are coves like this, one after another, all down the coast, with great dinosaur humps of rock in between. One cove has dark-red sand. The rock is scoured with trenches and furrows, or in other places it's pockmarked and lacy, like bone marrow. A twenty-minute walk in either direction and there's not another soul around.

Ran into Joni Mitchell at the bakery lady's today! She was wearing turquoise and silver rings on her fingers and had a bad sunburn on her chest. Long straight blond hair and a long upper lip, with a cute overbite. There was only one loaf of bread left and she really seemed to want it, so I let her buy it. Then the red-haired guy with the turban, his name is Carey I think, came in and scared her, grabbing her from behind and lifting her up. She has a nice big laugh. I was relieved when they ignored me. I can never bring myself to say fan stuff to musicians or actors. It feels so intrusive.

I told Nick about Joni, but he doesn't like her songs that much. "Her lines have too many words," he said. I felt like holding up his notebook, but refrained.

———

Something has happened that I don't understand. The moon was full, it was the middle of the night and I was having a nightmare. I only remember the end of it, when there was a huge bee circling my head, dive-bombing me, trying to fly into my eyes. It wasn't a regular bee, it was a killer bee and I was very scared. I had a little paddle in one hand that I was using to fend off this attacker. I woke up with that incredible sense of relief you have when you realize it was only a dream, and now you're safe in bed. Then I noticed that Nick wasn't beside me.

He's gone out to pee, I thought, and lay in my warm sleeping bag, grateful to have surfaced and escaped the killer bee. The light of the moon shone through the door of the cave, through my pretty batik curtain. Some of the wild dogs that roam the beach were barking, and from the sound of the surf, the wind was coming up. I remembered that we'd left the charcoal brazier outside and hoped the wind hadn't scattered any leftover embers.

Nick's side felt cool. He must have been gone for some time. I unzipped my bag to go looking for him.

When I stepped out of our cave the moon was so bright it was as if a big television were casting a blue pall on everything. It threw my shadow on the cliff wall. I smelled cigarette smoke and saw that the marine next door was sitting on the ledge, in boxer shorts. He had a brush cut; he was the only cave guy with short hair. Beano, they called him, because that's all he cooked, beans and rice. That's what he brought to the parties.

Hey Beano, I said, what're you doing up?

He lifted his cigarette.

Want one?

I did smoke, but I rolled my own and didn't like filtered American cigarettes.

Have you seen Nick?

Yeah, he said with his eyes fixed on the surf below.

Is there a party somewhere? I asked. But the night was perfectly quiet, except for the dogs.

He pointed behind him with his cigarette, toward the cave he shared with his sister.

Nick's in there?

He nodded and gave me a kindly look with lustrous eyes. Whatever he had been through in the marines, it seemed to have made him gentler than the others here, so intent on being pacifists.

I was slow to put it together. So, Nick had slipped out of our zippered bed and had gone next door, to sleep with . . . Sally, that was her name. Beano and Sally, brother and sister, the model family next door. What nerve, among other things.

This time Beano passed me his cigarette and I took it. I didn't know what to do—storm into the cave and drag him "home"? I was confused. Nick and I had sex, lots of sex. I thought he loved me, and my body, at least he said he did. A deep sense of disorientation came over me. Everything was turned upside down, and I doubted it all, one hundred percent of it. Nick was not who I had thought he was, and so neither was I.

He could have at least warned me that he wanted to sleep with someone else. Was restless. It might have been negotiable. In theory.

Luckily there was a canvas tarp nailed over the entrance to their cave, thick enough to muffle any sounds. The dogs barked on, as if scolding the moon for being so bright. Beano and I didn't say anything, we just sat there smoking and watching the phosphorescent white foam of the waves as they broke down below. The breeze, all the way from Africa, was not as warm as usual; I began to shiver, so I left Beano and went back inside. I curled up in bed, pulling the toggle on my sleeping bag to cover everything but my face. Maybe they were just talking, I thought. She was quiet, but she seemed smart, knowing. Dark bangs cut straight, like Veronica in the cartoon strip. I decided I would give him the benefit of the doubt.

———

So began my enchantment, my inability to break free of the damaging spell that Nick's betrayal would cast. Not that we used words like betrayal, or jealousy. This was 1970, the height of the so-called sexual revolution, when possessiveness and jealousy were nothing but bad ideas, "bourgeois constructs." I felt wrong just being in their grip.

The next morning Nick came back as if from brushing his teeth, unrepentant and casual. No apologies, no explanations. "Where were you?" I must have yelped. I was next door with Sally, he answered with a touch of exasperation. I didn't know where you were, I said, I was worried. But Beano told you, he replied mildly; we could hear the two of you talking outside.

We.

He changed his clothes and took our soap, water bottle, and towel to head down to the faucet. I'll get the water, he said, and that was that. Even though he couldn't disguise a certain just-laid friskiness, his behavior made it impossible for me to cry or fight. And I was too off balance, too dismantled, to even locate my feelings, let alone act on them. When he came back I was back in bed, pretending to read. (*The Bell Jar*, of course.) He opened his notebook and began to write.

Later in the day I went down to the Mermaid, ordered a bottle of red wine, and slowly, methodically drank it. Joni was sitting at another table with the red-haired guy, playing back-gammon and drinking beer. They smiled at me and left me alone. At dusk, when I finally made my way back up the cliff to our cave, Nick was gone. I slept in my clothes. In the middle of the night, he came in, sliding into his bag and leaving it un-zipped so as not to wake me. But I was awake anyway.

After that we settled into a routine. On most mornings he would head off with Sally, to spend the day in another cove. Tactful! I would sit in the door of the cave underlining *The Bell Jar* or head down to the Mermaid. By sunset, he'd be back, sunburnt all over. I would then fuzzily cook dinner, usually some version of an omelet, in our new frying pan. I was like any other wife in a bad grown-up marriage. He never talked about Sally—and I never asked. Some nights he slipped out, some nights he stayed with me. I wasn't able to question this, and therefore I began to fall apart, slowly and erratically, like a building gutted by fire but still standing.

I assumed a late-stage Simone de Beauvoir stance down at the Mermaid, starting on red wine at eleven a.m. and drinking with anybody who cared to join me. I knew I should take a stab at revenge sex, but I didn't have the heart for it. I was too busy trying to breathe in a whole new element, the thin atmosphere that exists outside the boundaries of unbroken love.

The worst part was Nick's journal. I didn't go looking for it; that would have required too much initiative and spunk. But he tended to leave it conspicuously available. In my path, as it were. And there aren't many spots to hide a journal in a cave.

One day I found it lying open on the ledge near the entrance where we kept the matches and loose change. I picked up the familiar notebook, each page pebbled blue with ink, and read his patient, writerly descriptions of their lovemaking. The feel of her skin, the grip of her thighs, the oystery pliancy of her clitoris. Nick was a bit of an aficionado when it came to women's bodies. He seemed fascinated by the rest of Sally too, her un-talkative aplomb, the mystery of an American woman from the South. She had olive skin and those broody, deep bangs—the opposite of me. I read in his notes that she had dropped out of Juilliard, disillusioned by the classical music world and unsure of her own talents. She'd been living in Matala with Beano for two months now—an old hand.

Nick was the first man she'd slept with in a year, he noted. Imagine writing that down, I thought with a flare of hatred. Scuzzy little journalist. I was still reeling from this fresh knowledge that I had been living and traveling and making love with a stranger. My whole understanding of the world had been recalled, like a car in which a fatal engineering flaw has been discovered.

I knew I should leave Matala and Nick. Instead I settled into my lugubrious role as Cuckolded Hippie. Hoot from San Antonio was sympathetic and sat with me a lot at the Mermaid. He said I should move to Texas, where the ratio of men to women was better. Joni's smile when I passed her on the way to the faucet seemed knowing.

Then I got sick, my default strategy, with a cough that wouldn't go away. The caves were dusty, needless to say. I stayed awake at night when Nick wasn't there, coughing hard, hoping they would both hear me next door. But caves have thick walls, and in any case Nick was immune to guilt. I remembered him telling me that when he was little, cartoons upset him because they seemed so violent, and the animals in them were always hurting each other. So this new ability to administer homeopathic dosages of rejection day after day surprised me.

Why didn't I leave? It's the first question that women in unhappy situations are always asked, and can't answer.

A week or so went by like that. One afternoon I went down to the tap to wash my hair, to try to get a grip on myself in some small way. It was a humid day and the gush of cold water felt good on my scalp. Maybe now I can get it together to leave, I thought. I had a towel wrapped around my wet hair and was heading back toward the cliffs when I saw that a new couple had just arrived, with guitars. A welcome party was already under way around a bonfire on the beach. Carey had brought a bucket of beer from Delfini's, the joints were going round. Joni was there too, with a stack of silver bracelets up one arm and her dulcimer in her lap. Hoot hailed me over. Then I saw Nick and Sally in the circle too, sitting together. Okay, I thought, I'll do this anyway. They can't make an exile out of me. I took a sip of Hoot's joint and unwrapped my wet hair so the sun and the fire could dry it.

The new guy on the guitar was good, and knew all the words

to "Masters of War." I got into it, or maybe it was the dope; everyone was singing, the fishing boats rocked on the horizon, the sky was cloudless. Here I was on a Greek island, with Joni Mitchell. Then I looked across the fire and saw Nick leaning over, kissing Sally, as if I wasn't there. I was smoking a cigarette—Kents or Marlboros, I smoked anything now—and I flicked my lit cigarette at them and stalked away from the circle. But I didn't feel justified in my anger and hurt. I just felt foolish, swathed in jealousy like ugly clothes that didn't fit.

Maybe it was that night that I took to my pallet, with some cheap grappa to quell my cough. I fumbled in my pack for the razor blades I had furtively packed—an uncommitted hippie, I still shaved my legs. I'm not suicidal, I lectured myself, I just need to see my own blood, evidence that I exist. So I used a razor to nick a dotted line across one wrist. Nothing more than a bracelet of blood beads. It stung, like the nightmare bee.

And that did help.

Nick had left earlier that night to go down to the cafés, but I guess he had forgotten something—matches, or money. As I was busy with my handiwork, he came back and interrupted me. He made an exasperated sound, then took away the razor blades and my Swiss Army knife too. And then he left. No doubt he thought it was cheesy and manipulative of me, and he wasn't going to rise to the bait.

Free love meant that you could be attracted to other people, you could sleep with them, and it didn't necessarily change anything. The birth control pill also took away consequence. But every molecule in my body seemed to have been reorganized by his faithlessness and I didn't know how to proceed.

Eventually, I got to sleep. Nick was there in the morning when I woke up. I never did it again, but for me the cutting had broken the silence.

———·–·———

The next day Sally and Nick and most of the other cave people took the bus to some religious festival in a town near Mires. Sally set off in a straw fedora with a black feather in the brim. Nick took his notebook with him, which was too bad because I had now surrendered to reading it whenever possible. It kept me looped into their story. Turns out that Sally had been briefly addicted to codeine when she was at Juilliard; this would increase her appeal for Nick, I knew. I always felt a bit suburban in this regard, even though I was broken in other, less glamorous ways.

When they got back later in the day, the "wolf-women" announced that they were throwing a mythology-themed "Europa party" in their big cave on the third tier. These were two new arrivals who had brought a new vibe to Matala. They'd been on the road for more than a year, and were tough, brown, and fearless women. The previous winter they'd lived up in the hills of Jamaica, near Negril. I got talking to one of them— Carolina, with her knotted hair bundled up in an African sort of turban—and she let slip that they weren't just wolf-*like*. At night, when they were in the mood, they turned *into* wolves.

You mean, metaphorically. No, she said, I mean biting and growling and having a tail. Her washed-out blue eyes for a moment looked like husky-dog eyes, and I believed her.

The two of them moved into a cave that everyone thought was too big and rough to inhabit. Magically, they scrounged up a broken-down couch from the village and fashioned a rusted lamp into a kerosene torch. They organized moon-howling parties with candlelit headdresses. They were edgier than the hippie girls, adding some drama to Matala's laid-back scene. They also liked to throw theme parties like this one, making special raki cocktails with fresh pineapple.

So I put on some kohl eyeliner and showed up at their cave. Everyone else was back from the festival, in a party mood. Nick and Sally were there too, but it was so crowded it was easy to ignore them. Hoot made me dance with him, in his whirly-armed way. The new guy, Ferrous, was playing guitar; things felt good. Then the two wolf-girls started dirty dancing with a local soldier who had somehow been included. He got an erection and was horribly embarrassed, until the girls tugged off his pants. Everybody started clapping as he stood there with a stiff cock, grinning and red-faced. Carolina danced around his erection as if his penis were a little god in a shrine. Then he pulled up his pants and fled the party. But that was when things turned; other couples started making out, and more clothes came off. One guy I didn't recognize was standing in one corner, holding a glass with nothing on but a T-shirt, his cock at half mast, kind of hopeful-looking.

Not eager to be a wallflower at the orgy, I was about to leave when I saw Nick and Sally embrace and then slide onto the ground, until he was on top of her. Wow, this I can't handle, I thought, and headed for the door. I had to detour around them but they didn't seem to see or notice me. It was dark outside. I stumbled on the path and then, voluptuously, I let myself fall, and roll down, down the side of the cliff, scraping myself a little until I came to rest at the base of the cliffs on the cool sand. I lay there, fully abject, hoping someone would see me and assume that I was dead.

Soon enough, the wild dogs came sniffing around, poking their wet noses into my face until they got bored and moved on. I lay there for a long time until I was shivering. I heard a group of kids leaving the party cave, still noisy, but they took another path. My efforts to be conspicuously shattered and derelict were not having an impact. So I got up, brushed off the sand, and went back to our empty cave.

The next day I went down early to the Mermaid to begin my solo drinking. I had moved on from *The Bell Jar* to *The Autobiography of a Yogi*, by Paramahansa Yogananda, a book about spiritual enlightenment and not in any superficial self-help way. It was harrowing, in fact. I dearly wanted to be razed like that, obliterated, suffused with a shower of white light across the top of my brain. The thirst for transcendence was keen.

On Sundays Delfini's offered pancakes, for the homesick Americans. I was wondering how raki would go with pancakes when the door opened and Joni Mitchell came in. She was wearing a sort of patchwork jacket with nice ivory linen pants, and bare feet. She had her leather sandals in one hand and a notebook—a six-ring one just like Nick's—in the other. No doubt she'd heard about my predicament.

"Hey," she said. "Want some company?"

She sat down and lit a cigarette. One of my few remaining rules was not to smoke before noon. But I inhaled her smoke happily. Gauloises, thick and strong.

"Is Nick off somewhere with Sally?" she asked, getting right down to it.

"Yes," I said.

"I think it's bullshit."

"What is?"

"This free-love thing. It's bullshit. It's only free for the guys."

"I don't know," I said. "It's not like monogamy has a great track record."

"But don't you find," she said, drawing hungrily on her cigarette, "that if you love someone, you don't want them to sleep with anyone else?" She squinted against the blue smoke. Her cheekbones were amazing. "You just don't. Whenever I do it myself, at least I know it's hurting someone."

Carey came out of the kitchen with a plate of pancakes and a pitcher of honey. He put a black coffee down in front of Joni. The two of them kissed and she wiped a fleck of something off his cheek.

"What time are you off?" she asked.

"Another hour. It's market day in Mires, so we're closing early."

"We can go to the red cove this afternoon."

"Cool." Carey went back to the kitchen.

"How long are you staying?" I asked Joni. I decided that I liked her company. There was something about her that reminded me of home, of Canada. Her complicated, aggressive shyness. I poured a little red wine in her water glass.

"I don't know. Every day I keep meaning to leave." She laughed quite boisterously. "I'm supposed to be back in L.A. working right now. There are people there waiting for me to cough up more songs, put out another album. But I don't like the way music works when it turns into a business."

"I love *Ladies of the Canyon*. I play it a lot back home."

"Really? That feels like another person now."

"Can't you just make the sort of record you want to make?" Joni laughed and drank her coffee.

"Trust me, it doesn't work like that," she said. "Can I have a pancake?"

"Help yourself." She reached over with her fork, silver bracelets jangling.

"I know it's crazy here, but L.A. is even crazier. Although there's someone there I do miss." She lowered her voice. "Despite this one," she said, with a nod toward the kitchen.

"Who is it?"

"A musician. We were living together. But it's kind of hard for musician guys with me, because . . . I'm good too, you know?" She shrugged. "Not my fault."

"Men are fragile," I said firmly. The raki was kicking in.

"Graham isn't. And I'm difficult, I know I am."

"Well, I'm not difficult enough," I said, but she didn't pick up on that. My mood lifted. I began to feel the expansiveness that comes with the company of a smart, frank woman. Joni was just struggling to be herself, to stay herself, and so was I. Maybe there was something even freer than free love.

"I'm going to give you some advice," said Joni, "because I've seen the two of you around. Also I don't much like Sally. With her Juilliard, I-don't-play-folk-music thing.

"You should leave Nick, and leave Matala," she said, drawing on her cigarette. "He's not good for you. He's attractive and smart, but he's not going to let you thrive."

These sentences filled me with a sense of conviction. Yes, Joni Mitchell was right, and I would leave the next morning on the six a.m. bus. We raised our drinks and clicked them.

"To jealousy."

Shortly after, Carey came out of the kitchen and they left for the red cove. I ordered more wine. It would be six hours before Nick was home. Another eighteen before the bus to Iraklion left.

W e had no alarm clock, but I trusted myself to either wake up, or maybe to not sleep at all. The bus left from the far end of the beach at six a.m. sharp. In keeping with the new terms of our relationship, I didn't discuss my decision with Nick, nor did I keep it a secret, as I began to organize my things for packing. I would leave him the can opener and cooking knife, for instance. I'd catch the bus to the night ferry to Athens and then make my way back to England. Maybe I'd find someone to hitchhike with in the Athens hostel. Back on the road, I might recover myself. I knew the hard part would be shaking off this dreamy martyred spell and leaving Matala. Momentum would take care of the rest.

Luckily, the roosters began crowing before the sun came up. Nick happened that night to be asleep beside me. In the dark I got dressed, rolled up my sleeping bag, and tied it to my pack. Nick either slept on, or lay there in silence. I scrambled down the cliff and hustled across the beach, jog-walking as the heavy pack thumped up and down on my shoulders. I'm doing it, I thought with a spurt of joy, I'm leaving. Then I heard a sudden guttural roar, like a tractor starting. No. The sun wasn't even up! By the time I got to the little square that marked the end of the road, the bus was already over the first rise and out of sight. The sound of the engine took a long time to fade.

Perhaps it had been empty; it often was. But the driver was adamant about keeping to his schedule.

Well, I thought, I tried. I gave it a shot. I felt I only had it in me to make the effort once. Maybe destiny had other designs on me. I trudged back to the cave in my "good" shirt and jeans, unrolled my bag, and lay down beside Nick without saying a word.

Later the next day, I saw we needed flashlight batteries and went through Nick's coat to find some change. While I was rummaging around, the cursed journal fell out of his pocket. My rule had been, if it's not open, don't open it. But if it flips open, I get to read those two pages.

It was the most recent entry, about this and that, nothing lurid. Then he began a fresh paragraph, a single line.

"Rose tried to leave today."

B ecause I didn't manage to leave Matala, or Nick, we simply picked up where we left. There was the matter of our non-refundable plane tickets home, after all. So two weeks after I failed to catch the bus to Iraklion, Nick said goodbye to Sally. I gave Hoot and Beano a hug. Then we rode across the island, took the night ferry to Athens, and got back on the road. We had heard that sleeping on the roof of the Guhlane Hotel in Istanbul cost 24 cents a night, and the only ID you needed was your signature on a clipboard.

Why did I stay? To begin with, I was then, and would always be, a too-accommodating person. People-pleasing on the surface. Underneath, anger-lava. I blame it partly on a solitary childhood—my older brother was in school, my father working long hours—with my intelligent and depression-prone mother. She made the most of motherhood and housewifery, she was relentlessly creative, but the job used only fifteen percent of her. And depression is terribly preoccupying. It narrows you, shuts you down. When I was very young I think I adapted to her emotional absence—to an impression of love as absence. Or at least, something less than intimacy came to feel like a safe and familiar place to me. Which in turn meant that I cultivated a protective absence in myself too.

So I can't heap it all on Nick. At the age of twenty-four, important parts of me were missing.

In the Athens hostel we met someone who was headed for India and wanted to get his blue Volkswagen van to his brother in England. Could we drive it back for him? We gave him $200 in Travelers Cheques and he handed us the keys. The entire undercarriage could have been upholstered with Turkish hash, but that never occurred to us. Hippies trusted one another upon sight. If you had long hair and sandals made from old car tires, you were good. Nick and I were tired of hitchhiking at this point, plus we could save money by cooking meals and sleeping in the van. Although I wasn't keen on more cooking, it did give me pleasure to buy a cheap nesting set of toxin-leaching aluminum pots.

By 1970, the hippie circuit in Europe was as well mapped out as a Michelin tour of three-star restaurants: Amsterdam (cafés where you could smoke dope), Ibiza and Formentera (beaches, artists, Euro-bohemia), a rent-free week or two in the caves of Matala or a pension on Hydra, followed by the obligatory trek to Istanbul (cheap hash and bus rides to India). Some kept on heading east, to spend the winter on the beaches at Goa. The more enterprising had already made the pilgrimage overland from London to India, in vans or retooled school buses painted in psychedelic designs, and had come back home with carpets, jewelry, and Indian shirts to sell at the Portobello Road Market.

Or, they didn't come back.

As with all faintly domestic dwellings, I was quite taken with the van. It had a dangerous kerosene-powered stove in the back, otherwise taken up by a plywood platform and foam mattress covered in a batik Indian bedspread. There was one curdled pillow, and the rear window featured orange burlap curtains. The handiwork of some long-departed girlfriend.

The curtains reminded me of my childhood in Burlington, in a suburb defined by the whole concept of covered windows, with their mysterious apparatus of gliding tracks, boxy valances, and nylon sheers. A proscenium arch for the theatre of family. My mother had once reupholstered our living-room couch, an unfathomable skill. So a van with burlap curtains spoke to me.

A couple hostel kids, Scooter and Naomi, came along for the

DON'T I KNOW YOU? • 63

ride to Istanbul and to share the driving. Scooter had worked as a roadie for Three Dog Night, and Naomi was studying Sufi dancing. They were on their way to the beaches of Goa for the winter. I was a little nervous about Naomi because she was pretty and dark-haired, but she was too flower-child for Nick's taste. Scooter was a weedy, bearded, affable guy who was used to long rides in cramped spaces. I was grateful for their company because things hadn't settled down between Nick and me. He was writing less in his journal because I had asked him to please not leave it in my path. I suppose my snooping had contaminated it. But he was thinking what he didn't write.

Nick and I planned to go as far as Istanbul, then make our way to England to deliver the van in time to make our flight back to Toronto. But secretly, I had decided that I might keep heading east if things weren't right between us. I would go to India too—go all the way, for once. My habit was to turn back, always. I had turned back in Morocco. Had bailed on Portugal. I said no too often, out of fear and caution. This time maybe I would buy a seat on one of those psychedelic buses with no shocks and just keep going. Rip up my ticket home.

Then Nick would be sorry. Then he'd really feel it.

Nick seemed exactly the same as he had been before we came to Matala, just friskier, like a dog who'd had a good run off the leash. After a few days, the rhythm of traveling enclosed us and carried us forward. We never spoke of Matala. But in the pictures he took of me with our Kodak Brownie, on some beach or beside a fountain, I had a wary and ironic shadow in my eye, a new look.

After Athens, the plan was to drive through the day and night to Istanbul, with Scooter and Nick taking turns at the wheel. I didn't have my license. So we hurtled through Thessaloniki, with a stop for lunch in a café that played deafening

Greek music, sinuous and sobbing. We still weren't used to urban clamor after the weeks on Crete.

As night fell, Nick was at the wheel. We were moving through rural Turkey, where the main highway was a two-lane unlit road. No gas stations, no 7-Elevens. Very few cars. The four of us were quiet, lulled into a road trance as the dotted lines on the asphalt flowed into the cones of our headlights and then were swallowed up by the blackness behind us.

Green runaway pigs. That was my first thought. Low, round green creatures were scurrying across the road, and we were about to mow them down. Nick swerved the van onto the shoulder, where our headlights caught a mud-coated truck on its side in the ditch, its big rear wheels still spinning. Then we saw a figure lying crumpled on the road. Had we hit him? The green pigs, we realized, were cylindrical tanks, probably full of propane, that had fallen off the truck when it had either driven off the road or been hit by someone else who had sped away. Someone ahead of us on the road.

The man on the pavement was making low, grim sounds. I knelt down and felt his neck; he was alive.

"Hello! Hello, excuse me? You've been hurt but we're going to help you," I said, like a lifeguard ordering kids out of the pool. "We're going to take you to a hospital." That seemed unlikely. We had no idea where we were. The man's eyes were open, beseeching, but he did not respond.

"*Om mani padme om,*" Naomi chanted, unhelpfully.

Insects whirled in the path of our headlights. The absolute country silence was alarming, except for a ticking sound as the truck wheels revolved. Nick reached into the cab, turned the ignition off, and poked around looking for identification. Naomi got the bedspread out of the van and tucked it around the driver while Scooter carefully, carefully rolled the runaway

green tanks of propane off the road. Our man wasn't bleeding, which seemed more ominous. I consulted a tiny pastel map
of all of Europe, and saw that Istanbul could still be hours
away.

This is what you get when you drive a car, I thought angrily.
Even someone else's. Next thing you know, you're cleaning up
after things like this. A car means consequences; you become
part of the whole mess.

Then the Turkish man turned his head and I saw there was
a ragged gash on his forehead, and his black hair was matted
with blood. His eyes were open now but unfocussed. Gingerly
I tested his limbs. They seemed to work.

"We shouldn't move his neck," said Scooter. "It can, like,
screw up his spine forever." Nick was still searching through
the glove compartment of the truck, looking for the man's papers. For the comfort of print.

"Nobody's going to turn up with a gurney," I said with
newfound authority. Naomi was doing some sort of deep-
breathing exercise to center herself. "We either leave him here,
or move him into the van." Using the blanket as a sling, the four
of us bundled him into the back of the van, where he moaned
on the foam bed and I guiltily found myself worrying about
bloodstains on the sheets. His skin was ashen.

"Don't worry," I said, "we're going to find a doctor. You'll
be okay." He closed his eyes, but I could see his coat collar jerk-
ily lift and fall, like a shivering mouse.

"Use one of my T-shirts to wrap his head," I told Naomi.
"They're on the back shelf."

Dodging the green tanks on the shoulder, we set off in fearful silence. Nick drove, trying to be as gentle as possible when
he changed gears. Scooter was using his thumb in an attempt
to measure kilometers on our map.

"We never buy decent maps," I said to Nick in a tone of despair. This was a touchy subject between us, how much money to invest in maps. I wanted individual ones for each country; what was the point of a map where France was the size of a Chiclet?

"There's one road to Istanbul, and we're on it," said Nick. His knuckles on the steering wheel were white. "You should be looking for road signs instead." I stared into the lonely cone of yellow from our headlights, straining to glimpse a light, any signs of a city, as we listened to the groans of our friend, who lay with his head wrapped in my good blue Biba T-shirt.

And if he died on the way? Would anyone believe that we hadn't hit him? He didn't smell of alcohol, and there was no evidence that he had skidded off the road. So someone did run into him, and then drove away. What would the police make of us? This was the same year that a young American, Billy Hayes, got caught trying to smuggle hash out of Turkey, and went to prison for the next five years—a horrendous experience he later described in the book that Oliver Stone then turned into *Midnight Express*, a lurid movie full of unpleasant stereotypes about the Turkish people.

We had already heard rumors that the Istanbul police were brutally cracking down on hippies. We didn't want to mess with them. They would search the van, and Naomi had smoked a joint on the way; there would be seeds, papers, evidence.

Anyway we weren't supposed to have to deal with these sorts of problems—we were just doing our thing, in various foreign countries, peaceably. Neither birth nor death was supposed to be on the agenda. I'm on the pill, for God's sake, I found myself thinking, irrationally.

We came to the outskirts of Istanbul. Highway signs appeared, one with a stick figure prone on a bed. We followed the signs through gray sleeping streets to a hospital that in no way resembled the overlit institutions of home. This cur-yellow, two-story building could have been the back door to a food-processing plant. Our man was still alive, and marginally less pale. When we tried to carry him, he swayed to his feet instead, shivering. We helped him through the doors into Emergency, where the nurses accepted him nonchalantly, like a pizza delivery.

I felt an odd lurch of the heart leaving him there. In a way, it was the most intimate encounter with a local we had had for months. The look in his eyes when I had held him on the road.

By then it was three or four a.m. We groped our way through the entrails of Istanbul until we found ourselves in an empty parking lot beside a white building with a domed roof—a planetarium? It seemed like a safe place. We tucked the van up against one wall of the building, punched the lock buttons, and settled in to sleep.

Naomi and Scooter sprawled over the bare foam mattress, having left the blanket and sheets behind with our friend. In the front seat, unwilling to curl up together, Nick and I tipped our heads back and fell into exhausted sleep.

A voice, high, nasal, and very loud, was keening in my ears. Now someone else is hurt and calling to us, I thought. Why are there so many injured Turkish people everywhere? Then I woke up: It was dawn, and the muezzins were broadcasting from the top of the slim minarets directly above us. We had accidentally pitched camp at the base of the Blue Mosque. As Naomi and Scooter rolled down their windows a guard spotted us and headed our way, hand on his nightstick.

"Turn the key," I said to Nick. "Go, go!"

We wheeled out of the lot into the first stirrings of dawn in the city, and a teeming market. There were plenty of freaks in the crowd, hippie girls peeling oranges and thin-chested guys in drawstring pants. We pulled over to one and asked him where to find a place to stay.

"Go to the Pudding Shop, on Divan Yolu, two streets over, and ask anybody there," he said. "Want an orange?" said the girl, whose eyes were rimmed in kohl. We took it.

The Pudding Shop was Istanbul's Carnaby Street, the place everyone went as soon as they hit town, for silty Turkish coffee, rice pudding, yogurt, and news of where to head next. By the door was a message board advertising bus rides to India for $35. I wrote down the days and times. Travelers heading west after a winter in India hung out at the Pudding Shop too, bringing back a whiff of the real thing—the Eastern vibe, their eyes clear and shining with it. They weren't going back to grad school, or fighting in Vietnam. They weren't getting a law degree or planning a wedding. They lived in palm huts on the beach at Goa or begged and meditated. Or they set up three-stool roadside cafés, where they served crepes and fresh coconuts for a couple hours a day and then closed shop. They seemed in no hurry, and always knew where to buy the most resinous hash or the best hand-knotted carpets without getting ripped off. They knew which beaches you could camp on and where the police were hassling people. Some were just long-haired hustlers in djellabas, but a few were evidently in possession of bliss. At least, they had the charisma of having achieved a degree of ease in the world. I was so far from that.

In Istanbul I felt myself in the suburbs again, on the outskirts of a new consciousness. This was where the new world and its strivings bumped up against the indifferent East. It was one thing for us to believe that we could easily shed the conventions of the West, coming from Canada, where the mortar was barely dry in the walls. It was another thing to wander through the Grand Bazaar of Istanbul, imagining that we could change anything about a world this rooted and strong and deep. The hippies looked slightly silly here, like bugs or monkeys, creatures out of their proper habitat. The "revolution" made more sense in the countryside than in cities, built on history, catacombs of human memory.

But in 1970 the young mistrusted history. We wanted to shed our human past in order to be lighter and more transparent—more like the pop icons of the time: butterflies, rainbows, and daisies. We wanted to become innocent, weightless citizens of nature.

Istanbul made me homesick for history—a history I didn't even have. It would have been easy to keep going back in time, to sign myself up for a magic bus. But I caught a complicated, seductive scent of what lay east of Istanbul, and wasn't sure I was up to it. And this time Nick wanted to turn back too.

Scooter and Naomi stayed in Istanbul while Nick and I drove alone across Europe, bypassing Paris without comment, picking up hitchhikers sometimes, to London, where we delivered the van to the owner's brother. He did check under the seats for drugs. We spent a few days in London, doing normal things together, even scoring rush seats to see a production of *Hair*. But when we collected our mail at the American Express counter, I saw that Sally had written Nick a postcard. He pocketed it to read later.

There was also a letter from my friend Jane saying that she'd just found a big apartment on Queen Street with a third bedroom. Were Nick and I looking for a place to rent when we got back? *No,* I replied, with one line on a postcard of the Tower of London and its guillotines: *Nick and I have broken up*. I gave the card to him to mail.

The next day we parted on a London street, almost casually. I made my way to the airport alone and flew home to Toronto. The moment I pushed through the subway turnstiles on the way to see my parents, my heart began to race and a feeling of panic overtook me. When I got home, my older brother greeted me at the door in his slippers; our parents had just left on a trip to the Corning Museum of Glass in upstate New York, and he was taking care of the dogs. His marriage was on the skids too, he said, almost cheerfully. Then he gave me an Ativan, my first.

I had never had a broken heart and for a long time I couldn't recognize what was wrong with me, or why home didn't feel the same, would never feel the same. I kept seeing the green runaway pigs, the propane tanks as they rolled across the highway to Istanbul—that moment just before you grasp what is about to happen to you. I went to doctors and made them listen to my heart. They gave me ECGs. Nothing turned up.

That was the year I started doing book reviews for a local newspaper—eight paperbacks a week culled from the picked-over jumble on the editor's desk. I lugged them home in a cardboard box, and found I had opinions on everything—the I Ching, concrete poetry, pop-up books, erotica, a new edition of the Rand-McNally atlas. I filled my days with reading, and the sight of my words in print reminded me that I had a voice after all.

By spring I wasn't over Nick, but something had shifted: The world was a book I still wanted to open.

The Rehearsal

The slightly round-shouldered boy onstage could be a drifter panhandling at a stoplight, except for the expensive guitar strapped around his neck. As he tunes it he looks down, and his long hair swings right across his face. Then he walks to the lip of the stage, shading his eyes. It's late on a February afternoon in Toronto, 1971, and Massey Hall is empty but he's looking for someone out in the darkened auditorium.

Sitting near the back is a middle-aged man with a square, handsome face. He's wearing black zip-up galoshes and hasn't taken off his overcoat or plaid scarf. Now and then he cranes his neck back toward the lobby doors. He has a strange feeling that his ex-wife, Rassy, might show up for the sound check too. He half hopes she will. It's been years since they've spoken in person.

Neil spots his father and waves.

"Dad, could you hear that okay?"

"Oh yeah."

"The guitar sounded too loud to me."

"Isn't it supposed to be too loud?"

He laughs. A voice comes over the PA.

"Neil, try backing off the mike a little."

"Man, this hall is so live," he says in the direction of the voice. "I sound like Meat Loaf or something."

"Do you want to try it standing up instead?"

Neil gives the voice a lopsided, glinty smile. "Standing up?"

"Oh right. Sorry."

When Neil turns around, Scott can see the outline of the back brace he has worn since the operation, except for when he performs. He's being more cautious now, trying to let his body heal properly. There are physical things he wants to be able to do around the ranch.

Another voice comes over the PA. "Like the rug?"

Neil looks down and for the first time notices the rose and blue Turkish carpet. "Oh yeah. Nice."

"And if you start keeping time in those boots, it'll help muffle the sound."

"Cool. Thanks, Ed."

No one sees the doors at the back of the hall open, as a young blond woman in glasses slips into the last row. She takes out a notebook and a pen.

His father watches Neil gingerly lower himself onto the wooden chair, tune his guitar, and begin to sing.

Sailing heart-ships through broken harbors
Out on the waves in the night . . .

This was the reason Scott had set the alarm for five a.m., to get his daily column out of the way early so that he could sit here alone in the dark and listen to his son. Neil's voice, sweet and sharp at the same time, carried so much feeling even when the words stayed mysterious. It had taken him a few years to figure out that song lyrics don't work like paragraphs in a story. They mostly trace feelings, in the way that a map records the names of towns and cities. But now he thinks his son is a good writer, very good in fact. Maybe he'd learned a thing or two from his dad, sitting for hours at the old Remington, typing on the yellow three-carbon sheets of copy paper the newspapers used back then.

Five columns a week. When you have to write a column every day, you get economical. And you can't half care about the words; they're either on the money or not. But what is clarity, in a song? Sometimes he doesn't know what the hell the lines mean in some of Neil's songs. *When you're old enough to repay, but young enough to sell?* It doesn't seem to matter, the phrases still turn a key inside you and the feelings come. Like Blake's poems, childlike and deep. Although he's not sure Neil read much poetry when he was growing up. All the books were in his office, off-limits whenever Scott was working. Which was most of the time.

The opportunity to give his son *Songs of Innocence and Experience* had come and gone long ago.

As for the hair, his hobo hair, Scott had taken a pass on that early on, and so had Astrid. She was always careful not to act like his mother. She never criticized Neil. The split from the boy's mother had been bad, but Astrid and Neil got along pretty well now.

Anyway, his hair had always been goofy, even as a kid. Better hanging in his face like this than the damn pageboy he wore back in Winnipeg when he was in that school band. The Rogues. No, the Squires. For some reason he remembers a word, the first one Neil latched on to as a baby: "dombeen." It meant pudding, celery, porridge, and sometimes cats. An all-purpose word. He could write a song called "Dombeen."

A few rows behind him, the woman in glasses writes in her notebook. She has moved closer to the stage but sits a tactful distance from Scott.

Now the lighting guy is trying out different filters, from warm to cool. They're going to film tonight's concerts and the director, whose horn-rim glasses are duct-taped on one arm, prowls around the wings looking worried. Nobody can see Neil's face on camera, he says. How can they get him to put his hair behind his ears?

Neil sits patiently on the edge of the stage, knocking the spit out of his harmonica. He was never a complainer, Scott remembers. Even when he had polio as a boy and was in terrible pain at times, he didn't make a fuss or cry, he just got quieter. After the first bad day in the hospital, all he said was "Dad, this is the worst cold I've ever had." Scott had been the same himself as a boy, when he came down with the Spanish flu the year so many people died of it.

Generally speaking, the Youngs were good at not crying. That was reserved for stories, or songs.

Neil stands, hitching up his jeans. He's too skinny, Scott thinks. And he looks like he's already shouldering a lot for a twenty-five-year-old kid. True, he and Rassy had gotten married around the same age, but that was back when people magically became adults overnight. They turned twenty-one, found jobs, bought houses, had children, wore ties. Things are different now. The young stay younger longer. So do the older ones, or at least they try to. He's been guilty of that himself.

He walks out into the lobby to see if it's still snowing outside. The two Astrids, his wife and Neil's sister, will come later to catch the first show. Neil tactfully made sure that Rassy's ticket was for the second show. Scott still wishes they could all go somewhere afterward as a family again. Maybe to Ciccone's, their old spot, on King Street West.

He steps outside to a cold, clear sky. After coming down thick and cottony all day, the snow is starting to let up. He smokes half a cigarette, his eleventh of the day, and goes back to his seat. Someone else is sitting in the darkened auditorium, he notices, a blonde with a notebook. Probably a reporter. He moves to the other aisle.

Up on the stage, a tiny woman in white jeans and cowboy boots has appeared out of the wings holding a milkshake container.

"It's called a smoothie," she says, handing it to Neil. "But with yogurt. I hope you like yogurt." In Toronto, in 1971, yogurt was still an exotic import from unknown Slavic countries.

"Hey, I'm livin' on a ranch now," he says to the jeans girl. "Cows are my people."

"It has papaya too. It's supposed to give you enzymes or something."

"Thanks, tastes good."

He watches his son lazily flirt and wonders how things are going with the new one, the actress. But a movie actress with her own ambitions, trying to settle down with a musician away on tour, somebody whose father didn't exactly stick around—that's not going to be easy. Even if Neil has turned out to be more of a homebody than Scott ever was. Not many twenty-five-year-olds want to buy land, or can, for that matter. Three hundred and forty thousand dollars he paid for the ranch, in cash. But it was a smart move, Scott thinks, not to get too caught up in L.A. Although you can smoke a lot of pot out in the country too.

Land. The best thing he ever did when he came back from the navy, Scott thinks, was to buy those acres up around

Omemee, through the vet land deal. Neil was eight or nine, and he spent the summer days fishing off the Mill Street Bridge. Then there was the one long season at Lake of Bays, when all their friends visited. Laughter and drinks late into the night on the porch. That's what he thinks about whenever he hears Neil sing "Helpless"—those summers up north with everyone there.

That was before the newspaper column, when all he wrote was fiction. It felt good being able to raise two boys just by writing short stories and sending them off to magazines. Getting rejections along with checks in the mail from the *Weekend* or the *Saturday Evening Post*. Some for $3,000—a lot of money back then. Surely Neil has some good memories from those days in Omemee, before his dad disappeared.

He doesn't regret leaving so much as the fact that he didn't talk about it to the boys. He should have said, "Remember, you can come live with me whenever you like." He assumed they knew that. Anyway, frank talk wasn't the custom then. Now he knows that when a father leaves a son at the age of thirteen, everyone can seem to carry on fine, but it changes things pretty deeply. It meant, for one thing, that over the years they got in the habit of being out of touch, and so they have to work around that. Not that Neil seems to hold it against him. It's never come up in conversation, at least.

Onstage, Neil is singing "Cowgirl in the Sand," his voice cutting through the words with an almost bitter sound.

> *Old enough now to change your name*
> *When so many love you is it the same . . .*

When Astrid gets here, he will definitely suggest they all get together afterward, at Ciccone's. To catch up. A lot has happened since Neil left town five years ago, in that goddamned

Pontiac hearse—the cops had to call him in the middle of the night when they found it abandoned in L.A., with parking tickets due. Scott was sure that going to California was a foolish move and that Neil would be home before winter. But two weeks after he arrived Neil had somehow found himself a band and paying gigs. The next thing he knows, the first CSNY album is out and sells a million copies. Then his son—his skinny, chaotic, floppy-haired son—is playing Carnegie Hall with people like Jack Nicholson paying a lot of money to hear him perform.

That was when it hit him. He was standing on the street in front of a Carnegie Hall poster with a red Sold Out banner across it, and the words "Tonight. Neil Young—Folk Singer" at the top. Scalpers were selling tickets for $100 (you couldn't buy an obstructed seat for that now). As the tears came he stared at the poster and wondered how life had brought the two of them to this point. Later, sitting in the audience four rows from the stage, he felt too self-conscious to cry.

After the show, backstage, he stood apart from the people swarming Neil. Jack Nicholson came over to him. He had long muttonchop sideburns. "Your boy is very special, I hope you recognize that. You should be celebrating!" he said, clapping him on the back.

Scott did recognize it. He just didn't show it. That's why now, in the rehearsal, the sound of Neil's voice wraps around his heart like a lasso.

The snow has stopped well before the first concert, and Massey Hall is full of almost too-reverent fans. They applaud the smallest moment, including a request from Neil onstage not to take photographs when he's singing.

"It kinda distracts me from what I'm trying to do here," he drawls. "When the song is over and something's happening, like, people are applauding, then you can take your pictures, okay?" They laugh and applaud again. He's wearing yellow work boots and a plaid shirt that hides his back brace.

Scott sits near the front with the Astrids on either side. Maybe it's the hometown effect or the acoustics of Massey Hall, but Neil's voice sounds especially strong, and he attacks each number with a somber force. He seems to be singing to them from far inside the songs. Most are unfamiliar.

"I've written so many new ones on this tour, I don't know what to do with them, except sing 'em."

It's funny how so many musicians adopt that country inflection, Scott thinks. Nobody from Omemee really talks like that. Bob Dylan, Neil, both sounding like sheep farmers when they're actually downtown kids.

Scott is shocked to see his quiet, comical, thin son pouring out so much grown-up passion. Then Neil starts talking about a song he's just written about the old foreman who manages his ranch. "That's right, I live on a ranch now," he murmurs apologetically, "and this guy kind of came with it. Louis Avila is his name." He starts to sing the song, his voice soaring like a big bird floating on thermals.

Old Man, look at my life, I'm a lot like you . . .

Astrid looks sideways at her husband and smiles. Scott knows he's singing about someone else, but it feels partly about him too. Not that he's so old! Anyway, he knows that's how a good song works; each listener feels the words are a private message, aimed directly at him.

He wonders if the people around them are thinking that

it's a song about his father and he feels a storm of things inside—pride, embarrassment, relief. His son does love him after all. Breaking up the family wasn't done much back in the 1950s. It was unusual. And he could have managed it better.

Then the concert ends and he's on his feet with the rest of the audience. Something in his chest that has been tight for a long time unfurls.

The three of them go backstage.

"Good show," says Scott to his son, immediately regretting the silly, British-sounding phrase. He puts his hand on Neil's skinny arm.

"Thanks, Dad," says Neil. "It felt good. Hope it wasn't too loud for you."

Then people begin to swarm around Neil, and they say goodbye. The tiny woman in the white jeans is there, flushed with excitement. Out in the lobby the audience for the second show has begun to arrive. Scott lingers, in case his ex-wife turns up. In the crowd he recognizes the blond woman who was taking notes at the rehearsal. A journalist just out of college; now he remembers talking to her about his hockey book. Before Neil was famous. She sees him, smiles, and starts heading his way. What the hell is her name?

"Mr. Young," she says, holding out her hand. "It's Rose. Rose McEwan. We did an interview last year."

"Yes, I remember. How are you?" He keeps an eye on the people streaming in. He doesn't want to miss Rassy.

"You must be so proud of your son tonight," Rose says, not letting go of his hand. "Wasn't he fantastic?"

"Yes, yes he was. Very impressive indeed." Why did he end up sounding like a naval officer in these situations? "Are you writing something for the *Star*?"

"No, for *Rolling Stone*, actually. Just a little sidebar on 'the hometown concert.'"

"But it's *Rolling Stone*, good for you." She was quite pretty, he thought, despite the big glasses and the cowboy shirt.

"I did something for them on Ronnie Hawkins and the Band."

"Rompin' Ronnie? No lack of material there."

"A little too much, actually." They laugh.

"Do you have time for a drink or something?" She touches his sleeve. "I'd like to talk to you about tonight."

"Yes, well, I'm with some people . . ." Just then his wife comes up and slips her arm in his. He introduces them. Astrid gives Rose a cool smile, one she is practiced at. Scott is handsome, with a fine head of hair, and women like him.

"It was very nice to meet you, Rose," she says as Neil's sister catches up and the three of them head for the door.

Rose stands alone in the lobby. She feels a little bruise of rejection, then dismisses it as unprofessional. Tomorrow, she'll call him at the *Globe*, set up something. She has the feeling there's a lot he wants to say about his son, that no one ever asks him.

Scott leaves without ever catching sight of Rassy, and they hurry through the cold night air to the parking lot, where he scrapes the ice off the windshield of their car.

"We can stop somewhere for a drink if you like," his wife says on the way home, with a hand on his knee. Some sort of celebration seems in order.

"No, we should probably head home while the weather's clear." He looks over at her, grateful for her company and the gleam of her dark hair—the way she dressed up for the occasion and now is perfectly happy to call it a night. The way she handled that Rose woman. Sidebars in *Rolling Stone*? When was the last time he saw a girl's byline in that magazine?

He should write something about tonight, though. He feels like rushing to his typewriter the minute they get through the door. Instead they drop off Neil's sister and head home, where they pour a nightcap. They sit on the couch side by side to watch the news.

Later in bed, he keeps hearing Neil's voice, twisting and bright like a small flame inside him. For years he's carried a heavy feeling of having failed his son. It's lifted now.

Astrid stirs beside him.

"Neil was wonderful tonight, wasn't he?" Her low, unwounded voice.

"Yes, he was."

Her arms go around him, her breath is warm on his neck. Down in the city the second show would be over and people would be leaving Massey Hall, fanning out into the snowy night, satisfied. Neil might be backstage with Rassy right now. Or heading down to Ciccone's for something to eat.

Early tomorrow, before the column, he would type a few notes about this miracle of an evening. The night his son came home.

The Bill Murray Effect

The year I turned thirty, I spent the summer working in a Kingston, Ontario, restaurant where my friend Zalman was the chef. His wife, Rose—another Rose, obviously—made the desserts, including a legendary Spanish flan. I was the "salad girl," washing greens in the deep zinc sink, and sometimes I worked out front too, taking cash or making the fancy coffees (the words "latte" and "barista" were not yet part of the language). Zal and Rose were dear longtime friends who were hoping that Roberto and I would stay together.

But the breakup was already in motion, like a car rolling back down a hill in neutral. You didn't want to get in the way of it.

They had invited us to rent the small apartment at the back of their farm for July and August, with the idea that this sojourn in the country might salvage our relationship. A plan that was not working out so far. I had an assignment from *Outside* magazine that was overdue, and the writing had stalled.

It was hard for Roberto, a news photographer from Colombia, to find much work in the small city of Kingston. The mood at home was sullen, and my response was to book extra shifts in order to stay out of the apartment. Communication was not our strong point.

During lunch shift one August day, one of the waitresses came into the kitchen with a bottle of white wine. "This is for you," Sherry said with a slight eye-roll, "from the boys by the window."

The hungover guys. They had ordered two double espressos from me when I was out front earlier. I went back into the dining room to thank them, and this time I recognized one as Dan Aykroyd, of early *Saturday Night Live* fame. The fish in a blender guy. I knew his family had a cottage on a lake north of Kingston. But I didn't recognize his friend, who looked strikingly ordinary. It turned out to be Bill Murray. He had just finished his first season on the show and wasn't famous yet. This was pre-*Ghostbusters* too. He was just a guy with nice brown eyes and a roundish nose, hanging out with his TV buddy.

I thanked them for the wine. The three of us kibitzed back and forth, and then Bill Murray asked for my phone number. Oh, that would not be appropriate, I said with a flirtatious smile, swatting him. I didn't bother to explain that I was living with someone, my waning boyfriend. Then I went back to the kitchen and my sink full of lettuce. At this point, I believe I made a decision, although I wasn't ready to admit it at the time. The fog of denial, when you are avoiding a breakup, can cover many sins. I dried my hands, wrote my name and number on a piece of paper, folded it inside a fresh hamburger bun, and put it in my apron pocket. As if I had no plans for it.

When I finished with the lettuce, Zal asked me to take over

at the cash, which I did, just as Bill Murray and Dan Aykroyd came over to pay their bill.

"If you don't have a phone, that's a whole other matter," said Bill Murray.

Which is when I took the hamburger bun out of my apron and tucked it into his shirt pocket. He acted like this was normal behavior for a cashier in a restaurant and I thought we were just playing out our little scene. It was fun to flirt with someone so nimble, really fun, but by the time I left work later on I had forgotten all about the exchange.

I took the bottle of wine home for another silent knife-clicking dinner with Roberto.

"Any luck today?" I asked. He had pitched a photo essay to the *Whig* about the women in solitary confinement at the infamous Kingston Prison for Women.

"No," he said, and did not elaborate.

The next morning the phone rang.

"It's Bill. Want to catch a ball game tomorrow night?"

Bluff called. I dithered and said I had to work. I also explained that I was currently, technically, involved with someone.

"Fine. No problem. So just meet us for drinks," said Bill Murray.

Well, why not, I thought. I'm an individual. People meet other people for drinks all the time.

"Tell me when you get off work and we'll pick you up outside the restaurant," Bill Murray said.

The next day I told Roberto that I'd be working late, and put some eyeliner in my purse.

That summer I commuted everywhere by bicycle, including the twenty-kilometer ride from the farm to the town and back. I had long blond hair, wore Gloria Steinem aviator glasses, and had just come back from a five-month cycling expedition in

South America with Roberto, so I was thinner than usual and in good shape. But South America had done us in—it was just too hard, too isolating, a ridiculous undertaking. We had made it up and down the Andes in Ecuador, but we couldn't make it through dinner in a restaurant. The only problem with breaking up was that the trip, both the hardship and the beautiful strangeness of it, had fused us. Five months in a tent is a micromarriage.

Roberto was a decent, kind man—a keeper, really. Although I had run away from him at first, now I was utterly confounded by our falling apart. I had decided that it showed a deficiency in me, an inability to love someone who really cared for me, and was deserving of my love.

So I was waiting for something to happen when Bill Murray turned up, live from New York.

The next day, after my shift, I stood with my bike at the corner of Princess and George feeling silly and mildly felonious. A vintage roadster pulled up beside me. It was an eye-catching cream-colored convertible, some rare model I couldn't identify. Aykroyd was at the wheel with his TV pal beside him.

"Hop in," said Bill Murray. He had a faint constellation of acne pits on his cheeks and lots of wayward brown hair.

"I thought we were going for drinks," I said.

"We are," he said. "Hop in."

"What about my bike?"

"Not a problem," said Aykroyd, who was quite tall, with a sturdy farm-boy build. He stepped out and slung the bike into the back of the car. I got in beside it and they began to drive out of town.

"I thought we were going for a drink," I said again after a while.

"We are," Bill said. "A country drink." We were now moving

through the outskirts of Kingston, where all the boarding kennels, storage places, and car dealerships were.

"I can't be too long," I said nervously.

"Don't worry, it's not far."

We drove north into stony, rolling farmland. Late-afternoon
light slanting over cornfields. Perhaps I'm being kidnapped, I
thought placidly. It seemed uncool to ask. It was also, I noticed,
a fine day in late August, with goldenrod nodding in the ditches.
It felt good to be out of the kitchen and the omelet-y smell of
the restaurant. This is an adventure, I told myself, just go with
it. Lighten up and live a little. (Years later, this sentiment would
be recognized by others who have been similarly hijacked as
the Bill Murray Effect.)

A half an hour later we turned onto a gravel road that took
us to a cottage—a white frame house with a sun porch, and a
separate smaller bunkhouse. Nothing fancy, just a typical Ontario family cottage on a lawn that slanted down to a broad,
shallow-looking lake. Close to shore, reeds poked through the
surface of the water like a five o'clock shadow.

"I'll start dinner," said Aykroyd, heading over to a charcoal
barbecue. "Make yourself at home."

"But I'm expected home for dinner," I said.

"We'll get you back, no problem," said Aykroyd, scraping
black gunk off the grill. "Why don't you guys go for a dip while
I put the chicken on."

Bill Murray changed into swimming trunks—roomy ones,
probably borrowed. I didn't have my bathing suit with me, but
I was wearing a Danskin body stocking, dark-green, under my
summer dress, and I figured I could swim in that. I also had on
a pair of candy-cane-striped red-and-white platform sandals;
it was the first generation of platform sandals (unless you
count ancient geisha-girl, bound-feet versions). I wouldn't nor-

mally wear heels with a bathing suit, but in this case I had no choice.

We walked down to the lake, waded in, and paddled around, orbiting each other and talking. The lake was a little weedy but the water felt cool and welcome after the drive. I like being in the water and I'm a good swimmer; I did a dolphin dive to impress Bill Murray. There's a kind of amusing shark-fin thing I can do with my elbow too. Being in a lake felt less datelike, and safe. I told him about a synchronized-swim group I was part of at summer camp, where we performed to a loud, scratchy recording of the thunderous piano theme to *Exodus*: *Duh DUH . . . duh DUH, duh DUH duh duh . . . duh-duh*. Very dramatic. So the two of us lay on our backs in the water, and sculled our toes together as we sang the theme to *Exodus*. Then we paddled back to the shore and sat in the early evening sun, drying out.

I told him that I wasn't really a salad girl in a restaurant. I was "sort of a writer." Which was true—especially the "sort of" part. I wrote weekly book reviews for the *Toronto Star*, and was working on an article about our South American adventure. I'd published a couple things in *Rolling Stone* too, but that little window had come and gone. Not too many women wrote for them.

Bill Murray talked about his first year on *Saturday Night Live*, and living in New York City. "There's a certain amount of pressure involved," he said mildly, like someone who had very little prior experience with pressure. Also, this was 1975, when the streets of New York were more dangerous, and the subways were like something out of Hieronymus Bosch: hellish, hot, and noisy.

"It's a lot to take on in one year."

I found it easy to talk to this not-quite-handsome stranger

with the round nose and the slightly pitted skin. He didn't make jokes, at all; he was sincere and straightforward. He could have been the secretly sharp guy who pumps gas at the local summer marina. He didn't go on about himself or the show—he was more curious about what I was up to. He had the knack of tuning in to other people quickly, getting past the small talk to go deeper, but in a lighthearted way. There was a zone of intimacy he was skilled at creating without making you nervous.

Meanwhile, I could smell the chicken on the barbecue. Aykroyd was playing some R&B on a boom box.

I had the impression that I wasn't the first roadhouse girl that these boys had scooped up, but I didn't care. Nobody was putting the moves on me, and I was surprised by how genuine Bill Murray was. There was a formal kindness about him. Plus, I had only seen him on TV a few times, not enough to be starstruck or tongue-tied. He was no star, yet. Just as I was no writer. We were still in the lobby of our lives.

Pretty soon I found myself talking more seriously, about books, writing, and what I really wanted to do. His listening silence and his questions were encouraging.

But then, as usual, I got nervous—nervous about what would come next, nervous about how good it felt to be talking like this, nervous about lying to my blameless boyfriend. I talked to him about Roberto.

"So give the guy a call," Bill Murray said, "tell him the truth. Tell him you got kidnapped but you're okay, and you'll be home soon."

We had moved to the kitchen of the bunkhouse now, ready to eat dinner (three oversized chicken drumsticks coated in blistered red BBQ sauce). Aykroyd pushed the big black rotary phone over to me.

"I'll turn down the music," he said.

"Hi," I said when Roberto finally answered, frosty-voiced. "Sorry to be late. I'm just having drinks with Dan Aykroyd, you know, the guy on *Saturday Night Live*, and his friend. They came into the restaurant the other day, remember I told you?"

There. The damage was done. "I've already eaten," Roberto said, then he paused, and hung up.

Aykroyd served potato salad out of a cardboard container, and the three of us ate inside because the mosquitos were starting. John Lee Hooker played on the boom box. They were easy, taciturn buddies, a couple of guys who could be out there rocking on the porch, enjoying twilight.

"This is all delicious, thank you," I said primly as I picked at the deli salad. Roberto's cold, angry voice had stayed with me, and I couldn't eat much. Aykroyd poured a couple shots of tequila. I passed one to Bill Murray, and drank another glass of wine instead. Maybe tonight is the night Roberto and I will finally break up, I thought. Maybe I can fly to New York with my new friends and become a highly paid television writer. Stranger things have happened.

They didn't complain about skipping dessert when I said I had to get back home. "My life is complicated right now," I said as they cleaned up and put my bike back into the roadster for the drive to the farm. Clearly they had hoped for a longer, more interesting evening. But this was how the dice had rolled, and that was okay with them too. It was the zen thing; the only possible, sustainable response to fame.

The long shadows were still golden. The air had just an edge of coolness, an edge of autumn. Riding in the car with these two undemanding swains, my hair whipping around in the breeze and one wheel of my horizontal bike slowly spinning in the air, I realized that it had been too long since I'd felt this way. Hopeful.

They dropped me off on Abbey Dawn Road at the top of the long gravel driveway into the farm. Bill Murray helped me hoist my bike out of the car, and we said goodbye. He crooked his finger under my chin, tilting it up in an ironic movie moment. "You're one hell of a woman," he said in a John Wayne voice.

Really? For a second I believed him. I hope I blushed. Then I got on my bike and headed down the road toward the lights of the farm and my last night with Roberto.

Just beyond the little bridge over the creek, I passed the horse meadow, where I could see an orange dome tent pitched in the far corner. Our South America tent. Lantern light glowed through the nylon walls. I cycled past slowly, surreptitiously, hoping he couldn't hear the gravel under my wheels. It was obvious that Roberto had decided to skip the fight we were about to have and make the first move.

Good, I thought, good for him.

Bob Dylan Goes Tubing

One morning Eric and I came back from town to find a strange car parked under the white pines beside our cottage. An old Citroën, the kind where the chassis goes up and down hydraulically. Yellow. Nobody we knew drove a Citroën.

Eric's son, Ryan, ran down the long switchback of wooden steps that led to the water. "There's somebody out on the lake," he called up, "on the air mattress."

We shaded our eyes. A pale, small, but visibly adult figure was lying on the mattress, slowly paddling with his hands toward the diving raft.

"I need the binocs," Eric said, and went in to get them. Standing on the deck he studied the figure.

"This is really weird, but whoever that is looks exactly like Bob Dylan." He passed the binoculars to me. He was right. A pale little guy with a pencil mustache, in a Tilley hat, was on our air mattress.

"See? Dylan, only older."

"Well, he is older."

The figure paddled closer. Eric waved and called out. "Hi there! We're back."

I waved too. It could, remotely, be some friend of a friend, dropping by on his way up to another cottage. Our place, a rental, had no landline. So sometimes people just turned up.

"Yeah, I'm back too," the Dylan person called. Then he started singing in a slightly hokey *Nashville Skyline* voice, "Back here on Kashagawigamog."

That was in fact the name of a northern Ontario lake, but not ours. Ours was Sturgeon.

"What do we do now?" Eric said.

"Invite him up, I guess. Offer him a drink. Although, it's early."

Eric cupped his hands. "Come on up and join us if you're heading in."

"Sure thing," the floater said, having reached the raft. I got a towel from the pump shed and took it down to the dock. Bob Dylan—no question, it was him—slung the mattress up on the raft and did a credible breaststroke over to our dock, keeping the brim of his hat dry. He held on to the edge with thin white fingers.

"No ladder?" The nails on the baby finger of each hand were extra long, and filed square.

"Let me give you a hand."

I leaned over, careful to keep my scoop-neck shirt from gaping, and Dylan grabbed hold of me like a big ropy eight-year-old. He was pale as a grub with a dot of chin hair and a riverboat-gambler mustache. But his blue eyes were still strong and clear. They met mine, took me in. He whisked the water off his arms with his hands as he stood up.

"Water's real nice, once you get in."

Dylan was wearing a pair of old-fashioned wool swimming trunks with a narrow white belt. Wet, the suit revealed a springy crescent of cock underneath. His skin was so white it looked translucent, but he had biceps—from playing guitar, probably. His forearms had energy too, and drew your eye.

He wrapped himself in my blue towel.

"Want to see the boathouse?" said Ryan, who had run back down the stairs again. He showed Dylan Eric's old green Chestnut canoe hanging from the rafters, and the aluminum boat we use for fishing. Ryan was nine and didn't know or care who this skinny stranger was. Our seven-year-old daughter, Ceri, was staying with her grandparents in Quebec and he was getting bored on his own.

"The canoe leaks," Ryan said, "but we can go tubing. My friend Trevor has a Chris-Craft with a Merc one-twenty."

"Sounds good," Dylan said, using his finger to close one nostril as he blew out the other one to clear his sinuses. Then we all climbed the eighty-seven wooden trestle ties up to the cottage, where Eric was waiting for us with the map spread out on the kitchen table.

"Okay now Bob, you're here," he said, pointing to Sturgeon Lake, a liver-shaped body of water northeast of Huntsville, "and Kashagawigamog is quite a ways over there." Kash was closer to Bancroft, in Haliburton.

"Guess I kinda overshot it," Dylan mumbled. "Nice ride up, though."

I was staring into the fridge without registering anything.

"Can I offer you something? Orange juice? Gin and tonic? We have beer, of course. Canadian beer."

"Sure, that all sounds good."

"Or how about a nice cold Stoli with some lemonade?"

"Fifty-two gypsies went down by the wall/and none of them came back," he sang. "Give it to me in a cup/and let the Queen dance with the Jack."

After some dithering, I mixed Dylan a Red Needle—scotch and cranberry juice with lots of ice—and opened a couple Coronas for us. Ryan was back into his video game. Bob downed his drink and fingered peanuts from a dish as he studied the map, using a felt pen to circle some of the names that caught his fancy.

"Arnprior," he murmured, with a faint lift of the mustache. "Irondale. Madoc. Madawaska."

Meanwhile Eric stood in front of our CD collection sweating over what to play for Bob Dylan.

"Rose, where's that bootleg unmastered copy of 'Brown Sugar'?"

"No!" I cried, leaping over to the CD player. "Play . . . play the Robert Johnson box set, did we bring that?"

Dylan looked up from the map.

"Got any old Valdy?"

"Valdy." Eric swiveled on his heels to me with panic-stricken eyes. "Now, let me have a look."

Valdy is a West Coast Canadian folksinger who enjoyed a little plateau of fame in the 1980s, and then disappeared from view. While Eric inverted his head to read the labels on the lowest shelf, Dylan turned on the radio. CBC's book show was wrapping up.

"Good old Shelagh Rogers," said Dylan, putting chunks of cheddar on a row of crackers. "Turn 'er up."

"Really?" Eric said. "You follow Shelagh Rogers?"

"The boys on the bus listen to NPR and CBC all the time. When you're on the move it's good to have something that's always there, right? Something regular."

"Huh," Eric said. He was staring at a CD of Glenn Gould, the Goldberg Variations. Too manic for this time of day, and a little show-offy, he decided.

Ryan came in and said that Trevor and Angus were coming by to go tubing and did Bob want to go out with them? We explained tubing to Dylan—being dragged around the lake behind a powerboat while clinging to a large inflated rubber donut with handles. Like tobogganing down a hill, only over water.

"Sure, I'll give it a shot," Dylan said, wiping crumbs off his little mustache. Ryan got him a life preserver and we went down to the waterfront to watch the big Chris-Craft chug up to the dock. As they all roared off, the brim of Dylan's hat flipped straight up in the wind. He looked happy. Eric waved and turned to me.

"What do we do when Dylan gets tired of tubing?"

"Let's worry about that later." I hung the towels out on the line, lay down on our bed, and fell asleep. I wasn't used to drinking before lunch.

Dusk was coming on. We had cocktails and listened to Lucinda Williams singing "Passionate Kisses." I held off pouring myself a second one. Dylan stood at the big front window scowling at the horizon, which was a bloody red.

"Look at the sun," he said, "goin' down over the sea." He spider-walked one hand down the windowpane. "The sky is erupting now, and I must take my leave." He went into the guest bedroom. We heard him rummaging around in the dresser and then he emerged wearing an old pair of Ryan's pajamas, blue flannel with a Smurf motif. He held a toothbrush in his hand.

"Okay if I drink the water?"

"Go ahead, we just had it tested."

For several minutes he scoured his teeth over the kitchen sink, brushing and spitting methodically. Then he flossed, making the thread *pock* rhythmically. Rinsed.

"Think I'll sleep down by the lake tonight," he said, before he banged out the screen door with a striped Hudson's Bay blanket over one shoulder, and Ryan's cheap guitar in his hand.

I stood at the window. Wrapped in the blanket, Dylan settled on our yellow plastic chaise at the end of the dock. I had a good view of him through the birches, in the early lavender darkness. He took out a pack of American Spirits, lit one, broke up several more, and threw the crumbs of tobacco to the minnows that dimpled the surface of the water. Farther out on the lake, a pair of loons, long-bodied, black, and plump, left a placid W behind them. This was the time of evening when the fish fed and unseen bugs disturbed the water, as if a light rain were falling.

Then it was truly dark. Eric made a fire in the woodstove. In his room, Ryan had fallen asleep over an old *Spider-Man* comic book. I covered him and turned off his light. He had Eric's habit of sleeping with both hands shoved under the pillow.

A little later, I slipped out of bed and down the trestle stairs to give Dylan a flashlight and some bug repellant. He was still awake, playing the guitar softly.

"If you hear rustling in the woods, it's just raccoons," I told him. "They won't bother you on the dock."

"Frogs are jumpin, toads are croakin'/seems like everything is broken," he crooned in his cigarette-frayed voice.

"Good night, Bob. Sleep tight."

"Hey Ro, you too."

We watched the moonless night sky for a moment. The

stars were all out, coming at us in smithereens. Coldness radiated off the dark water. A shooting star slipped across the blackness.

And so, without a word of explanation, Bob Dylan became a guest at our cottage. Every morning he got up first—we would hear him plunge off the dock, thrash out to the raft, and then swim back again. Later on he'd often take a trip into town to buy the local Chelsea buns. And most afternoons he went tubing with Ryan and the boys.

"It's not too different from being on the road with the band," he said, "just more fun."

Sometimes we would stand on the dock with the binoculars, watching him bump over the waves behind Trevor's boat, and think, Bob Dylan is tubing on our lake. It was pretty surreal. But Canadian summers are so short that everything about them feels dreamlike. Like something separate and lovely, bound to end. We were only renting the cottage and didn't socialize too much on the lake. As usual, I was trying to get some writing done, without much success. So it was just the four of us that August—me, Ryan, Eric, and Bob Dylan. And it was good at first.

The cottage was old-fashioned, with partitions between the three small bedrooms that didn't go all the way up. With Dylan next door, Eric and I had to make love like hostages, scarcely moving. I began to develop a taste for it that way. One night, not long after his arrival, we had flipped our covers down to get at each other more quietly when we heard Dylan talking in his sleep.

"Someone's got it in for me," he said, clearly and loudly, "they're planting stories in the press."

"Just let me check on him," I said to Eric. I slipped into his room and there he was, an aging poet in Smurf pajamas, his white feet uncovered. Now he was mumbling. I put my hand on his brow and he soon settled down. I tucked him in. He looked so young asleep.

The next morning he emerged with a rumpled face, unsmiling.

"Bad night?"

"Seems like sleep's the only place I'm not alone," he muttered, topping his Chelsea bun with a half inch of cold butter.

"Did you hear the loons?"

"Yeah. Good tune. D minor."

"Your oatmeal's ready, Bob." Like me, he preferred it with a lot of maple syrup in a wide soup bowl, so it cools quickly. We sat down at the table. The day was overcast and chilly, and the lake looked too rough for tubing. Eric was in the porch playing Monopoly with Ryan, crowing about having acquired eight hotels.

"Want to play?" Ryan asked Dylan, who sat down with them. They gave him a silver candlestick from the Clue game as his marker and he shook the dice long and hard when his turn came round. I could have slipped away then to do some writing, but I decided to make a lamb stew instead and started chopping up onions. In no time, Dylan had snagged three railroads, as well as Park Place and Marvin Gardens.

"Wiggle, wiggle, wiggle," Dylan sang, zipping his candlestick around the board, an unlit cigarette hanging off his lip. We let him smoke inside, but he usually didn't push it.

"Hurry up and roll," Ryan said morosely. Eric, who didn't like board games, gazed out the window at the choppy gray lake. He was looking a little fed up, I noticed. Sooner or later we were going to have to do something about Bob Dylan.

"We should go down and put the chairs in the boat-house." I looked pointedly at Eric. "It looks like it's going to storm."

"I'm sure he'll leave soon," I said when we were down by the lake and out of earshot. "He just needs to rest."

"But what if he doesn't? What if he ends up coming back down to the city with us?" Eric gnawed at the side of his thumb.

"Somebody's going to track him down eventually. He's world-famous, for God's sake."

"Plus, the guy likes to eat, in case you haven't noticed. When you factor in gas for the outboard, and all those cartons of American Spirit I bring back from town, it starts to add up."

"He's rich. Money probably never crosses his mind."

"Well, it should. It crosses mine." Eric was already nervous about the money he would have to raise for his next film project.

"Let's give him a bit more time. It's good for Ryan; he's teaching him chords on the guitar. We could have nipped it in the bud on the first day, but we can't kick him out now. It would be rude."

"And I don't appreciate the way he goes around doing those imitations of Paul Simon singing 'Graceland' when he can tell by our CD wallet that we like him."

"That's just how he is."

"He gets away with murder playing Scrabble—you didn't even challenge 'zydeco'! You wouldn't take that shit from me. Why are you defending him?"

"I'm not defending him, I just think he's fragile right now. *Empire Burlesque* was not a big seller. And I like it when he sings for us."

"Right," Eric snorted. "When he can remember the words."

If you asked him directly, Dylan wouldn't sing. But after supper he might sit down with Ryan's guitar and ease into a song. One chilly evening we made a bonfire outside. Dylan wrapped himself in the Bay blanket and sang "Farewell, Angelina," followed by "Tangled Up in Blue." He played with his head bowed, his voice hard-edged, like an old sharpened knife. That night he made up a song for Ryan called "The Man in the Loon." It was about a boy who fell into the lake as a baby and was raised by a pair of loons, so he grew up thinking he was a bird, and could swim forever underwater.

"Slept in a rowboat/swam through the reeds/livin' in the river/where the crawfish feeds."

Later on he sang that Beach Boys song "In My Room," changing the chorus to "In My Loon." Ryan played along on his little Casio keyboard. "Now play 'Surfer Girl,'" I asked, excited. But then Dylan put the guitar aside, ground his cigarette into the dirt, and went off to bed like a small king, his blanket sweeping the pine needles behind him.

That night in bed, Eric turned to me. "Were there any messages at the marina when you went to town? Hasn't his manager or somebody tried to reach him?"

"Nothing." A mosquito hovered. I let it land on my arm, and smacked it. "We're it, I guess."

"Anyone else would at least buy the odd bottle of wine," Eric said, rolling away. "Talk about out of touch."

"He's just lost."

For some reason, Ryan got the best bed in the cottage. Well, I knew why. His mother and Eric had split up when he was two, and I sometimes favored him over Ceri, to win his affection. The bed had a new mattress encased in zippered plastic that rustled whenever he shifted in his sleep. Our bed was bigger, but old, and it sagged. The law of physics meant that Eric occupied the middle, so on hot nights I would often move to the screened-in porch to sleep on the sofa-bed. I liked to feel the cushions against my back, and my feet solid against the upholstered arms.

I was settled in with a duvet on the porch one night as a ribbon of cool air flowed over me. I could feel the presence of the lake, like a sleeping dog. The call of the loons was so clear and loud, notes breathed into a bamboo instrument. Sometimes the sound of laughter from a party on the other side of the lake would carry over, but that night it was perfectly quiet. I listened to everyone in the cottage breathing—Eric, almost a snore. Ryan, turning often and rustling his plastic. I couldn't hear anything from Dylan's room. Then I heard someone get up and use the bathroom.

"Ryan?"

"No."

Dylan, wrapped in the blanket, came onto the porch. His feet were long and narrow and white. I could smell tobacco and the strange lanolin cream he used on his hands and nails. Bag balm, he called it, something farmers used on cracked cow udders.

"Quarter moon, Ro," he whispered. Through the trees I could see the bone-colored crescent.

I thumped the edge of the sofa. "Sit here."

Shivering, Dylan tried to keep his blanket from slipping off while he lit a cigarette.

"Mind?"

"Be my guest."

He sat down on the sofa.

"Can't sleep?" he asked.

"It's cooler on the porch."

"Yeah, the air is sweet."

I tucked my feet under Dylan's bony ass. The smell of his cigarette was rough and pleasant—sometimes tobacco smelled so good. I brought my knees up, uncovering my feet. He took them in his cool hands and absentmindedly stroked them, as if they were a cat that had found its way into his lap.

"I can only really sleep on the bus," he said. "It doesn't feel right if I'm not moving."

His hands felt so alive on my skin. A kind of swarming intelligence came off them. He put out his cigarette in a saucer on the windowsill. A loon breathed its shaky note. Dylan's hands stroked further up my leg, like a masseur, following the line of the calf muscle.

"Swimmer's legs," he said.

"Not anymore."

"I like to watch you move around this place."

I let that pass. He shivered.

"Here," I said, lifting up the duvet. "Get warm." He slipped like quicksilver out of his blanket and under mine. He was smooth as the handle of a knife, slim as a boy, cool as china. His mustache didn't scratch when we kissed. I froze for a moment, listening for Eric's near-snore, which rasped on, and Ryan's rustling.

"You are a jewel," Dylan breathed into my ear. "A precious shining jewel."

The skies were turning a harder, more brilliant blue, and the water was almost too cold for swimming. The mist that rose from the surface of the lake took longer each morning to lift.

Our porch encounter was never repeated, or mentioned. Eric suspected nothing and he even began to warm to Dylan as they worked through his Johnny Cash collection. One day they found a Valdy record, *Country Man*, at a garage sale in town, which thrilled them. As for me, on the rainy afternoons when Ryan lay on the couch reading old copies of *National Geographic* and the two men were listening to "Girl from the North Country," I couldn't have been happier. All my men at peace, under one roof.

Then one Sunday morning when we were still in bed, I heard the engine of the Citroën turn over, stealthily, and catch. Followed by the whine of the car in reverse as it backed down our gravel road, swishing past the tall poplars.

"He's gone," I whispered to Eric.

"I doubt it. Probably just went to town for smokes."

"It's Sunday. Nothing's open this early."

We got up, expecting a note, or possibly a check, but there was no sign of anything. I went into his room where the bed was neatly made, and Ryan's sock monkey with the X's for eyes leaned up against the pillow. In the kitchen the box with the last Chelsea bun was gone.

"He fucking took my bun," said Eric. Then he checked the shelf of albums. "And Valdy too."

When Ryan woke up, we told him Bob had to leave early, to catch a plane and go back on tour. He was disappointed; they were in the middle of learning "Never Can Tell" by Chuck Berry.

"He's on the road most of the year," I said to Ryan. "Next time he comes through town, I'm sure he'll look us up."

"A hundred bucks we never hear from him again," said Eric.

But I am a romantic. I didn't need to see him again.

A few days later, as we were packing up to go back to the city, the marina lady came by in her boat. "A letter came for you," she said, handing Ryan an envelope addressed to him care of Warners' Marina, Sturgeon Lake. He finally got that right, at least. It was written on stationery from a Best Western in Boise, Idaho.

"What's it say?" I asked. He read it out loud.

Ryan, Didn't want to wake you up but thanks for all the rides. The Chuck Berry chords are E, B flat, D, only bar chords sound way better. Tube on, Yr grateful Bobby. It was folded around a hundred-dollar American bill. Just what Eric now owed me.

"I already figured out the chords," Ryan grumbled. Then he began deflating the inner tube, sitting on it as the air whooshed out.

Somehow, when we got home, in the muddle of unpacking we lost track of Dylan's letter. I looked everywhere for it, and nothing turned up, except for the little candlestick marker from Monopoly. It wasn't a good idea, we decided, to share the Dylan episode with friends. Whenever we tried to broach it, they would look concerned.

So our time with him became a family secret—something that might or might not have taken place, like the mirage of summer itself.

I n January, Dylan put out a new album called *Madawaska*. When I heard the title, my heart raced. Eric brought home the CD and I scanned the list of titles on the back. Maybe I was afraid of, or hoping for, something called "Precious Jewel," or "Swimmer's Legs." The music was traditional bluegrass, with fiddles and two women singing harmony with Dylan on the title tune. *"And all along the Madawaska/I've been thinking of the night/When the moon rose up in splendor/and your step was young and light.*" A simple song, like "Red River Valley." Eric played it twice, and neither of us spoke. The next song, fast and driving, was an intricate narrative about a stable of famous racehorses that burns to the ground.

"No sign of *Country Man* at least," said Eric.

I got up in the middle of the night, and played *Madawaska* again, with the headphones on. The moon wasn't full that night on the porch, but the rest of the lyrics felt true. I took it as evidence, at least. Everyone craves evidence that a time was real, even for five minutes.

My Star

Everywhere I went in Cannes, she was there, wearing something black and minimal, exuding mystery, her famous falcon eyes hidden by dark glasses. One night she deliberately sat in front of me at a screening; I could tell by the self-conscious way she moved her head. On my way to the bathroom the morning before the first film of the day, there she was again in the lobby of the Lumière with the same faint, complicit smile. I couldn't get rid of Charlotte Rampling.

Eric says it's happening more often now—stars stalking ordinary people. Especially in Cannes, where celebrities still wield an unironic glamour. Here they remain facts, like the stars in the sky.

My first time at the festival I came on my own as a journalist, freelancing for the *Star*. I did what you do when you are one of the four thousand media who descend on Cannes every spring—I raced from screening to screening, wept over my faulty Internet connections, underslept, and binged on films until my eyes felt like melting wheels of full-fat cheese.

But this time I was there with Eric, whose first feature, ᐃᕗᐃ (Inuktitut for "that place above"), had been accepted in the festival's sidebar program, *Un Certain Regard*. It's a drama set in the high Arctic about an oil-seeking American geologist (played by Rob Lowe) and the Inuit who try to thwart him. Very little dialogue. One of the Inuit actors, Aipalovik, has come with us to Cannes for the premiere. His name means both "evil god of the sea" and "entertainer," he explained with his lopsided smile.

Aipalovik has been to Sundance (where he was cast as an indigenous zombie in the horror movie *Inukshuk*) but never to the south of France. He is thirty-four, placid and handsome, with a sparse black chin-beard that seems to be especially attractive to the women here. He wears only cargo shorts with Teva sandals and finds everything interesting, which makes him an excellent traveling companion. Aipo used to work as a driver on one of those polar-bear-viewing buses for tourists, and before that he hunted caribou. So the empty white spaces of travel are familiar to him.

This time I wasn't in Cannes on assignment, which means I could take advantage of a quaint French tradition—the Spousal Pass, or as it is diplomatically known (to cover mistresses too), an "Accompaniatrice" pass. Technically it's only for the media who want to bring their partners, but we managed to wangle one. And I didn't mind playing the wife card this time around; I was secretly pleased, in fact.

My laminated white Spousal Pass, worn around the neck, allowed me to file past the lineups of sweating critics with lowlier accreditation. Aipalovik had a limited-access blue pass, for instance, which was embarrassing. Eric tried to get him upgraded, but the French officials wouldn't budge. (They still call the Inuit Eskimos here.) Aipalovik just shrugged and took it in good humor. He spent his time in lineups flirting with the women around him anyway.

In the first week, Charlotte Rampling's taste in films uncannily mirrored mine. She sat two rows away from me in Godard's *Maudite Langue*, and we both stood to applaud, while some booed. We were in aisle seats opposite each other in *Sheep Stealer*, Nuri Bilge Ceylan's four-hour pastoral epic. Also, we both made a point of staying for all of the closing credits. The theater is often deserted by the time they stop rolling. Then I let her leave first. Her small smile on the way out acknowledges our ritual.

Charlotte was in Cannes for a special retrospective of films by the Italian director Liliana Cavani. Most notorious among these is *The Night Porter*, in which the actress plays a Holocaust survivor who, years later, runs into her captor (played by the epicene Dirk Bogarde) in a Viennese hotel. They embark on a sadomasochistic affair complete with full frontal nudity and Nazi trimmings. Roger Ebert called it "as nasty as it is lubricious," but the film acquired a cult status, and it was a typically brave choice by Rampling. Odd pairings seem to appeal to her. The last movie I saw her in was *Max, Mon Amour* by the esteemed Japanese director Nagisa Oshimi. She plays the wife of an English diplomat and embarks on a very credible affair with a chimpanzee. Rampling's performance was note-perfect, as usual. Subversive seduction is her forte.

As the press conference for Liliana Cavani wrapped up, Aipalovik and I joined the crowd out in the hall waiting for Charlotte and her costars to emerge from the salon. I threaded my way to the front, worried that she might be scanning the crowds for my face.

The doors swung open and Charlotte appeared with her little retinue. Although she looks tall and regal on-screen, in real life she is rather small with delicate facial features. No puffy duck lips for her. She wore a modest black dress with no jewelry, and seemed as composed amid the frenzy of Cannes as she is on-screen.

"Charlotte! Over here!" the photographers called out, as their devices clicked and whirred. Some carry stools so they can shoot over the heads of the crowd. "Charlotte—Presse Internationale!" yelled one man as the actress walked away. She turned and paused, offering a wry smile as if to say, yes, all right, if it's international.

I must admit I got quite caught up in the moment. I felt like crying out, "Charlotte! Over here—Spousal Pass!" I think that might have amused her.

In the evening, after Aipalovik left us to join a bevy of publicists having drinks on the lawn of the Grand, Eric and I strolled back to our hotel. The owners were a charming young couple with impeccable manners, who sang out *"Bonjour!"* or *"Bonsoir!"* at our every encounter, in that formal French soprano. Back in our tiny room we drew the drapes against the noise of the Petit Majestic, a café where festival-goers spill out into the streets, drinking and talking until dawn. All night long the noise of the crowd sounded like heavy surf, almost soothing. The sea was only a few blocks away, but it is an orderly body of water. Like the teacup-sized dogs carried in their handbags by the Cannoise women, it is not really "nature" anymore.

Eric and I developed a nightly ritual in Cannes. First I would call Ryan and Ceri; my mother was staying with them and they needed to complain about her cooking. Then I would set out our earplugs on either side of the bed, tenderly place our two mobile phones in their charging cradles, and drape a T-shirt over Eric's new laptop, whose green lights pulsed like something small, alive, and breathing. The TV and the air conditioner also had little red eyes. This constellation shone over us as we slept.

One morning I skipped the 8:30 a.m. screening to go to the market and buy some food. You cannot snack in Cannes; you must sit down at a table in a restaurant and spend a proper hour or two, so I try to keep our mini-fridge in the hotel stocked, mostly with fruit. The strawberries here are small but potent as a drug.

In fact, my favorite Cannes moments were when Eric and I sat on our balcony at dusk, poured two glasses of rosé, and ate fresh strawberries with Brie. Sometimes oysters too. The air is especially soft at that time of day, and the palm trees in the garden throw their jagged shadows on the ochre of the hotel façade. We toasted each other, our hard-earned life together (his first wife was a handful), and felt lucky to be there.

The Cannes market sells everything, not just food. I was standing at the stall that sells only bikinis—there is no cut-off age for bikini-wearing in the south of France—when I saw Charlotte across from me, sniffing a melon. Her sunglasses were enormous. She wore a trench coat with the collar turned up and the same black ballet flats as the day before.

Casually, I drifted down the aisle to the strawberry stall and paid for two boxes. She just as casually left the melons behind and began to inspect some dried lavender opposite me. I crossed the street and ducked into the doorway of a patisserie. *Bonjour, madame!* cried the woman behind the counter, snaring me, so I bought two Opera cakes. Through the window I could still see Charlotte looking around for me, perplexed. The lavender seller was waiting for her to pay when she abruptly abandoned the bouquet and walked away. There was a sad slump to her shoulders, or so I imagined. She carried an umbrella.

I dashed out of the store with my cakes and decided to follow her for a few blocks. I felt a little bad for having eluded her like that. And what was the harm, really, if she had some compelling interest in me? She was an actor, and actors study other people. The streets were thronged and the crowds swam around Charlotte without a second glance; her singularity, her charisma, only flared on-screen. I had to jog to keep up with her. Then, when I turned down rue Mace I spotted Aipalovik admiring the ball gowns in the windows of a couturier's shop.

"Ten thousand dollars for a dress," he said when I joined him. "But it's finely crafted, isn't it? The little crystal drops on the bodice." He looked a bit worse for wear. Eric said that when he had left the bar at the Grand the night before, a big-boned American girl was touching Aipalovik on the arm and laughing whenever he spoke. His years as a hunter had made him attentive and highly observant, which the women here are not accustomed to.

I explained to Aipo that the French actress Charlotte Rampling had been following me for several days.

"Why would she follow you?"

"I don't know, but I was just at the market and there she was again."

"Perhaps she was buying food."

"No, no. She was looking at lavender. No Frenchwoman would buy lavender, it's for the tourists. She's obsessed with me for some reason."

Aipalovik pondered this. "You know, when I'm hunting, I keeping thinking I see caribou in the distance. But it's usually not the case."

"This is different. Come with me."

I led him to the Majestic, where the minor celebrities stayed (the A-listers stayed out of town, at the absurdly deluxe Hotel du Cap). A white Rolls with tinted windows had pulled up and was disgorging new guests. It was always a kick just to walk through the lobby to view the haggard and wealthy in their finery. The orange-skinned men with the $15,000 chronometers on their wrists, and the women of full artifice, looking embalmed.

"The rich often seem unhappy," Aipalovik observed as we threaded through the lobby. And there she was, standing near the bar, checking her watch with the tiniest of frowns. I plucked at Aipalovik's arm.

"Over by the floral arrangement, three o'clock."

Charlotte had several small shopping bags at her feet. I was irritated for her sake by the late arrival of her Accompaniatrice.

"Her beauty is subtle," said Aipalovik, "but powerful." We watched as she drew one bare foot out of her shoe, like a deer.

"And she has a wound," he said, his brow clouding a bit. "Look at her right foot." He has a big nurturing side, Aipo.

It was true; I could see a blister on her heel that had been rubbed raw. It was bleeding a little. Cannes is very hard on the feet, with all the walking and the cobbled streets. That's why I always carry Band-Aids in my purse. I put a flesh-colored Band-Aid in Aipo's palm and he glided across the room. Charlotte turned a wary eye to this new, unusual person, dressed like a river guide. But after listening to him for a minute or two her face softened. She smiled. That guy, he had the touch. Swiftly he peeled the wrapper off, picked up Charlotte's foot as one would a horse's hoof for shoeing, and smoothed the adhesive strip over the curve of her blistered heel. The deed was done almost before she could register what was happening.

But Charlotte wasn't fazed. She slipped her foot back into its black flat and opened her handbag, ready to pay him, whereupon he looked horrified and backed away. Just then a flustered young man in jeans and a silvery shirt came to her side, scowling at Aipalovik. She kissed the man and put a calming hand on his arm. She shook Aipo's hand. The couple went and sat at the bar as he made his way back to me.

"She smells like heaven. And those eyes. I understand now."

"Let's slip out while she's distracted."

"Being in the same vicinity as you does not amount to predation," Aipo pointed out, but I let it go.

The next night was Eric's screening. He was trying to be offhand about it, but he was terribly nervous, fidgeting so much in the morning films that I had to leave and slip into another one. But his anxiety was understandable. The day after the premiere, reviews would appear in all the industry papers and Cannes can make or break a film. Not to mention the fact that movies set in frigid landscapes have a bad track record at the box office. So we split up for the day. I was coming out of David Lynch's *Wild at Heart* when I all but collided with Charlotte.

Again with the all-black wardrobe, the almost mousy hair, the basilisk gaze. A face that teetered provocatively on the fulcrum between youth and age. The Band-Aid was still visible on one heel.

I lingered in the lobby, brandishing my presence, then went out into the sunlight and headed along the boardwalk of the Croisette, walking slowly. The sunbathers were out in force and the noon light dazzled on the sea. I stopped beside the golden Cannes carousel, where the ticket seller was a Jayne Mansfield lookalike, except that her one arm had been amputated below the elbow. The arm was neatly rounded at the end like a sausage. She could still swing a smart handbag from it though. I watched the carousel turn, empty except for two teenage girls. I could feel Charlotte close behind me. We were tethered.

That night Eric's screening seemed to go over well, but it's impossible to judge reactions at Cannes, where the audiences are either jaded or overly partisan. Rob Lowe was fantastic as the slick American colonizer, and people leaped up to clap at the end. That might have been as much for Aipalovik as anything else—he was irresistible on-screen. Eric sat rigidly beside me. His nerves made it impossible for me to fall under the spell of the story, but the images of the polar seas and pewter skies were still ravishing. The more the world behaves like a block-buster action movie, the more I long for silence and space on the screen. Watching the film also told me something new about Eric, his passion for this subtle landscape. It's always a surprising act of intimacy to see things through his eyes.

Afterward Eric's distributor hosted a reception in the Cannes apartment he rents during the festival. The Canadians all came out to support Eric and Aipalovik, some young French film-makers crashed the party, a few critics floated by scarfing up the appetizers, and at midnight everyone went out onto the balcony to wait for the fireworks to begin. The nightly display is always artful and protracted, like dinner in a Cannes restaurant.

When I went back in to fetch Eric there she was, talking to him. She must have slipped into the screening unnoticed. But why would she want to see a little Canadian film about the high Arctic?

This time her black dress exposed the tops of her shoulders and had a single row of jet beads. A DJ was playing loud disco, so she was bending in close to listen to him. Her hand rested on his upper arm. I stood back and watched Eric, who was flushed, animated, eager to please. I should have gone up to them but a curious passivity overcame me. Finally they gave each other European double-cheek kisses and they parted.

I crossed the room to my husband.

"Wasn't that Charlotte Rampling?"

"Yes," he said, still rosy-faced. "And she loved the film! She adored it. She called it a master class in stillness."

"Well, it's certainly a far cry from *The Night Porter*."

"She said she'd love to work with me sometime. Her agent's going to send me a screenplay she's been working on, with the guy who wrote the biopic about Rodin's mistress, what's her name . . ."

"Camille Claudel."

"They've got their investors all lined up, and now they're looking for a director. Someone under the radar, she said. Can you believe it? Charlotte Rampling!" His face shone like a child's.

My reaction was intensely physical. The blood roared into my head until the music seemed to come from some room far away. I drained my glass.

"I'm sorry, but working with her is out of the question," I heard myself say in a firm unspousal voice. Outside, the fireworks had begun, pillowy explosions.

"What are you talking about?" Eric said, taking the glass out of my hand as a waiter swam by with a fresh bottle. "Why not?"

"It's just—I've been watching her operate. She's trouble, Eric. You've never been good with trouble."

"Really? I ran into the director of that chimpanzee movie she was in, and he had nothing but good things to say."

He looked at me then with an expression of confusion and concern but my words were already there between us, irredeemable. Aipo will back me up, I thought. Aipo gets it.

Then our host came over with an American producer who wanted to congratulate Eric. I left them and joined the others on the balcony. Charlotte stood at the rail with her young man, watching the lights burst against the blackness of the sky, out-shining the stars. Pink, silver, blue, then blinding flashbulb bursts of white, with gunshot sounds. A paparazzi dazzle. The display seemed to go on forever, then escalated into a final thunderous salvo as the people around me exclaimed and applauded. It really was a spectacular show.

I clapped too. But inside my head it was absolutely quiet and still, like her.

Jimi and Agnes

My son came across this online," Rose said to her editor at the *Star*. "It's amazing how some people spend their time." She showed Ellen a video of three men sitting around a Ouija board in London, England. They were trying to have a conversation with Jimi Hendrix but the spirit world wasn't cooperating. "Maybe that means he's still alive," one of them joked. The marker immediately scooted over to YES. "So where is he living now?" they asked. The heart-shaped marker, gliding on its three felt-tipped legs, searchingly spelled out the word T-A-O-S. Taos, New Mexico.

"Now, take a look at this."

Rose opened up a fansite called *Where's Jimi????* featuring many photographs of black men with Afros who bore little resemblance to the legendary guitarist. But one picture stood out. It was a snapshot of a thin, dark-skinned figure with a corona of gray hair getting into the passenger seat of a car driven by a mannish-looking old woman. In the parking lot of a Winn-Dixie near Albuquerque.

"What are you suggesting," said Ellen, who had a weakness for some of Rose's crazier story ideas, "that you jump on a plane to New Mexico and try to track down Jimi Hendrix?" Both of them were thinking about the story Rose had written about the academic who had "proven" that the lost city of Atlantis once flourished off the coast of a small Bahamian island. Unsurprisingly this turned out not to be the case, but Rose's story became the second-most-popular feature in the paper that year.

People no longer read the news in search of what's true, Rose concluded. They'd rather have an opportunity to believe in something.

Ellen was studying a budget sheet on her laptop. "If you come up with a Plan B for another story when this one turns out to be a hoax, and how can it not be, I'll talk to Ken about it. He's a huge Hendrix fan, as you know."

Ken was the newspaper's publisher, and Ellen's ex-husband. They had a bantering Bogart-and-Bacall relationship that Rose liked to be around. Ken also took pleasure in assigning stories to Rose that she had absolutely no interest in or knowledge about, like Brazilian soccer scandals. But sometimes she would come back with fresh perspectives on these mysterious subjects. He would read her copy, chuckle, and say things like, "How can you not know that about the world?"

Rose felt lucky to have landed somewhere with friendly editors who indulged her ideas and still cared about commas. But it wouldn't last. A job in print journalism was soon going to be like working as a blacksmith, or a calligrapher. Sixty people had been laid off at the paper only the month before. Finding Jimi Hendrix alive could save her neck.

What she hadn't mentioned to Ellen or Ken was her hunch about the identity of the old woman driving the car. Very few people could have recognized her, but Rose was sure she did—

it was the distinctive profile of the minimalist painter Agnes Martin. Born in Saskatchewan, now in her late eighties, Martin had spent much of her life in seclusion, living in the New Mexican desert, although her work continued to attract international attention.

Ever since Rose had seen an exhibit of Martin's work in the Whitney she had developed a peculiar attachment to her paintings, which are nearly all the same: pale luminous canvases, like windows, empty of narrative and covered in a faint grid of pencil lines. They have a powerful, wordless presence and are almost impossible to reproduce.

The polar opposite of journalism.

The house was a plain white adobe affair out in the desert with a rodent's skull for a doorknocker. Rose lifted the little head and let it fall several times. When Agnes Martin had refused to answer her emails, she decided to just fly there and show up. A gallery in Taos had given her directions. If worse came to worst, Rose thought, she could always write a piece about the "energy healing fields" near Sedona, Arizona. Someone had recently died there in a peyote ceremony.

It was dusk, abruptly cool. In the distance, lavender light still pulsed above the mountaintops. The door opened and an "oh" escaped Rose. She had expected someone taller than the man who stood there, ash-haired, slightly stooped, wearing an emerald-green brocade jacket over the frill of a white shirt. His long fingers were covered in silver and turquoise rings, and a bone cuff circled one wrist. It was Jimi Hendrix.

He showed no surprise at this unexpected visitor, said nothing whatsoever, and led Rose through a velvet curtain into a room where Agnes Martin sat with her legs planted at the end of a long wooden table. Large and squarish, she wore black robes with men's oxfords. Her thinning silver hair was gathered in a little bundle of braids at the back of her neck. She looked like some strange Shakespearean king.

"I didn't say yes," Agnes said coldly, referring to Rose's letters. "I didn't say anything at all."

"I know. I decided to take a chance and come anyway. Sooner or later the story about the two of you is going to get out there, after the Winn-Dixie photo. Better my paper than the British tabs, perhaps."

Agnes and Jimi exchanged a sorrowful look.

The two of them had just finished a meal and were drinking mescal from thumb-sized clay cups as the last smudge of mauve faded in the sky. One wall of the room was entirely glass. Jimi lit a line of votive candles at the bottom of it and poured some mescal for Rose. They were sorry to see her, they explained, but since she was here, she could sleep in the paint shed and they would talk in the morning. The cot was made up, and there was a chamber pot underneath.

Then they both stood.

"Good night, Ms. McEwan," Agnes said. "We get up at six a.m."

The altitude gave her dreams, mostly anxious scenes involving airport lineups and slamming taxi doors. She dreamed that she and Eric were still together, going somewhere in a car, and between them on the seat was the rodent-skull door knocker. Rose was flipping through the CD wallet as Eric drove and the road unspooled ahead. She played some old Bob Marley and things felt all right between them. Then a rooster crowed, a real rooster. She woke up shivering with one sheet wrapped around her in a room full of paint tins, dog food, and garden tools.

She took a jacket out of her suitcase, and in the pocket was the letter from Eric, still unopened. Her address on the front in gold print. Probably the invitation; her stepson and daughter had already received theirs.

When the sky began to lighten she got up and went outside. A white El Dorado she hadn't noticed the night before was parked in the yard, like a big grazing animal. A dog asleep on a nest of blankets whumped its tail but did not stir. She looked at the horizon, an undulating line of soft mountains, like ground-down molars—nothing like the straight lines of Martin's paintings. Rose felt her gaze moving out and out, a neglected muscle stretching.

At the end of the yard was another adobe structure, with a skylight. She peered through the windows. There on scaffoldings and easels were Martin's paintings. With a trespasser's glance toward the house, Rose pushed the door open and stepped inside. There was something erotic about entering rooms like these, where private people did their work.

A large canvas stood on a table against one wall. A third of it was covered with faint horizontal pencil lines under a wash of yellow. These paintings about nothing, Rose realized, apparently made of nothing, still had to cross the line between half-imagined and finished. Despite its emptiness the canvas still gave the impression of being cluttered.

Rose went over to a stack of paintings in the corner and flipped through them like record albums in a rack. Gray, gray, blue, cream. Fields of color, they revealed little. Perhaps she was too close to them, too greedy for their meaning. It was like peering into the folds of a brain to find the location of a particular memory.

"That is old work," said Agnes, blotting out the light at the door. "I use the canvas backs for sketching."

"I'm sorry, I didn't want to disturb you."

"Well, there are no secrets here anyway. It is all simply looking and doing, and looking again."

"This one—can you tell me about it?" Rose flipped to the half-finished canvas.

"There is nothing to tell," Agnes said, waving the question away. She was wearing a man's blue denim shirt and a long Mexican-looking skirt with embroidery along the hem.

"But I don't associate you with yellow."

Agnes went over to the splayed canvases and shut them like a book.

"I often begin with yellow. That is a secret, I suppose."

"Do you paint directly from the landscape, or do you use photographs?"

"Jimi and I may drive up into the hills and I will either paint or sketch. I sometimes draw the mountains, work on the rest, then take away the mountains altogether. Only light interests me in the end."

Behind the door was a small canvas distinct from the others, painted in thick strokes of black, purple, and white. It seemed to represent two swirling figures. Rose went over to it and held it up.

"That one is Jimi's," Agnes said.

"Of the two of you?"

"Yes. I'm fond of it. James could paint, if he chose to."

"Well, he's quite accomplished as it is."

"Yes. I wish he thought so."

"He doesn't?"

"No. All that media nonsense overtook him near the end

and he tends to dwell on that." A rooster crowed again from the yard.

"But he likes to cook," she said, walking out of the studio, "and breakfast must be ready." Rose followed her. The dog came up and sniffed Martin's skirt. It was seven a.m. and already hot.

After breakfast the three of them took the El Dorado into town for supplies—eggs, bread, mineral spirits, more mescal and wine, and many small hot peppers. The shopkeepers greeted Jimi by name and gave Rose a warning look that said *Yes, he's safe with us.* Then they drove up into the hills, left the main road, and turned onto a trail of two hard-baked ruts. "We're going to do some work," they said.

The sky there seemed to behave like a lens that overfocused everything; Rose found the effect almost hallucinatory. She sat in the back (like a dog, she felt, although not unhappily) and said nothing. Jimi drove. Agnes was beside him, wearing a fisherman's canvas hat. Jimi played a CD—"Caldonia" by Louis Armstrong. He sang along with it, his frayed, slouchy voice full of space like Armstrong's.

Caldonia—Caldonia—why won't you be mine . . .

Utterly absorbed, Agnes looked out her window at—what? Rose saw only empty sky and featureless desert. Her eyes wanted to close.

They came to a stony, gently ascending riverbed and turned into it.

"Our cobbled road," Agnes said with a rare smile.

The riverbed took them up to a flat, high pinnacle of land—a mesa—where they stopped. Silence, and suffocating heat. Agnes looked pleased and put her hand on Jimi's arm. Rose got out of the car and stood looking at the 360-degree view. It made her dizzy, as if the horizon far away were the lip of a great waterfall. The light was merciless, the heat pressed upon them, and Rose felt a stirring of panic. There was nowhere to shelter here, only this old car and this strange couple. For a moment she wondered if she were still asleep on the plane and dreaming. Sometimes being a reporter felt like being a criminal on the lam.

"If you look carefully you can see the ranch," Agnes said, pointing. Rose squinted and saw nothing.

"Ah yes," she said.

"Did you bring the hard-boiled eggs, James?" Agnes said. "I'm hungry."

Agnes erected a folding easel and put a small canvas on it. She snapped open an old-fashioned doctor's satchel and began to take out pencils, brushes, and crumpled tubes of paint. Jimi came back from the car with a cloth-covered basket and a salt-shaker.

"Have you ever seen anything like the color of that yolk?" Agnes said, holding out the shelled egg she had just bitten into. "But nothing I could work with."

Rose wandered about, feeling disoriented. She put one of Agnes's clean paint rags under her hat to protect her neck from the sun. She was used to being rooted in her mind, on the screen and in her sentences. This was too much.

"Play for us, Jimi," Agnes commanded. He had taken out his guitar, a nail-polish-red Gibson Les Paul. Unamplified, the guitar sounded loose and tinny, like music coming from another room. He sang "Little Red House" in a smoky absentminded way, humming through some of the lyrics as Agnes stood at her easel with a pencil, her head moving from horizon to canvas and back again.

As she sat on top of the cooler listening to Jimi Hendrix sing, Rose felt she really should be making notes. This story would be big. She took out a notebook and uncapped her pen. "V. hot," she wrote. "Little Red House." Then she closed the notebook and lay down on the ground, draping the cloth from the egg basket over her face. She listened.

Jimi's voice, pitched a bit lower than in the old days, was so all of him, all at once, in every note. Like the bluest of blue on a canvas. Like a true pencil line. Rose lay there remembering the first time, long ago, she had heard that backward-sounding song "Manic Depression." She was in the bed of a man she hardly knew. Kevin? Kevin something. He was drunk and playing all his Janis Joplin and Hendrix records for her, letting the needle fall too hard. Then they had sex and fell asleep. A not so unusual night in those days. But the off-kilter surge of "Manic Depression," its churning plea, and the nakedness of Jimi's voice had made Rose get up out of Kevin's bed (carefully, so as not to wake him) and walk back home alone.

It was time to be truer to herself, she'd decided.

Under the cloth Rose inhaled the smell of the eggs and a lingering scent of bread. She began to relax, feeling the hard ground under her hips and shoulders. Agnes was making chicken-scratching sounds on the canvas with her pencil. Occasionally she would carve away at the angle of the tip with a penknife. Jimi noodled around on the guitar, making up a song about their rooster, Fidel.

To be inside art, not outside thinking about it. Rose had forgotten how it felt. Journalism did not work like that.

As Jimi played, unexpected images came into Rose's mind, like animals at dusk appearing at a water hole. An image of Eric wading into the lake at the cottage, hugging himself and shivering. The look on his face coming down the hospital corridor the night Ryan had walked through a glass door and cut himself badly. She couldn't reach him on the phone, and when he showed up hours later, he wouldn't say where he had been. That was the point at which she knew, but refused to believe it.

Then up rose another image of someone she worked with, a man with long sideburns and sleeves rolled tightly above his elbows as he pattered away on his keyboard. Rolf. This bland colleague sat in Rose's line of vision for most of the working day. Part of her landscape.

Sometimes her job was not to see.

"*My cherie amour,*" Jimi was singing, "*lovely as a summer day . . .*" This brought a twitch of a smile to the corners of Agnes's mouth. Her eyes kept flicking rapidly from horizon to canvas like a hummingbird that sips at a feeder, retreats, then darts back.

"Oh, it's wrong now," she said, stepping back and letting her painting arm drop. "You distracted me, James."

Hendrix put down his guitar, went over to Agnes, and wrapped his arms around her as he studied the canvas. Rose lifted the cloth off her face to observe them.

"It's fine, Ag. Just thin it out."

"It will show." She pouted like a girl.

"It won't. Keep going—this part is fine." He pointed to one corner of the canvas, a curdled white like cirrus clouds.

"Yes, that part is good."

"Go on."

"Play something different," Agnes instructed, already twirling her paintbrush in a rosette of paint on the metal cookie sheet she used as a palette.

"You start. I have to take a piss." Jimi ambled over to the other side of the car, out of sight.

"Paintings are jealous," Agnes said to Rose. "The moment I feel the tiniest bit of satisfaction with one, the painting immediately senses it and misbehaves."

"Is it like a sense of smell, that you lose the freshness of your vision after a while?"

"Yes. The first strokes are crucial. They come directly from the eye, not the brain."

Jimi came back over, jingling the car keys. "Let me show you something while she works," he said. "Cherie, we're going to the hoodoos." Agnes didn't turn her head.

They drove back down the riverbed to a point where it forked, and followed another branch. The banks deepened until they were inside a narrow, shallow canyon. I really ought be asking him questions, Rose thought. After all, this was prime time—alone in a canyon with the world's most legendary guitarist. Who had not died of an overdose after all. But she hated to break their companionable silence and the road required all of Jimi's attention. Rose looked at his hands on the wheel, studying the four or five rings he wore. One was a Victorian cameo, a woman's ivory face in profile. Another was a fang-shaped object, a bone or a bit of tusk.

"It looks like ivory," said Jimi, who had caught her glance, "but it's made from a hoof. Agnes had an old horse she didn't want to part with. When he died, she carved his hooves into birds and spoons, and this ring."

"I didn't know she made other things."

"She likes to sew my shirts too."

With a familiar feeling of power and illicitness, Rose began to turn the conversation in the direction she needed it to go.

"You two seem to get along very well."

"Yes, now. But not at first. She'd been living alone for a long time when I showed up."

All the windows were open and the cool air on Rose's arm felt good. She got her notebook out of her bag, and saw the unopened letter from Eric. But maybe it wasn't the invitation after all. Maybe it was a note, a drunken midnight note saying "Wedding off—please call!"

"Can I ask how you came to be together?" she asked Jimi.

He said nothing as he pulled off the road and stopped. Huddled before them was a forest of round, red dirt columns, a few twenty feet high, sculpted by the wind. Some resembled whirling Sufi dancers, cylindrical shapes that tapered at the bottom and fanned out ecstatically in the middle, then narrowed again. Others looked off-center, like half-thrown pots on a potter's wheel, mouths wobbling out of plumb.

"These are the hoodoos. It's supposed to be sacred ground—the Hopi have ceremonies here."

"I can see why." One of the columns was tall enough to cast a little shade and they walked toward it. Rose took a different tack.

"So how did you end up here, Jimi?"

"I came the long way round. When I 'died,'" he said, "I was flown to Zambia, where at least I wouldn't look out of place. For the next few years I lived in the countryside there and raised goats. I had a wife."

"Did you play music?"

"No."

"Why did you run away?"

Jimi ran a hand down one of the sand columns and was quiet for a time. "Just, things had gotten out of hand."

"You were so young. Only twenty-seven."

"All I wanted to do was play guitar, but the more famous I became, the more other things got in the way."

"Like drugs."

"Yes. In the end only heroin got me back inside the music."

"So you faked your death?"

"In a way. I mean, I did almost die. But I made a deal with the doctor who revived me, who had treated me before. She came with me to Zambia to get me through quitting."

"Really? She never told anyone, or wrote a book?"

"No, no," Jimi said impatiently. "She cared for me. She kind of loved me."

"But why leave Zambia?"

"My wife was very traditional. She wanted a lot of babies and a man with a big herd of cattle. A guitar player who didn't play anymore wasn't her idea of a husband."

They stood under one of the hoodoos and she touched the silky, wind-abraded bark. A tree of stone.

"So I came here and disguised myself at first. It worked. America is full of fugitives anyway. I found a little house to rent outside Taos."

"Alone?"

"Yes. Then I bought a guitar and began to play again."

Rose waited patiently, saying nothing.

"One day in town, I went into a gallery and saw two of Agnes's paintings. They struck me, like an old blues song that doesn't sound like much at first, but the lines stick in your head. A week later I went back to see them again and Agnes was in the gallery, hanging something new. We spoke. Later that day I went back to her house."

"So the two of you are . . . ?" Jimi laughed.

"We're together. Let's leave it at that." He reached in his pocket for the keys.

Rose felt the door of their conversation close. They got in the car, and Jimi drove at jarring speeds back to their earlier spot. Agnes, her hat jammed low on her brow, stood in the same place, looking at the same horizon line. The canvas now had an urgent radiance. It was heading toward finished. Her face looked smooth and lit-up too.

Jimi walked over and she turned to him with delight, as if noticing a new blossom in her garden.

"Cherie, this is good," he said. She nodded.

"Well, it was your distraction that took me there."

Jimi kissed her hand and Agnes gave him a look so full of love it scalded Rose. She turned away and began to gather up the remains of lunch.

Music, sweet music—wish I could caress . . . caress . . .

On the way to the ranch, Rose watched the violet layers of dusk drift onto the tops of the hill. She was thinking about the time, in her twenties, when two of her friends, Eva and Richard, had broken up. They were the first of their crowd to live together, and the first to separate. Eva moved in with her for a few months, a long winter when Rose faintly resented the fact that Richard couldn't come round anymore. She and Eva did gloomy girl projects, like making candles. Then one night Richard turned up, ostensibly to retrieve some records. Eva was playing Dylan's "Blood on the Tracks," over and over. Richard sat wordless at their kitchen table. When "Tangled Up in Blue" came on, Rose had to flee the apartment, jogging to the 7-Eleven for milk they didn't need. The song was too bitterly true. When she returned there was no sign of either of them but the door to Eva's bedroom was closed, and the record was still playing.

They stayed apart, but after that night Richard was back inside their circle. The two of them could be very funny together, at parties. And years later, when Eva had her surgery, he walked her dog every day. True love is hard to vanquish.

Sitting behind Jimi and Agnes in the El Dorado, driving into darkness, Rose made some decisions. She would tell her editor that Hendrix was nowhere to be found—the whole thing was a hoax—and that Agnes Martin on her own was not enough for a story. Too old, too difficult, and her paintings were impossible to reproduce. The paper was always happy to kill an art story anyway. She'd pitch the Sedona energy fields instead. Ellen would go for that.

As soon as they got back to the house, Jimi began preparing dinner and Rose went to the shed. She shivered; in the desert the nights were suddenly cold. Sitting on the cot under the single light, she opened the letter. A stiff RSVP card slid out. The gold lettering was a bit much, but at least the wedding would be in Philadelphia, not Palm Springs, where Judy's parents now lived. Then she turned on her phone to call Ryan and Ceri. "Are you sure?" said solicitous Ceri. "I'll rent a car," Rose answered. "We should all go down together."

Exfoliation

Steam filled the darkened room, along with the smell of eucalyptus.

"Just close your eyes." Her voice was low, with a pleasant accent, neither American nor British. The tips of her long blond hair swung against my shoulders. She stroked my jaw to let me know she was about to begin, then covered my eyelids with damp discs of cotton.

The room was narrow, like a berth on a train. Lying there I remembered why I don't like facials. It has to do with the claustrophobia of the small cubicle, the disorienting fog of heat and steam, and the upside-down face of the aesthetician, with a smiling red slash and teeth where her forehead should be.

She removed the discs and I looked up at her. Her pale skin was poreless and faintly powdery, like fresh drywall. My face was bathed in her warm odorless breath. I had an urge to flee, to run out the door in my smock and paper slippers. But in three days I was going to a wedding, the wedding of my ex-husband, Eric, and I wanted to look my best.

A thick magnifying glass on a metal arm swung over my face and her eyes grew huge, like fish swimming by the glass of an aquarium. She ran a finger along my jawline, where a line of small white bumps lurked.

"Guess it's been a while since we've seen you."

"Yes. More than a year, actually." Do not feel shame, I told myself.

"Okay, lots to work on here." She swiveled away to turn up the steamer and prepare some new unguent. The air in the room grew thicker and whiter. The two of us floated in our little heaven.

She gathered her hair back into a low ponytail with a scrunchie so it wouldn't get in the way, and bent over my face, like someone in prayer. Her blue eyes were tilted up at the corners. Inverted, this gave her a slightly sad or rueful expression. I tried to read the name tag pinned on her uniform. G— something. Gwendolyn? Gwyneth? Gloria?

Settling on a stool behind my head, she poured a lotion into the cup of her hand and began to smooth it on my face, stroking up from the jaw. It felt cool, menthol and tingly. The feel of her hand triggered a little swoon of tenderness in me. How long had it been since anyone had touched my face like this? The agenda-free caress: we never get enough. As G began to paddle away at my jawline and Balinese music wafted into the room through a vent in the ceiling, I went over the chronology of what had happened with Eric one more time.

The marriage had survived so much, with adulterous skirmishes on both sides. Sometimes we were just looking at each other across a great distance, two people on opposite banks of a cold rushing river. And whenever he was working on a film, everything in our lives went on hold, including me.

But we had lasted. How many other married couples had

stayed together, among our friends? Two or three. One co-dependent toxic pair, an okay one, and a loving, thriving, enviable couple. Until the woman got cancer, and died.

In fact it was when Eric and I were getting along smoothly and Ceri and Ryan were settled in school that the trouble hit. "Looks like we're in it for the long haul," he had said to me on our tenth anniversary, raising a glass. Our Elmore Leonard version of tenderness.

G's hair brushed my face. "I'll start with some extractions and then I'll work on the puffiness," she said. "I like the hijiki mask, myself, for circulation and lift. It's Japanese seaweed with lots of antioxidants. Plus some alpha-hydroxy."

"Sounds good."

I found the pseudo-scientific language of skin care silly, unquantifiable, and almost religious. But I wanted to put myself in her hands.

She got to work tweezing the side of my nose with her index fingers, pushing out tiny pencil-points of black. This was the fun part, really. Everyone likes squeezing zits, whether they're yours or someone else's. Grooming stirs deep reptilian brain pleasure. As she squeezed, an image came into my thoughts, of that lifeguard . . . Doug. From Guelph. I worked with him at summer camp when I was seventeen. He had big welty pimples and pitted craters on his back, like Richard Burton's face. During afternoon rest period a bunch of us would lounge around behind the staff quarters, on the broad, satellite-dish rocks of Georgian Bay, and Doug would let me work my way through the moonscape of his scarred back. A sweet, peaceful interlude.

Most of my friends are single now, or divorced. One widow, about to remarry. When Eric and I were together, still dealing with his son's anger after he divorced, sometimes I wondered what our friends thought about our marriage. Did they wish they were us, or were they grateful to be living their uncoupled, unencumbered lives? People stay in a marriage for many reasons. Fear and inertia, or choice and love. In most cases a bit of all four.

"So how's your week been so far?" said G as the steam hissed companionably.

"Not too bad. Getting ready for a wedding in a few days."

"Not yours!" she said, rearing up in delight.

"Oh, no. Just someone I know."

"We'll make you outshine the bride," G said, nipping away at my jawline, at those tiny hard white ones.

"Well, I'd be very happy if you did," I ventured, "because she's marrying my ex-husband."

G didn't know what to say to this. But something about the whole cleansing routine was disinhibiting me, as they say in the geriatric world. Out with all the toxins, I thought, including those little black dots of impacted memory.

"It turns out they'd been sleeping together for some time," I said with a sort of chuckle. "While we were together."

"Huh, wow," said G. "Not good!"

"No, not good indeed. I think it had been going on for years. But I never did manage to sort that part out."

"Did you know her? The bride?"

"She was his therapist, actually." Another cackle escaped me. Really, the whole saga was hilarious. "I even saw her a few times myself, to discuss our relationship." G tactfully sat back for a moment, then bent again to her work. The skin of my face began to sparkle with a pleasant pain, as if I'd been lightly slapped.

"So what was she like?"

"I found her humorless and arrogant. But attractive, in a blowsy sort of way."

"What kind of therapy did she practice?"

"Cognitive-behavioral."

"Which is?"

"Short-term, results-based. It's about changing your mental habits, rather than talking about Mum and Dad. Although some of that might have been a good idea too."

"I'm sorry. That must have been sooo hard for you."

A therapist line: she was good at this.

"As a matter of fact, it was." Two tears swelled in the corners of my eyes, and rolled down my temples. G swabbed them away with a cotton disc.

"I had my suspicions for a long time before he told me. Occasionally I'd flay away at him, interrogate him. But he said I was just being paranoid, and feeling old. We'd been together for twenty years, after all. Two kids, his son and our own, a daughter. And unfortunately I saw him as someone who was incapable of lying. He used to be so transparent when we first met, an open book."

"That rings a bell," said G with a thin, lopsided smile.

"He couldn't even hide a parking ticket. But then somehow he caught on. He learned how to lie right under my nose."

"Oh yeah." Half her mouth smiled.

"I mean, I can lie, like most women I'm pretty good at it, but I didn't think he was capable of it. I was almost impressed that he had pulled it off."

"Men are such douchebags," G said, shooting a tiny black projectile out of my cheek. She finished the extractions, which left a trail of stings on my skin, like a hot rain falling. Then she began massaging my face, drawing her hands up my neck and gently paddling away under my jaw.

"Gets the lymphatic system active and draining."

"What about you?" I asked, straining my eyes up to find hers. "Are you married?"

"In a way," she said. We laughed. "My husband's a musician, so he's away a lot, on the road."

"Oh, that's a tough one. My ex is a filmmaker, and he was always on the road a lot, either in production or on the festival circuit. I used to travel with him sometimes—we went to Cannes one year—but it's hard, without a role of your own. I just miss sitting around on the couch with someone."

"Marriage and couches, man, they go together."

"He had to spend six months in Belgium when we first moved in. That's when I fell for someone who *was* around all the time. But he happened to be married."

"Oh yeah. As in, married-married?"

"Right. So that messed us up for quite a while. But I always claimed it was Eric's fault, for leaving me alone so much in the beginning."

More tears, which G tenderly swabbed away.

"We were careless with each other, that's all." I sighed. "It's a miracle we made it as far as we did."

"Why did you stick it out?"

"Oh, you know. Love." At this G snorted. "And I knew he'd be a good father. Which he is."

"That's huge. Seeing my husband with the children is such a turn-on for me."

G was using a brush to paint a gritty white paste on my cheeks and forehead.

"What products are you using?" she asked.

This was a question I always dreaded.

"Well, I buy all those toners and cleansers, then they sit on the back of the toilet and I never use them. I wash my face with soap, usually."

"O-kay . . ."

"Glycerin soap. And I use Kiehl's moisturizer." Kiehl's was

old-school, a New York pharmacy that used to make little vials of patchouli oil in the hippie days.

But G didn't criticize. She kept painting away.

"I think you'd find that exfoliating once a week would make a big difference."

"I'll try," I said meekly.

Somewhere on the floor above us, a phone rang, and high heels clicked across the floor.

"Chris is always asking me to go on the road with him," G said. "But I hate being 'the girlfriend.' You go to the club, the guy on the door stares at the clipboard for a long time, and you say, 'I should be on there, I'm with the band,' and finally he gets bored looking for your name and waves you in. You're always feeling not, like, official. Then I sit around backstage eating all the vegetables on the snack trays."

"Yeah, those trays with all that celery! Celery's a non-food."

"I can live with the celery. It's actually very hydrating and high-fiber. But if I start giving the guys feedback on the sound mix or whatever, I feel like that girlfriend in *Spinal Tap*, the one who wants to make the band wear costumes based on their zodiac signs . . ."

She turned around to rinse her brush in the little sink. I could feel the potion on my face tightening, as if I were wearing pantyhose on my head.

G's brows lifted and her red mouth smiled.

"But he really, really likes me to be there in the audience. So I try to go."

She consulted a sheet of paper on the counter and ticked off two items on a list. My tears were now blocked by the drying mask.

"After our daughter was born, I stayed home and started writing a blog, with recipes and parenting stuff, which amazingly kind of took off. My traffic was insane! I do believe that domestic life can be, like, a spiritual path."

"Or not," I said cheerfully.

"Then I realized that I was still home all day long, only working harder! So I hired a nanny, and I signed up for an Ayurvedic skincare course."

"The balance thing?"

"Right, and that's when things really fell into place. The products are natural, and it's one on one, you know? Which is extremely rewarding."

"Well, the work suits you. You have a lovely touch."

"Thank you! It's so nice to get feedback in person. There's too many haters online."

"So do you ever fight around the kids?"

"Oh, no. We consciously put the kids first. Well, we try to."

"I think we expect way too much from marriage."

"This year I started to make some of my own lotions and masks. It's like cooking, only for your face. Here's my website."

She took a sky-blue card out of a drawer and put it on the counter beside my glasses and earrings. Now that the close work was over, she pulled off the scrunchie and shook out her blond hair.

"So how did you find out?" G asked. "About her."

"It wasn't any one thing. Small nothing moments that I look back on now and think, how stupid could I be, why didn't I pick up on that?"

"Whenever Chris gets a crush on someone I can always tell," said G. Now I was able to look at her right side up. She had a perfectly oval face and her smile was thin, wide, and wry. A little rueful. "He starts kind of posing in the mirror when he's getting dressed. Fussing about what to put on. Or buying something too hipsterish."

"My first clue was when I went to see a friend who was dying. She asked me how things were with Eric, and the words just came out of my mouth. 'I always feel jealous,' I said, 'although I have nothing to be jealous of.' As soon as I said it, I realized that it was true—he was somewhere else, really."

"You feel it in your bones," G said. "Like a cold draft. It's awful."

"Marriage is kind of a performance, right? You both agree to play your roles. That's part of the security of it, knowing what comes next. Then one day you realize that the two of you are just running the lines, and nobody's home."

"So tell, about the big reveal."

"What?"

"The moment, the moment you found out."

"We were sitting at our kitchen table. We had been to a friend's birthday party. I was a bit drunk, and that's when I tend to hammer away at whatever's bothering me. I was railing away at him. And somehow her name came up."

G trundled her chair to the side of me and held up an appliance that looked like an electric toothbrush. She pressed a switch on it and a thin, powerful shaft of light shone out.

"I'm going to do a few passes with this—it helps stimulate the production of collagen, which pushes new cells to the surface. You might feel a slight tingling." She began moving it over my face, as if writing on it.

"He had bumped up his therapy sessions to twice a week, and so I made a joke, like 'you're spending more time with her than me.' Then, drunk, I said, 'You might as well be sleeping with her.' And he didn't say anything."

"Bingo."

"His face got really pale, and he kind of gathered himself

up. It was obvious that he'd been preparing, rehearsing, for this moment."

"What did he say?"

"He said, 'I do have feelings for her.' Nobody says that! Like something out of a nineteenth-century novel. It broke my heart. What he meant, of course, was 'I love her.'"

"Uh-oh," said G, sweeping back and forth with the light.

"I realized that I had to catch up quickly, like a film on fast-forward, to something that had been going on for some time. The odd part was this rush of relief I felt, that my sense, my feeling of being *unpartnered* wasn't something that I had imagined. So I wasn't crazy after all."

"You're really pinking up here," said G admiringly, patting my cheek.

"Anyway, I guess you know what I'm talking about."

G turned to the sink and rinsed her hands. She dialed the steamer down a notch. The Balinese music sounded like soft mallets on bones.

"Oh yeah."

"So, tell."

She sighed. "It involves some names."

"Feel free to change them," I said merrily. "It's all the same story."

I hadn't felt so light for ages. Telling someone about my husband's betrayal was the best spa treatment I could imagine. And I felt a swell of affection for him now, for the two of us having come through it, both knowing exactly what the other one had endured.

"It was during the band's last tour of the American southwest," said G with a doleful timbre to her voice already.

"We'd been talking about starting a family. Chris wasn't

opposed, but the whole question of where we would settle, how often could he be on the road and all that, was on the table."

"How old were you?"

"Thirty-two."

"And you were acting?"

"Yeah. That was a problem. There were times when I was a little bit more famous than he was. And frankly, it bugged him. He wouldn't admit it, but it always came out when we argued."

"Careers are overrated," I said.

"Once, we were at some event and I overheard him saying, 'Gwyn's a great cook, but only when the camera's on her.'"

"Ouch."

"Yeah. And I began to notice that on the nights when it was more about me out in public, we'd come home, and . . ."

"Ixnay on the sex."

"Right. What women used to do."

"Well, I've never been more successful than my husband, so I can't speak to that." I felt quite giddy. My broken marriage seemed like nothing more than a story now, one passed around circles of chuckling women.

"So you quit show biz?" I was getting the picture that G's career had been considerably more glamorous than mine.

"Yeah. I tried being a country singer for a while, which was fun—but it overlapped too much with Chris's career. Then I took some time off. I went to an ashram in India for a couple weeks, which was, like, life-altering. That's when I decided that I wanted to do something very modest, but intimate. Service, you know?"

"Like in AA."

"Anyway, that's when I realized that I wanted to work on people's skin."

I was sorry, at this point, that my skin wasn't more well tended, for her sake. But on the other hand, I had given her a weedy garden, a challenge. And our time together had been intimate, more private than anything I had experienced for some time.

"I think we're done here, Rose," said G. "I'm going to give you a few samples of that mask, it seems to be working for your skin. And remember—exfoliate, at least once a week. Getting rid of dead skin will make a huge difference."

I made a silent vow to follow her advice.

"You're very good at what you do," I said. I patted her arm. "I think you've found your calling." I gathered up my things. The tipping would happen upstairs.

"Thank you." She gave me a wad of foil packets, free samples of masks and moisturizers. "And I won't say have fun at the wedding."

"I'll try not to throw a drink in anyone's face." We laughed and she gave me a little hug.

"You'll be fine," she said, swiveling a round mirror toward me. "Take a look."

I flipped the mirror to the unmagnified side, and braced myself for redness, or at least that slightly raw, post-facial look. But my face was calm. The green of my eyes had deepened. And my skin looked fabulous.

Don't I Know You?

Was it the moon? Something was shining down on Rose. She could also hear a sharp, staccato sound, like dishes being shattered or a broken toy falling down stairs. No, she realized, it was laughter, human female laughter. Someone out laughing in the moonlight.

"S'my favorite organ, the liver," came a voice, a little slurred, with some sort of English accent. "Just hanging out there under the ribs, doing its thing, not a poncy showboat like the heart. And look at the size of it! You could make a bloody nice handbag out of this one."

More laughter, and that metallic clatter again.

I should be working, Rose thought. But on the tops of her feet, she felt a mild, cool weight. That must mean I'm horizontal, she thought. Very good! If she was lying down, there was a strong possibility that she was asleep, and only dreaming.

Then came a dim but unsettling sensation, a kind of stirring and probing deep inside her. As if she were a bowl of batter with bits of eggshell in it, and someone was trying to fish them out with his fingers.

The stirring went on, until another feeling, more urgent and ruthless, broke through the membrane of her consciousness: pain. It glittered and writhed, a corkscrew twisting through her. Pain like a state of unbearable intelligence. If she were dreaming, Rose told herself, it was time to wake up and take action, take steps against this noxiousness.

But she was a stone that could not rise.

Then the corkscrew withdrew. Rose became aware of a new bubbling sound, a silvery cascade of notes that carried her along like a twig on a current. After a while she recognized this dancing, bright articulation—it was music. Bach's Goldberg Variations, to be specific, Glenn Gould's version. She knew every note; it was the soundtrack for her daily stretching routine. There was the faint sound of Gould autistically humming in the background, so she was not inventing this.

Where in the world was she, Rose wondered, that the moon was shining down on her while her guts felt like the keyboard of a piano being played by Glenn Gould?

"What a tough bugger it is too," the English voice continued. "You can drink bourbon morning noon and night for years till your eyes turn the color of piss . . . then lay off for a week and bingo, the liver's ready to go again, fresh as a daisy."

This time the laughter was masculine, turbulent, a dark and moist convulsion in the chest.

"But the brain, Christ. I don't trust that tapioca. All you have to do is bump your head on the bathroom cabinet and it'll turn on you. It's just like some chicks, the brain—cheat on 'em once and you'll be paying for it till you drop."

Rose wanted to agree about the cheating part but her lips refused to move.

"F'rinstance, and this is between us, ladies, I haven't really been the same since I fell out of that fucking palm tree," the voice said. "I'll be in the OR, tackin' up a hernia or something, nothing fancy, and suddenly my mind'll go blank, yknow-whammean? Like I'm looking down at someone else's dinner."

More moist rumblings, like swamp gas bubbling up from some primordial place.

"Some bloke from a newspaper once wrote that I keep a picture of my liver on the wall at Redlands," said the voice. "S'not true, of course. S'bollocks as usual. But they did make a little video of my liver when I was in Switzerland, doing the blood thing, so I took a peek at that. And it was bloody fuckin' impressive, let me tell you."

Again with the wet, rattling cough.

"Sweetheart, my hands are tied up here, d'y'mind tipping that bottle to my lips? And help yourself too."

"Maybe after lunch," said the gentle voice.

Swallowing sounds, protracted.

"So, yeah . . . my liver was brown, a kind of nice dark chocolate brown, and it was the shape of . . . that big rock in Ah-stry-lia, what's it called?" the voice asked. "The famous one, you know . . . oh, damn this palm-tree brain . . ."

There were feminine murmurs, too soft to be deciphered.

"Ayers Rock, yes, thank you Cynthia, you are a clever one! Yeah, so my liver in this video looked like that big red fucker."

The voice, like the music, began to sound familiar to Rose, but the name that went with it kept drifting away from her. Kevin? No. The voice aroused a certain feeling, though, a friendly feeling, as if she were on her way for a drink with a solid old chum who had just turned up, someone fun from her past. But the pawing sensation in her guts continued, and fought against this warmer current.

The stirring became an irritable tugging.

"I keep forgetting how *complicated* it is in here," said the voice. "It's all higgledy-piggledy, like some sort of bloody casserole my mum would make."

"There it is, in the lower quadrant," said a woman. "See? You may need this." A slapping sound was followed by a new and more terrible pain. Rose's sense of herself shriveled, like an insect that had blundered into a flame.

"I've got you now, you little cunt! Get the fuck out!"

There was a tweezing sensation, then the pain ended abruptly.

"Oh, it's a biggie," said the voice, sounding pleased, "but the margins look clean. Nothing spreading into the pelvic cavity that I can see. Looks like a hemangioma to me."

Rose heard a wet plunk. "Take this down to the lab, but bring it back later. I've got plans for it." Again with the loamy chuckle. The female voices giggled.

"Doctor?" said the gentle voice beside him. "There's still a bit left in the bottle."

"Pass it here."

Lengthy gulping sounds ensued.

"Y'know, some pe'le say i'z a bad idea, to drink while you're performin' surgery on other pe'le. But! I pers'nally don't agree with that. I do *not* agree with that! Because, if I'm really in the *groove*, really sort of *feelin'* it, y'knowwhammsayin, another bit of the Jack just puts me even *more* in the groove. Am I right, Cyn?"

"Shall I clean up the cavity for you?" said the gentle voice. "She's bleeding quite a bit."

I'm bleeding, Rose thought. Pay attention!

"Oh yeah, Christ, that's not good, be my guest. Mop away." Rose felt herself being massaged from the inside.

"One more clamp . . . that's got it I think. Good call, ladies."

A fit of coughing came and then subsided. "Y'know, the sight of blood still puts me off. Guts, bones, crazy shit that glistens, that I can take. But if I have to get a needle, some sort of tetanus thing when I fall and cut myself, I don't even want to see the blood climb up the syringe. Which is pretty funny, right?"

The gentle voices murmured words that Rose couldn't make out.

"Whoa, look at the hemoglobin levels, better top her up. Hand me that bag, Cyn. It's O type, right? What the hell, A's fine. Ahanh! Just kidding. Now where's the portal . . . annnd in she goes."

A warm surge came over Rose, as if she were a loaf of bread being baked. It felt sexual.

"That'll get her back out on the dance floor."

Rose was getting used to having someone else's hands inside her. You just had to relax into it, like a hard yoga pose.

"Bet you a bottle of Macallan it's benign, even though it's an ugly-looking sucker."

"Doctor, do you want Heather to close for you?"

"No, for chrissake, I can *close up*, you think I can't close up? It's like the intro to *Gimme Shelter*, I can do it in my fuckin' sleep!"

Rose sensed nips, tiny nips. What was the name of that Frida Kahlo painting of herself wild-haired, bleeding in a hospital bed, the red spilling over the frame? *A Few Small Nips.* They didn't so much hurt as tingle. She was floating right under the surface now, but she didn't want to wake up.

Then she recognized the voice and knew why she was horizontal. She was being operated on by a seventy-year-old rock star and there was a bottle of bourbon going round the OR.

Oddly enough, she was okay with this.

H ey, sweetheart," said the frayed voice, "how're ya doin'?"
Rose opened her eyes. The moon was gone. She looked
down; she was in a hospital gown, under stiff, thin sheets, in
a hospital bed. The figure sitting beside her wore green scrubs
but his little cap had a skull pattern on it—skulls on skull, as it
were. All up one hairy, muscular forearm he wore beaded Ras-
tafarian bracelets. His hair was gray and pubic-kinky, escap-
ing from the cap. His face was like something exhumed from
deep in the earth but his brown eyes were warm—surprisingly
clear and healthy eyes.

"I feel like I've been run over by a garbage truck," she said.

"Good, good, that's what we like to hear. It means you're
alive and your body's pissed off."

Cautiously she shifted so she could look at him more directly.

Keith Richards, her surgeon.

"I'm sorry, I hope you don't find it rude, but I have to
ask . . ."

"Yeah, don't worry, I'd be asking questions too."

"Are you . . . like, trained at this? I mean do you do this
often?"

"Depends on whether the band's rehearsing, but lately I've
been operating once or twice a week. I did an open heart a
couple weeks ago, which turned out pretty well. Not perfect,
but the guy survived, more or less. Liver's my specialty, though."

"Where did you learn how to do this?"

"When I was in Switzerland. I met this cat who was into
'expressive surgery,' he called it. The jazz version, you know?
He was a cardiologist but what he really wanted to do was play
in a band." Keith rolled his eyes.

"I get a lot of those. Anyway, I taught him some chords. He wasn't bad actually, decent sense of time, and then he let me watch him operate."

"Wow."

"He told me, just do surgery the way you play guitar, and you won't have a problem. It's all in the hands, right? Which turned out to be true. I mean, you have to have good backup in the OR. It's like bein' in a band that way. But if you kind of *feel* your way through the body, it usually works out."

Rose's mouth hurt at the corners, where her dry lips had cracked.

"Really? You improvise?"

"Well, I did practice. There was this junkie in the clinic when I was there, who was down to eighty pounds and they let me operate on him." Keith whistled.

"Oh man, I'll never forget the look of that liver—it was like roadkill. But I kind of chipped away at it, cleaned it up the way you would your rose garden in the fall, and three hours later, the guy's got a hepatic unit like a newborn baby's. He wakes up feeling great, kicks his habit in a week, and now he's this celebrity meditation guru."

"Who?"

"Sorry, can't say. Anyway, when the operation was over I was standing there with the scalpel thinking, This is my new instrument."

"But doesn't being a surgeon interfere with the whole music thing?"

"That's kind of seasonal anyway. Bit like being a fisherman. I mean, Mick's always got other stuff going on, he's off getting his brows done or whatever. Buying new leggings. If I put all my eggs in that basket, I'd be fucked. This way, when we tour, I hang up the knife and don't book any OR time. But if the band's between gigs, I can do a little surgery and feel like I'm keeping my chops up, right? It's all about the hands."

"How does Mick feel? About you doing surgery on the side."

"He thinks it's a load of crap. He said he wouldn't trust his shih tzu to me. Which is a crap thing to say, because operatin' on animals is no piece of cake. I tried it once on Hooker, my black Lab, and never again!"

An image of Frank, her aging wheaten terrier, came into Rose's thoughts and made her eyes tear up. Her neighbor with the cockapoo was taking care of him. She didn't even tell her ex, and certainly not the kids, that she was going in for surgery.

"But Mick doesn't like me having a life of my own. He just wants me to get out there on stage, stay upright, and be more or less in tune." His chest rumbled. "I think he's jealous. I think he'd like to do surgery himself."

"Has he tried? I mean, do you guys all have special permits or something?"

It was one thing for rock stars to snag the best table in a restaurant but she'd never heard of them getting backstage passes for hospitals.

"No, but he'd probably pick it up fast. Mick's a detail guy, very neat. Good motor skills." Keith made sewing gestures. "But he's got a low fucking boredom threshold, and there's a lot of drudgery involved in operating. Darning socks sort of thing. Mandrax is good for that part."

A nurse came in, her stockings making a slithery sound, and gave Rose two white pills in a small paper cup. Just holding her head up to swallow them made her ribs ache.

"But I do like the liver," Keith went on, sitting on the end of the bed as he absentmindedly massaged Rose's feet through the sheets. "I've operated on quite a few close friends, actually."

"Anita, you mean? Did you do surgery on Anita Pallenberg?"

"No. Although we did fantasize about it." He gave a warm chuckle.

"That woman had the constitution of a Clydesdale. But I did, let's see . . . Eric Clapton, and Nick Cave, and funnily enough, Pavarotti—he had early stage bile-duct cancer and I managed to nip that in the bud."

"So if my . . . tumor turns out to be benign, should I worry about something worse, down the road?"

"Nah, your chances stay the same as anybody else. I think our bodies like to grow stuff, like mushrooms in the forest— it's their artistic side coming out. Cancer is just creativity run amok," he said, fishing in her bedside drawer for any stray codeine pills.

Rose felt a wave of fatigue. She didn't want to have a creative body. She wanted a dull one that behaved itself.

"I hope you don't mind me saying, but I think you need to use more anesthesia when you operate," Rose said. "I could sort of feel you inside me when I was on the table." The phrase made her blush. "And I could hear you kibitzing with the nurses."

"You're joking! Oh that's not good. I'll speak to the anesthesiologist, or whatever you call him." He gurgled. "You don't want to be conscious for the sloppy bits."

"It's okay. It wasn't torture, it was just weird. Especially since your voice sounded so familiar. I'm a big fan, by the way. I play *Main Offender* all the time."

"Yeah, thanks. Good one, that."

"So . . . it was confusing, that's all."

"Look sweetheart, I've had surgery too. It's no picnic."

"What happened?"

"It was after I fell out of that fucking palm tree in Fiji. It was only seven feet off the ground but I hit my head, and had an aneurism. Nearly croaked. They flew me to the mainland, operated on my brain, and I was in a coma for weeks."

"Oh my God."

"World's worst hangover when I woke up from that. And I've had a few."

"Did you think you were dying?

"I had the tunnel thing happening. The white light . . . train come in a station sort of thing." He laughed. "Yeah, I was jamming with the big boys."

"How did it feel?"

"Silly. I felt pretty arsed about falling out of a tree, and not a very tall one either. I thought about Patti, how I'd miss her, and the kids. Plus the band, of course. Even Mick. Basically I felt embarrassed to be dying."

A slithery sound as the nurse came back in. Her name tag read "Shell." She wore dark lipstick and looked more like someone in costume as a nurse.

"Dr. Richards, the lab reports are in. Do you want to take a look at them now?"

"Yeah, I'll step outside with you."

Rose reached out for his hand, and he took it in both of his.

"I won't make you wait."

They left the room and Rose lay there trying not to care too much about her life. She wished she'd said yes more often in the past, yes to risky things that might have taken her down different roads. But she had been brave, more than once. Marrying Eric (a mistake, as it turned out, but the first ten years were good). Having Ceri. Not giving up on the writing.

An image came to her, of her thirty-one-year-old self. Her

blond hair was long and she was in a taxi, heading into New York with the manuscript of her first book, *Night Crossing*, beside her. No appointments set up—she literally pushed it through the transom over the door of Farrar, Straus & Giroux. "Your submission created quite a stir in the office," the letter began, when it arrived weeks later. It was a rejection but an encouraging one.

Rose looked back on her own innocence as if she were out walking a dog that had stopped far behind her to explore the woods until she had lost sight of him. And kept waiting, patiently, for his return.

Keith Richards and Shell came back into the room.

"I knew you were a lucky girl," he said, his face crinkling. Shell beamed too, as if they were a couple announcing a pregnancy.

"It's negative?"

"Yes. Harmless, but sizable, which explains the pain. You'll be fine now."

Rose wept a little.

"I was prepared for the worst," she said, swabbing her cheeks with a tissue. "I always imagine the worst."

"And now, we're going to toast you."

Another nurse brought in a trolley, with a silver shaker on it, an ice bucket, martini glasses, a jar of olives, a lemon, and a zester. Plus a glass dish that contained something mottled and oysterlike: Rose's hemangioma.

"Olive, lemon, or . . ."

Keith pretended to slurp the tumor down, and they all laughed nervously.

"No takers? They say it's like a Malpeque, quite briny."

Then he mixed some Grey Goose vodka with ice and made

a noisy show of shaking it up. He poured it into three martini glasses and added curls of lemon zest.

Rose sat up, smoothing her hair behind her ears. She had an urge to cut it very short, and dye it patent-leather black, or fuchsia, or both. Bangs with fuchsia tips. Her daughter would be appalled. But there was the rest of her life to live now, after all. The martini glass felt silvery cold in her hands.

Keith held up his drink and tipped his head forward like a monk. The fingers on his right hand were a little gnarled with arthritis, Rose noticed. But they had moved so gently inside her. She had a fleeting desire for something more—an appendectomy?

He met her eyes.

"To your continued health."

Before the World
Was Made

Our bus driver was a little red-haired guy with bushy ginger muttonchops. We were heading north out of the city into the faded high rises of Don Mills, on one of the routes where they still announce the stops live. "Chipping Road next," he said with his lips against the mesh of the microphone. Then he began to croon.

Down on Cyprus Avenue . . . with a childlike vision leaping into view . . .

He was driving like a show-off too, swinging the bus way out on the curves like a matador flaring his cape. Across the aisle from me was an elderly woman who gave me a fearful, what's-with-our-driver look. The only other passengers were two teenage boys with corpse-sized duffel bags slumped at their feet, and hockey sticks. But they didn't seem worried.

Ahead of us was a cluster of schoolgirls, long hair whipping in the wind, waiting by the curb. As cars honked the driver plunged across two lanes of traffic to pick them up. I'm not even sure it was a regular stop. The girls were dressed identically in white knee-highs, white shirts, plaid ties, and micro-short tartan skirts. When the door opened they came bubbling up the steps, all long legs and knapsacks—so much beauty, like five young Cate Blanchetts. As they moved down the aisle their unzipped parkas shed cold winter air on us.

One of them, ginger-haired like the driver, punched him on the arm as she went by.

"Hey Van, 'sup. Would you kiss-a my eyes?"

This caused the other girls, who had already staked out the back of the bus, to shriek with laughter. It was three o'clock on Friday afternoon and they were revved up for the weekend. Everyone on the bus seemed to be heading home but me.

I'd given myself a full hour to get to my interview on Castlefield Street, a long street on the Google map that petered out into blankness. The street view showed carpet outlets, appliance warehouses, and the headquarters for Flo-Q, a company that sold upscale bathroom fixtures and spa water features. The LinkedIn listing had said they were looking for a writer who could "bring sparkle" to their online catalogue copy.

Lately I've been writing fiction but my last novel, *Night Crossing*, didn't perform well. Too literary, my agent said. So my new plan is to use my "skill set" to get an undemanding job in "communications," in the "water-feature field" if necessary, while I get up every morning at five a.m. to write. I'm already 120 pages into my next novel, *Havoc*, which has thriller elements. I'm pretty happy with it so far. I just need this job.

We were crossing a bridge over a ravine, with a brownysilver thread of water twisting below. The Don River, presumably. The girls at the back of the bus were passing around a phone video laughing with self-conscious loudness as they fell against one another. The driver began to sing, gripping the wheel with both meaty, freckled hands.

And I'm conquered in a car seat . . .

Good voice, vaguely familiar, although it sounded more like a musical instrument—a tenor saxophone? The girls clapped. The woman across the aisle tucked her scarf more tightly around her throat. She was wearing a tailored wool coat and a proper felt hat with a little brim. I looked down at my puffy parka with the ski-lift tag still dangling from the zipper. They're almost impossible to get off.

The thing is, when you work at home, eccentricities can start to pile up. Maybe you leave the house in the morning without checking for toothpaste at the corners of your mouth. Or you bike to the corner to buy milk, then leave one leg of your jeans rolled up all day.

"Attention," the driver said into his mike, "would the people in the back of the bus please move up into my lap?" The girls whooped and the redhead ran up the aisle to perch on one of his thick thighs. He nuzzled her neck, making fart-noises like someone blowing against a baby's stomach.

Wow. How can he get away with this? I wondered. Maybe he's already given his notice, and this is his last day on the job. The hat lady now looked truly frightened. We were moving through fringes of the city past boarding kennels and scrap-iron lots.

"*I maaaay go crazy,*" the driver sang, "*be-fore that mansion on the hill . . .*"

"Too late for that," said the girl as she twirled his red hair into ringlets. "Where's your crazy little captain hat, Van?"

He reached into a briefcase at his feet and pulled out a brown corduroy cap with gold braid. She put it on. A bright-eyed, pointy-nosed girl who looked like a young Winona Ryder came up the aisle and started taking pictures of them.

I checked the time: less than half an hour left to make my interview. Out the window, Don Mills had vanished, replaced by farm fields with a scattering of sheep here and there, like soft gray boulders. The syringelike spire of the CN Tower grew smaller and smaller behind us.

I rehearsed what I would say in the interview. ("The taps and faucets we use every day can either enhance or diminish our quality of life . . .") and reminded myself to act fifty percent more animated than felt sane or normal.

I made my way to the front of the bus.

"How much farther to Castlefield?"

He looked up at me with his wide, flushed face and smallish green eyes. Squinting, he put a finger to the center of his forehead for a few seconds, then stabbed it in my direction like a fork.

"*Night Crossing*, right?"

Now I was frightened too.

"Underrated, man! The last third, with the Nigerian stowaway dude in the container ship? Fan-tabulous."

I couldn't speak.

"Hey, don't worry about Castlefield," he said, checking his mirrors. "You don't need that bath shit anyway. We're taking the scenic route today."

"I can see that, but—"

"Just loosen up, angel," he said, giving my hip a fist-bump. "The next one's cookin'."

"Are you referring to . . . my current book?"

"Yeah!" He gripped his forehead. "Gimme a sec—*Hassock. Hassidic* . . . ?"

"*Havoc.*"

"Right! But here's the problem." He eased up on the gas and looked at me again. "You okay with a little feedback?"

"I guess so." Anyone who said that was going to give it to you anyway.

"You're too on the beat. You need to stay *behind* it a little, know what I mean?" He drummed on the steering wheel to demonstrate. "Unn-chukka, *unn*-chukka . . ."

I nodded.

"There's a kind of a *choke* thing going on with you."

The road curved ahead of us. He accelerated, causing the schoolgirls to shriek and cling to one another. I braced myself against a pole. As we pulled past an eighteen-wheeler the trucker gave us a long, angry blast of the horn.

"And I'd rethink the title. *Havoc* sounds like something you'd buy at IKEA."

I could feel my face burning.

"I like the title." I said. "It sounds like a thriller."

The hockey boys had scrunched up a piece of newspaper and were kicking it up and down the aisle like a soccer ball. No longer trying to hide her panic, the hat lady was on her feet, yanking on the stop cord. We pulled over to the curb and the doors hissed open.

"Have a shagadelic day, ma'am."

Then the two hockey boys left, shouldering their duffel bags. I didn't want them to go.

"Thanks, Van," shouted the last one out. "Stay cool."

"*Ding-a-ling-aling, ding-a-ling-aling,*" he sang back.

Now it was just the schoolgirls and me. Outside, the fields had given way to a forlorn strip mall, where the late-afternoon sun flashed gold in the windows of a Blinds to Go outlet.

"Excuse me, is this seat free?" It was the Winona girl. "I just need to make a private call."

What, is sitting beside me like being alone?

She tilted her head toward her friends chattering in the back. "It's quieter here."

I took my briefcase off the seat. There was nothing in it but my three-page résumé and two magazines, for bulk. Winona sat down and applied a phone to her cheek.

"Rebecca? Can you hear me? I'm on the bus. So . . ."

I took my CV out and pretended to read it. *Honors B.A., English Language and Literature.* Maybe I should add "with a minor in bath fixtures." Winona held her phone and said nothing for quite a while. I could hear rushed, tinny words on the other end, an inflection of hysteria. She shielded her mouth with her other hand and spoke quietly.

"Are you, like, bleeding a lot?" The gulping sounds on the other end ran together. "Did Evan go with you?" The pitch of the phone voice rose.

"Sorry. Dumb question. What if I came over—I could bring you something . . . a chai latte?"

"*The cool room,*" sang the driver softly into the mike, "*Lord, it's a fool's room.*"

Outside, flakes of snow began to whirl down. I checked my watch; five minutes left to make it to my interview. Clearly, this was not going to happen, which filled me with a wave of relief and even optimism. My future was changing, right this minute! Of course, I could call Flo-Q and reschedule, but what would I say—that my bus got lost? The driver likes my writing?

"Hey don't worry, Becca," Winona said into her phone, "it'll be okay. But what's the story if your mother calls me, or like, the school . . ." More burbling. "Of course not, I'm not a moron. Call me later."

She hung up and looked down at her phone with a sigh.

"Is your friend going to be okay? Sorry, but it's hard not to overhear . . ."

Winona looked at me for a beat and decided I wasn't crazy.

"She had to have an abortion. She just got home from the clinic."

"Oh dear, I'm sorry. How old is she?"

"Sixteen. But she wants to be a vet, which takes like eight years. And her boyfriend's a total douche."

"Sounds like she did the right thing then."

We rode together, as I thought about how it could be the right thing and yet feel like just the opposite.

"I had an abortion once," I said. The words fell out of my mouth, I don't know why.

"You're kidding," said Winona. "Really?"

I ignored her amazement. I thought my generation had invented sex too.

The fact is that I rarely think about it, except around the anniversary, in early December. Or whenever I have to fill out medical forms. Then I remember that my "number of pregnancies" is not one, but two. (My daughter is in Hong Kong right now, doing an exchange semester in engineering. She thinks the bath-fixture job is a terrible idea. Eric's son is back living with him in Philadelphia, so I'm on my own for the first time in ages.)

"How old were you?" Winona asked.

"In my early twenties. I was using a diaphragm. A very unreliable method, by the way. You might as well use a tube sock."

"So what happened?"

"I picked a gynecologist out of the phone book because I was too embarrassed to go to my family doctor. Remember, these were the days before the pill, the days of secret shameful homes run by churches for unwed mothers."

"What about the guy? The father?"

"He was good about it. He paid for half. But we weren't in love—we weren't even a couple, and I had no job, I was trying to write. There was no way I was ready to have a child on my own."

"I don't think even people who have children are ready to have children," said Winona spiritedly.

The driver smiled at us in the mirror. He was happy to see his passengers getting along.

"We were so insouciant about abortion back then. It was almost a feather in your feminist cap. I remember a girlfriend came to pick me up at the clinic, and brought a bottle of champagne."

"That's sweet."

"It was. But in fact there's nothing merry about it. Afterwards the body grieves, whether you think you care or not." I looked at Winona and corrected myself. "Which is not to say that abortion's wrong. Nobody else should make that choice for you."

"Right. Cause it's like, our bodies . . ."

"Right. But it's not something you forget, either."

"So what happened with the guy?"

I laughed.

"Well, he sort of lost interest in me after that. I didn't blame him. It's hard to have casual sex when your body is plotting the future."

Winona laughed too. Her blue drop earrings swung.

"I still check him out online now and then. He ended up owning a vineyard near Niagara-on-the-Lake. Ice wine. Married, divorced. No kids. But he changed his status recently. He's with someone new, a young actress, and they just had twins."

"Yuck. Twins scare me."

"A boy and a girl."

Outside, fake-looking white flakes whirled around, melting as soon as they landed. We were back in rolling farmland with thin rails of snow in the creases of the fields.

"Where the hell are we?" I asked Winona.

"Oh, he never takes the same route twice. It's okay. He just likes to improvise."

The snow dithered away.

"But it did make me wonder, when I found out about the twins."

"Wonder what?"

I hesitated. Usually I am the listener.

"I wondered if I could have been pregnant with twins too."

We rode in silence for a while.

"Anyway," I said, "it was absolutely the right thing to do, for me. And it sounds like this was the right decision for your friend too."

"Her boyfriend told her that pulling out was better for the environment."

"Hah. Good one."

"She's super-serious about the environment."

"Well, he's right, technically. Unless you factor in the over-population it causes."

Winona's chin trembled.

"She doesn't want me to come over, but I think I'll go see her anyway. Should I?"

"Definitely. Is she going to tell her mother?"

"Probably not. Her mother's sort of a nutcase."

We looked out the window. Some fine-boned horses, their muscles shining copper in the low sun, grazed in a field.

"*Your original face,*" sang the driver, "*before time and place . . . before the world was made . . .*"

"So what's up with our driver?" I asked. "He seems to know you all pretty well."

"He used to be a musician, some sort of jazz person I think. Once he drove us right to our front doors. Another time he took the bus to an Il Fornello in Richmond Hill and we all ordered pizzas. I can't believe he doesn't get fired."

"Look at where we are, though. It's so incredibly green—it could be Ireland. It keeps on snowing, but the snow just disappears."

"His name is Van," Winona said. "Don't worry. It might take a while but he'll get us there."

I fell asleep for some time. When I woke up, the highway had narrowed to a two-lane road that wound through a landscape of billowing, waist-high grass. Winona and the girls were sleeping too, sprawled against one another, white ear buds in place. I could hear a murmuring leakage of music. For some reason the sun was higher than it had been, although it shone with a diminished intensity. The snow had stopped. Cirrus clouds brindled the blue sky.

Up in the driver's seat, Van raised his arms off the wheel in an exaggerated stretch that ended in a yodel. Honestly, what a show-off.

We were driving on the left side of the road now, and passed a sign that said DUBLIN 120 MILES. A cement structure came into view on the horizon. It was low and long, with small windows and a tall, ominous smokestack.

"We'll be making a quick stop here, people," Van announced. "Feel free to stretch your legs and use the loo."

The girls woke up and ruffled their hair, smoothed down their skirts. We followed Van out of the bus down a walkway between beds of daffodils and tulips. The day felt both spring-ish and autumnal, with cooler currents threading through the air. Clamorous birdsong came from somewhere, although there were no trees in sight. The air was extraordinarily clear, with a carbonated sparkle, like an alpine meadow on a sunny day.

The building was divided into two wings, "Ambulatory/Long-Term" and "In Transit." We headed down the "In Transit" one with Van ahead of us, walking fast. He had a shapely little ass, for a guy.

A nurse in a white uniform came toward us. She smiled—a small, complicit, beatific smile, like Meryl Streep in *The Hours*. She didn't speak, but her smile had the most powerful effect on me, as if it were passing right through my body.

I never wanted to leave this place, wherever it was.

At the end of the corridor Van turned into a room, where the air felt cold, almost refrigerated. The rest of us stood shyly in the doorway. We could see a woman propped up in a hospital bed with her long dark hair spread on the pillow. She looked young, pale, and very sad.

"Hey Julie," Van said. "Sorry I took so long. The bastards keep changing the routes on me." He took her hand between both of his big ones and chafed it.

"How're you doin', angel?"

Julie gave him a look, half-annoyed, half-grateful. Then she coughed a terrible cough, liquid, harsh, and deep. Van let go of her hand and went over to the window. He wrestled with the sash and lifted it a couple inches.

"Open up the window, I need some air," said Van, making funny little pig-snorts. Julie didn't laugh. Van pulled a chair up close to her head. She turned away from him.

Some of the girls had drifted into the room. They were the same age as the girl in the bed, no more than sixteen. I couldn't figure out Julie's relationship with Van. Daughter? Niece? Underage ex-lover?

The peace and sparkle of the gardens had vanished in this chilly room and I found myself longing to go, to get back on the bus. Van looked uneasy too. He took a vase of wilted tulips to a little sink in the corner, poured the brackish water down the drain, and refilled it. But most of the petals had dropped. Only dusty black stamens remained.

I went over to the other side of Julie's bed and she gave me a faint smile. Her face had the underwater look of someone on serious painkillers.

"Let me fix your pillows," I said. She curled forward and I gave them a few whacks, then stepped on a bar to raise the level of the bed a few inches.

"Thank you." She gave me a searching look. "Are you here . . . to see the twins?"

Twins again. "No, I'm just here because of our driver," I said. "He hijacked us."

"They're right across the hall, waiting to transition. You should see them before they go, they're gorgeous."

A nurse came in, a different unsmiling one. She looked at all of us disapprovingly and strode out, the soles of her shoes squeaking.

I went to the window. This wing overlooked a manicured expanse of grass that might be a golf course. The view was picturesque but static and depthless, like a film set.

Van leaned over Julie and said something into her ear. Then he tried to organize the nest of her sweat-dampened sheets. She coughed into a tissue and added it to a crumpled pile on the table beside her. There was blood on some; Winona saw it too, and gave me a look.

A humidifier in the corner of the room hissed out an opaque

white V, like a lighthouse beam. Julie had a grip on Van's arm and now he had panic in his eyes.

The unsmiling nurse returned.

"I'm afraid I have to ask you all to leave, it's time for a perfusion."

"Hey, we're done here anyway," said Van brightly. He fumbled for something in his pocket.

"So Julie baby, I'm leaving you some tapes." He put a couple old-fashioned cassettes on her lap and waggled one of them.

"You're singing on this one. You sound fantabulous. When you're better we'll work up that tune you always thought I should do. The Crystals song."

Julie said nothing. She shut her eyes. Van tapped the edge of her bed.

"But I should go. I gotta go now. I'm running two days late."

Winona rummaged in her bag and put a plastic Starbucks card on the night table. Julie opened her eyes.

"It's got at least fifteen dollars left on it," Winona said.

"Thank you," Julie said. "But we don't have Starbucks here."

"But they're everywhere."

"This isn't everywhere," said Julie. "In case you haven't noticed."

The other girls were out in the corridor, spying on the other rooms.

"That girl is not a happy camper," Winona said to me, stopping at the open door of the room across the hall from Julie.

"Rebecca!" she said. "What are you doing here?"

A girl in a blue cardigan and skintight jeans leaned over two bassinets.

"I was just visiting the twins," she said dreamily. She smiled at us.

I stepped into the room. Rebecca waved me closer.

"Aren't they beautiful? They're so much bigger than the last time."

The babies, wrapped as tightly as cocoons, had blond hair, quite a bit of it. I watched the one in pink, her eyes moving beneath their lids as if following the action in a dream. The other baby made a comical series of grimaces, like a fast-forwarded training video on how to master facial expressions. I let the one in blue grip my index finger, a fierce grip that could support a chin-up. He held my gaze and I felt my face soften. Time eddied peacefully around us. *In another place.* The baby's solemn eyes were a milky blue, like my mother's.

Julie's nurse came in. The baby's hand uncurled.

"Oh, you're not supposed to be in here. These are in transit."

"In transit? What do you mean—are they all right?"

"Of course," the nurse said with a sharp look at me. "But visiting hours are over now."

"Rebecca, hurry up," said Winona, "or we'll miss our ride."

"Just a minute." Rebecca freed one small fist from the swaddling so the baby could suck on it. Which he did, noisily.

In the hall Winona and I stopped at a fountain, taking long sips from the arc of water. A sign on the door beside us said HYDROTHERAPY and I pushed it open. The tiled white room was empty except for a high-sided porcelain tub with hoselike attachments and a portable set of steps leading up to the lip, like a tiny Mayan shrine. Aha, I thought. The water feature.

A sound came from outside. Someone honking a horn.

Winona took my arm and stroked it like a cat. Rebecca caught up to us and took my other arm. We walked down the corridor like that and out into the peculiar sunlight, where Van was already behind the wheel.

Shovel My Walk

I f it snows overnight, the silence in the early morning has a different quality, as if a duvet has fallen over the city. I lay there wondering how deep it was. Then I heard the scrape of a shovel, like winter clearing its throat. Our neighbor Barry was already out there, even before the snow had stopped or the plows came through. Sometimes it's a lovely sound, shoveling. Sometimes not.

It was mid-January. I was still in bed, dragging my heels about getting the ad copy in for Flo-Q's new line of indoor wave pools. "No more sand in your suit" didn't do it for Leanna, who oversees me. She doesn't like me calling her boss. "We're cocreators" she always says before slashing away at my copy. I gave her a little cartoon that I'd drawn, of a couple in bed beside a big standing wave in the lap pool. The wife is saying "Surf's up, at least." Too negative, Leanna said. She was right.

I turned on my phone, then turned it off. I've been trying to stop tracking my novels on Amazon. The last time I checked, *The Bludgeoning* was in 789,470th place. Which is not the bottom, by a long shot. I repeated this to myself: "Not the bottom." My therapist, Katrine, has instructed me to take every negative thought I have and turn it into a positive one, like doing origami. Newsprint into bluebirds. I've also started a gratitude journal. "I'm grateful to have started my gratitude journal" was the first entry. How can I be sarcastic even with myself? I know it's important to take the exercise seriously, but it feels like I'm joining a cult of one.

Gratitude does work, though. I can feel my thinking shift ever so incrementally toward the light, an ocean liner changing course. And whatever works, I want. Eric's affair (I mean, his recent remarriage) is still livid in my mind, like some ghastly patterned wallpaper that you can't not see every day as soon as you open your eyes. And I'm still waiting to hear back from that e-publisher about *Havoc*.

I should be starting something new, but I don't have the heart for it.

Another thing I realize is that writing is a mirror you can't trust. On Monday the words look supple and fit, a fine dancing partner. On Tuesday the same words look contrived and flat. Who cares? *Blah, blah, blah.* On the other hand, I do not trust people who never doubt, who just plunge on. They seem like babies.

I should get up and shovel the walk, I told myself as I lay there ruminating, the term Katrine prefers. The new mother across the street might be wrestling her stroller out there right now, her child encased in clear plastic like a bunch of bananas. And sometimes Barry clears our walk too, if I don't beat him to it.

I do like my new sheets, though. Navy flannel. Part of my positive embrace of winter. What is flannel, anyway? Is it shorn from some flannel beast, a sheep specially bred by IKEA? And

I don't mind the way the gray light enters my room at this time of year in such a diplomatic way, easing me into the day. Especially when I do not get up until ten. Leanna doesn't care when I get up as long as I deliver by four thirty. That woman has an easy job.

So that's how my day begins, normally. But, and I want to get this down before it fades, this morning was different.

I rose at 9:20, and drew the curtains. More than a foot of snow had fallen. The cars parked across the street looked like desserts, white *îles flotantes* of meringue. Only Barry next door had already shoveled his way to the sidewalk, and was throwing down seedlets of blue chemicals to melt whatever was left. Affable Barry has had heart surgery and smokes, a lot, standing under his porch light. I do worry about the morning when he doesn't step out of his house to light up another cigarette, because he is often the first person I see when I leave the house—if, indeed, I leave the house—and the last person who sees me when I come home alone at night. I would miss Barry.

What was that song that Ryan wrote in high school, about our previous neighbor, a Portuguese man who insisted on pouring concrete over his yard even in the most lethal heat waves? "I Fear That My Neighbor Has Died." Good song. I miss him, and Ceri too. Why did I encourage them to live in other countries?

I was about to step into the shower when I heard the doorbell ring. My Victorian house has a wonderful arrangement— a brass ring on the outside that you pull. Through a series of Rube Goldberg mechanisms linked by a cable, this causes a coiled metal strip to spring open and strike a brass bell that then rings loudly in my hall. Everyone, even the jaded postal person, admires the bell. It probably goes back to the year the house was built, 1896. In the nineteenth century, our midtown enclave of cottages and brick houses became the living quarters for the working men who built the rest of the city—a neighborhood where cabbage soup was a staple. Hence the name, Cabbagetown. Now, of course, the houses go for a million, even semidetached.

When you're young, living in a vintage house confers character. You buy some history for yourself. But as you get older, the parallels between your aging house and your own decline can become oppressive. Your life becomes a list of repairs and maintenance. *Replace back stoop. Change furnace filter. Book physio.*

I wrapped my Chinese silk robe around me and answered the door. A tall broad-shouldered young man with an impressive nose and a *joli-laid* face stood there, dressed like a crossing guard, holding a large snow shovel.

"Cool bell," he began.

"Yes. It's very old."

"Clear your walk?"

"I don't know. How much?"

"Twenty bucks, including the side lane and access to your bins."

"Why do you look so familiar?"

He shrugged. "I'm on TV sometimes." Being recognized seemed to pain him. His eyes were a little too close together but the overall effect was handsome somehow. Then it clicked.

"You're Adam Driver!"

He pulled off his tuque. Unruly dark hair, a couple Cindy Crawford moles. Large head.

"Bingo."

"*While We're Young*! Loved you in that."

At this Adam Driver looked relieved, because I didn't go straight to *Girls*. I had just seen him in the movie *Inside Llewyn*

Davis, a slightly softheaded film about a singer/songwriter trying to make it in New York, who fails. He plays a more successful musician who is willing to do whatever sells, including a ridiculous song called "Please Mr. Kennedy." A small part, but he stood out, as usual. Any scene he's in gets big fast.

"And I *love* Justin Timberlake," I said, a little too enthusiastically. "But you were great. It's like you have your own dialect when you act. The way you kind of subvert the normal rhythm of a sentence."

This too-detailed, show-offy feedback nevertheless made him smile. His eyes warmed. Then we both realized that I was in a robe, it was very cold, and snow was sifting into the front hall as we spoke, building a tiny dune inside the threshold.

"Okay, shovel away, Adam. Just ring when you're finished."

"Cool."

I closed the door. Have a shower, I thought, but don't wash the hair. There was an unopened round of Brie in the fridge, and half a loaf of decent bread left. I took the cheese out of the fridge to come to room temperature. Adam would be hungry after all that shoveling.

From the upstairs bedroom, I peered through the slats of the blinds. Barry was out smoking next door, watching this young stranger work. Adam hurled the snow methodically, first left onto the front yard, then right, off the curb. Left, right, always moving west. He had unzipped his big parka. He wore those heavy cuffed garbage-man gloves. I guess this is how he keeps in shape, I thought.

I got into the shower, with its brand-new generous multi-stream Flo-Q head. Standing under the torrent of hot water, I couldn't help coming up with more copy. "Shower Yourself with Love," or perhaps just "Get Wetter." But Leanne did not like innuendo.

Afterward, wrapped in a towel, I went to check on Adam again from my office window. He was already halfway to the green organic bin in the lane. Neat margins. God, it's great to watch a young man use his body. His parka was off now and his yellow snow pants were held up by crossed suspenders over a thick sweater. Snow pants can be sexy.

I put on my second-best jeans and a little black tank top under a blue striped men's shirt. Mutton dressed as lamb? What the hell.

Then I went down, sliced the bread, cracked the packaging on some biscuits, and arranged them around the Brie with the cheese knife. I went to the door just as Adam was ringing the bell.

"Look at you," I said idiotically when I opened the door. I pretended to assess the bare sidewalks. "Great job!"

"It's still fresh," he said. "Not too heavy."

"Come on in and have a bite, Adam," I said. "You must be starved."

"I could eat," he said, a little embarrassed.

"By the way. That scene in *What If*, where you play Daniel Radcliffe's horndog roommate? Fantastic."

"The nachos scene?"

"Yes! You sit down across from Daniel with this huge plateful of food and you say—"

At this Adam got into character. " 'I've just had sex . . .' "

" 'And now I'm going to eat some . . .' "

And here we both shouted the word.

" '*Nachos!*' "

"Which could have been such a throwaway moment."

"Well, I can thank the writer for that one."

He unlaced his boots and put his parka on the newel post of the banister, then followed me into the kitchen.

"Hmm, Brie," he said, already paving a cracker with it.

"Not nachos, but close." I chuckled. "I suppose we could reverse the order."

What was I saying? Was I suggesting to Adam Driver that he eat my cheese, and *then* we have sex? Wasn't it enough that he had shoveled my walk for a very reasonable price? But when stars are involved, even minor ones, desire always escalates. It's like a street drug.

"Ha-ha," Adam said. Perfectly at ease, letting it go by gracefully.

He looked out into my yard, where I had neglected to take in the patio furniture. Like a 3-D printer, the round wrought-iron table had duplicated itself in a lacy layer of standing snow. It was very pretty and somehow French. Adam ate and gazed at the snowscape. He had a wide brow and his face was dominated by that nose, but changeable. There was a latent fury in his expression, even when he smiled. I poured him a tall glass of coconut water and he drank it down in one go.

"Gotta stay hydrated," he said. He tilted his chair back. "So, I'm going to work this side of the street, then do Sackville, then knock off for the day."

"Sackville's got deep front yards," I said helpfully.

"You're right. Maybe I'll only do one side."

I felt relaxed with him. Fatal. I tapped the back of his hand on the table.

"I know everyone must ask you this but . . . what's going to happen with you and Lena Dunham in the next season?"

I could see that I had now disappointed him. This was probably why he was shoveling walks in Toronto. To be not Adam Driver.

"Sorry, can't say. Embargoed. But I'm in four of the episodes. That I can tell you."

"And Lena . . . ?"

He made a *voilà* gesture with one hand. "Just as you would imagine. Creative. Open." He laughed. "Super open."

"She's handled her success pretty well, I think. For someone so . . ."

He looked at me mock-lasciviously. "Young?"

"Right."

"Well, young is just one factor, like being born in Ohio or . . . having a minister for a father," he said. "But it's not all-defining."

"I guess. Sort of."

He looked at me for a long moment. I had to break his gaze.

"What's your name?"

"Rose."

"Hello, Rose."

The doorbell rang again. I could tell by the shape through the pebbled glass that it was Barry, from next door. Reluctantly, I went to answer it. His shy bulk filled the doorframe. It was snowing again.

"Hi, Rose."

"Hello, Barry." We enjoyed our little formalities.

"I noticed that a young man came by to shovel your walk. Would he . . . be interested in doing ours?"

Barry, who was in his forties, lived with his mother, Ruth, a spry eighty-two-year-old who was always the first one out the door in the morning, to walk her little dog.

Adam Driver heard all this and came down the hall.

"Your walk looks pretty clean," Adam pointed out. Barry had cleared it earlier, so that Ruth could make her way.

"Snow's falling fast though," said Barry, "and I don't want to take any chances." He smiled and tapped his chest. "Somebody in Mississauga already died this morning from shoveling. It's the sudden intense demand on the heart muscle."

"He's just having a bite to eat," I offered, waving my hand toward the kitchen.

Adam stepped out the door to consider the job ahead of him. The snow was coming down thick and wet, already filling in the dark blanks of the pavement. When he came back inside there were flakes in his hair, perfectly formed crystals.

"Okay. But let's give it an hour," he said. He unwound his scarf.

"I'll light a fire," I said brightly.

"Sounds good," said Barry, retreating. "You'll have more to work with then."

I pulled out my phone and texted Leanna: DOWN WITH A BUG, COPY IN TOMORROW OK?

Adam Driver closed the door gently behind him, so the bell didn't ring, and brushed the snow out of his hair.

"I don't think we need a fire," he said.

Some time later, Barry knocked, waited, and rang the bell. Then we heard him below us in the laneway with the shovel, scraping cautiously, trying to make as little noise as possible.

The Reading

Rose felt a cold sore coming on. In the mirror she could see her bottom lip puffing up at the corner like a tiny Yorkshire pudding. It must be all the heat, she thought: the eucalyptus steam room, the Finnish sauna, the sulfur baths. She was almost homesick for the March streets of Toronto with their blackened pyramids of curbside ice.

This was her third day at Rancho Agua Caliente, just across the Mexican border—a reward she had given herself for finishing the novel, even though the book didn't have a publisher yet. Which could be tricky, after the dismal sales of her previous one, *The Bludgeoning*.

"Let me pay half," her ex had insisted. Having just learned that Judy was pregnant with twins, Eric was feeling both expansive and guilty. Rose accepted.

In her thick white robe Rose trudged down the hall to a reflexology session, already looking forward to the single glass of white wine she would allow herself for dinner at the raw-food buffet. She'd have to go early, to avoid sitting with Fanny the Manhattan broker. That woman was wound up.

There were three other white-robed women in the waiting room—the friendly inseparable sisters from Ottawa, who always did the pre-breakfast hike up the mountain, and an attractive older blond woman with luminous skin wearing horn-rim glasses. She was deeply immersed in a hardcover book. Rose squinted to read the title: something-something, by Ann Patchett.

At one point the woman snorted with laughter, pushed the bridge of her glasses up, and gave an audible sigh of pleasure as she turned the page. She had a long, thin nose. Even reading, her face was expressive, alive.

Then Rose realized that the woman with the book was Meryl Streep. For sure—that emotional skin. Her pale blond hair was caught up messily in a tortoiseshell barrette and she wore no makeup. On her feet were the too-big pink paper slippers that came in the spa welcome kit.

A smocked employee opened a door, releasing a cloud of aromatic mist, and summoned the two sisters inside. Rose was left sitting opposite the actress, who pulled a tissue out of her robe pocket and rubbed it under her red nose.

"Every time I go to a place like this I come down with something," she said to Rose with an apologetic smile. "Maybe being pampered is bad for your health."

"I know what you mean," said Rose. "All this pressure to relax has given me a cold sore." She pushed out her lower lip.

Meryl laughed. "I think I love stress, actually." She closed her book and crossed her hands over it. "You know? And I *hate* massage music."

"I brought my own playlist. Lots of Prince."

"Some klezmer would be good too. Very soothing." The actress extended her hand, her eyes dancing.

"I'm Meryl, by the way."

"Yes, I know, I mean, I recognized you, of course. I'm Rose."

"And what are you here recovering from?"

"I just finished writing a book. A novel."

"Oh, good for you! That's huge."

"But I'm having trouble getting rid of the voices," Rose said, pointing to her head. "I mean, of my characters."

The actress rolled her eyes. "Tell me about it. I've found ways to banish them, though."

"Really? Like what?"

"Well, I play tennis, really vicious tennis." She laughed. "I kind of *murder* the voices with my racket. And I sing in a choir, which helps." She unclasped her barrette and gathered up her hair again, closing her eyes dreamily. Her eyelids fluttered. "It reminds me that in real life I am not Adele."

Rose laughed.

"But you're so lucky," Meryl said. "You get to make your characters up. I have to take what they offer me."

"Don't you have your pick?"

"It's been better lately," she said, knocking on the table between them, "but it's still a boys' club, Hollywood, trust me." She poked her feet deeper into the pink slippers. "So what's your book about?"

Rose tried to inject some enthusiasm into her voice. Her doubt always clouded it.

"It's a thriller, sort of. About a woman, a writer doing research on some environmental activists who have this scheme to save the Great Barrier Reef. She's on a ship with them when they get hijacked by Somali pirates."

Well, that sounds ridiculous, Rose thought.

"What's it called?"

"*Havoc.*"

"Do you have a copy with you? I'd love to read it." She wagged the Ann Patchett. "This one's almost done."

"It's not quite published yet," Rose said, studying Meryl. She was maybe a touch too old to play Renata, her main character, she thought. But it wasn't out of the question.

"Well, what about a PDF? I don't mind reading on a screen."

The actress took a pen out of her robe pocket and wrote her email on the back of the reflexologist's card.

"You sound Canadian, Rose," said Meryl. "The way you say 'about.'"

"I'm from Toronto, actually."

Meryl clapped. "Toronto! I was up there for the film festival last year. I *loved* it. Don and I have fantasies of moving up there sometime."

"But the weather's not great. Even the summers."

"Oh, the weather's crap everywhere now," said Meryl, waving her hand like someone talking to a smoker.

A door opened and a pretty Asian woman with silver eyelids emerged.

"Rose? Hi, I'm Kumiko. Come on in."

As she went by Meryl, the actress gave her arm a pat.

"See you at dinner, Rose. Or maybe we could sneak into town, get some fish tacos. I'd love a cold beer."

"Sure. Me too. I'm in Room 344."

"Have a good session." She stuck out one leg with a delicate purple starburst on the calf. "I'm getting my spider veins done too. Zip-zap!"

Rose stepped into a small dark chamber and climbed onto the padded table.

"She's sooo nice." Kumiko sighed. "I wish everyone was like her."

"She does seem nice," Rose said, trying to be warmer and more vivacious than usual.

"We get lots of celebrities here, and some of them . . ." Kumiko bundled warm sheets around Rose, leaving her feet bare. She began pressing a point on the arch of her left foot and Rose felt a deep, gratifying ache.

"It's a bit tender there."

"That's your transverse colon. Don't overdo the brown rice here. People think you can't go wrong with brown rice, but it's extremely acidic."

She gave herself over to Kumiko's skillful prodding, and her spa-oppressed spirits began to lift. Soon she would be eating fish tacos with Meryl Streep.

Rose pulled her roller bag out of the taxi. It was March but freakishly warm. The front yard was pooled with melt-water, and the flotsam hidden under the snow all winter long had surfaced: ash-white dog shit, a stiff mitten, broken branches from the January ice storm.

She could hear her landline ringing as she unlocked the door. A dash-dot-dot long-distance ring. She put on her cold telemarketer answering voice and picked it up.

"You made it!" It was Meryl, already laughing.

"Hi! Yeah, I'm just back now. Sorry about the voice, I thought you were someone calling from India."

"Give me your address, I want to send you something I found in O'Hare when I was making my connection."

"Oh, wow. That's so nice." Rose spelled out her street and postal code.

"It's nothing, a set of place mats made of sweet grass, but I thought of you when I saw them. The thing you said over dinner, about Eric never wiping the place mats."

"Right."

Meryl lowered her voice. "Any more emails? About Chips and Vinegar?"

Rose winced. After two beers in town with Meryl she had overshared about the baby names Eric and Judy had already picked for the twins—Charity and Viggo.

"No. Just that one." Rose could hear a yappy dog barking in the background.

"Luther!" Meryl spoke sharply. The barking stopped.

"Listen, do you mind if I give Don your novel? He's a big snorkeler, he knows everything about reefs."

As Meryl talked, Rose tried to shrug out of her down coat, and got her scarf tangled in the phone cord. It was really time to ditch the landline.

"What's it like in New York now?"

"A *mass* of blossoms in the park. So gorgeous. It's good to be back home. But I miss our conversations."

"Yeah, me too." Rose doodled a crooked tree on the phone pad.

"And I've been rethinking what I said, you know, about the decapitation passage? It's not too much, not when you read it in context."

"I did do some research," Rose said. "Very few women have ever decapitated anyone. It's an anomaly. But it has happened."

"And for Renata, it does kind of make sense. After what she's been through. Such an interesting character."

"You think?"

"Absolutely. My only thought was, maybe the ending could be a shade tighter. Decapitation, news item, underwater shot of

Renata swimming through a school of fish, then zip-zap, end credits. Unless I've been reading too many screenplays. . . ."

"No, no, that could work." Rose was still in her coat, over-heating. "Well, I just got in the door, so—"

"Rose, listen, there's a benefit I've been invited to speak at, in Toronto, for ovarian cancer. Why don't I fly up for a quick visit?"

"Really? That sounds, that sounds great. When were you thinking?"

"Friday." Two days away.

"Which hotel?"

"Oh no, I'll just bunk in with you, if that's okay. I get tired of hotels."

A sheen of sweat broke out on Rose's brow.

"My place is tiny, but there's a spare bedroom you're wel-come to. No white robes, though."

Meryl gave a laugh that went up and down the scale. "Thank God we're out of there. And please don't go to any trouble. Just take me somewhere where they make a good martini."

"That I can do."

"I got you a little pedometer too, so we can see how many steps we take in a day. We'll walk everywhere. I can't wait."

They hung up and Rose felt a wave of anxiety. Why was Meryl Streep so interested in her? It didn't seem sexual. She obviously adored her husband. Her kids were all grown up, successful. Her other girlfriends were people like Oprah. What did Rose have to offer that Oprah didn't?

She moved through her house, looking at it with movie star eyes. The bedspread in the spare room needed cleaning, and those cheap vinyl shower curtains would have to go. She'd buy some memory-foam pillows, a vial of lavender, and a nice sleep mask. The actress was a light sleeper, she knew. Then

there was the question of where to take Meryl Streep in Toronto. The spice stalls in Kensington Market? The new aquarium? She studied a copy of *NOW* magazine that ranked the
city's restaurants, and settled on foie gras poutine at Yours
Truly on Ossington. There was a documentary playing at the
Bloor, about backup singers, called *Twenty Feet from Stardom*.
Which could be amusing for someone who lived at stardom's
ground zero.

So, dinner and a movie it would be. Like a couple on a date.

The airport limo door opened and Meryl stepped out bundled
in a mango-orange shawl and gray leather gloves. The sun
was shining, but the March wind had turned gusty, bitter. The
actress went through Rose's small pretty house, exclaiming, sigh-
ing, plucking at mohair throws, touching the paintings. She
went into the spare bedroom.

"My favorite pillows!" she said sprawling across the bed.
"How did you know? Plus all the books I could ever want. This
is *perfecto*." She plucked Rose's novel off the bookshelf.

"I'll read this in bed," she said, putting *The Bludgeoning*
beside the vial of lavender.

Later the poutine was a hit too, although they both longed
to have naps afterward. The movie didn't start for a while, so
they walked up Ossington, heads bent into the wind.

"What are cheese curds, anyway?" said Meryl. "Are they
the beginning or the end of the whole cheese process?"

"Yesterday Eric sent me a photo of himself, with pregnant
Judy," Rose blurted out.

"That's a bit weird. Don't you think? Did you ask for one?"

"No, of course not. I think it is weird."

"So what does she look like?"

"Dark bangs, big glasses, all covered up. Not his usual type. But she was his therapist before they got involved. All very taboo."

Meryl tucked her arm through Rose's. "We never really know who we're living with. Sometimes I look over at Donald when he's sleeping, and think . . . Who is this dear, unfathomable human being beside me?"

"At least he's beside you," murmured Rose. They'd had martinis before wine with dinner.

On the way to the cinema, they passed a dark shop front with a pink neon sign.

PSYCHIC READINGS BY SYBIL. HANDS, TAROT,
TEA LEAVES—$20.

Meryl peered through the window into a space that resembled all fortune-telling vestibules: dim, cluttered, with leggy plants in the corner and several cats slinking about.

"We've got some time to kill," said Meryl, opening the door. "Come on."

Rose followed Meryl into a room that smelled of aromatherapy oils, with a sign beside a metal ring on a cord that read PLEASE PULL FOR SERVICE. Meryl tugged on it. The cord spooled out and whipped back into place with a whir, like an old-fashioned outboard motor.

"What's wrong with a simple bell?" Rose muttered.

This made Meryl giggle. The color was high in the actress's face. She was the most excitable, responsive person Rose had ever met. Her laugh had an extensive vocabulary of beginnings, middles, and ends, in different tempos, and everything seemed to capture her interest. This caused Rose to feel more self-conscious about her own aloofness, her circumspection and Canadian monotone. But these qualities only seemed to make Rose more appealing to Meryl.

They whirred the cord again. One of the cats ran into the back room, where they could hear pot lids rattling, followed by the scuff of slippers. A hand parted the beaded curtain in the doorway and a striking older woman emerged. She had a cloud of white-and-ash curls, up-slanted greenish cyes, and remarkable cheekbones, porcelain and shiny. A fuchsia scarf was looped around her throat, warming her pale skin.

"Welcome," said Sybil. "You must be freezing. But this is what we get for driving SUVs."

Meryl pulled the shawl off her head and unbuttoned her coat.

"Yes, I'd like a reading," said Meryl with a creamy smile. "If this is a good time for you."

Sybil shrugged. "I'm always here working in the back, so any time is good. Tea leaves, palms, Tarot cards? Or I can do a combo for forty dollars."

"Whatever you feel like," said Meryl. "Whatever you think is appropriate."

"Let's start with the hands then." Sybil took Meryl's left hand and turned it palm-up.

"Huh," she said. "Interesting."

"What?" said Meryl, craning forward. Sybil gave Rose a sideways, diagnostic glance.

"Does your friend want a reading too?"

"Oh, we don't have time for two," said Rose. "Just pretend I'm not here."

"It's okay, we're together," said Meryl.

Sybil smiled a cool, broad smile.

"Then come with me," she said, slipping through the curtain.

Rose and Meryl followed her into a room lit by drooping strings of white Christmas lights. There were books on a sideboard by authors of a certain vintage, names Rose recognized—Primo Levi, Jane Gardam, Fay Weldon. A long-haired cat was curled asleep in an armchair.

"Minky has claimed the best one, as usual," said Sybil.

Rose perched on the arm and Meryl sat across from the fortune-teller at a gray Formica table.

"I like your coat," Sybil said to Meryl. "Max Mara?"

"No, Tom Ford," said Meryl, blushing. She was not the least bit vain but, as she told Rose, she had come to appreciate well-made clothes. And designers kept giving her things.

"It's a good length," said Sybil. "What's the point of a winter coat that doesn't cover your rear end?"

"That's so true," said Meryl, laughing a little nervously and laying both hands on the table. She wore almost no makeup, as usual, and had the same womanly hips as she did in *The Bridges of Madison County*. It gave Rose a certain satisfaction to see those squarish hip corners, just like hers. But inside, the actress was all youth and appetite—a fun gal, generous with her radiance. Rose felt more girlish and alive around the actress. Also, Meryl seemed to find everything Rose said hilarious.

"I don't know why Nutella hasn't caught on in a big way," Rose had said one night while they were lined up at the spa buffet. "Who could argue with chocolate and hazelnuts?" This caused Meryl to hoot with laughter.

"Nutella! You're right, it should be *huge*, like peanut butter."

Using a barbecue lighter, Sybil lit some tea lights under saucers of oil. A sharp scent filled the room.

"Bergamot and eucalyptus. Good for the nasal passages, commerce, and memory. But before we get down to work . . ." She cocked her head in a birdlike way and smiled at Meryl. Her mouth curved up at the corners, like a child's drawing of a smile.

"Oh, of course," said Meryl, rummaging in her eggplant-colored Kate Spade bag. She took some bills out of a pocketbook.

"I only have American."

"American's okay," said Sybil with a faint knitting of the brows.

"And no small bills, I'm afraid."

"Well, I'll do your feet too."

She tucked the money into a book and poured tea from a black iron pot into three thumb-sized cups.

"Assam and astragalus. Good for the immune system."

Rose sipped: liquid smoke. Delicious. She drank it down.

"Do you ever do the future, as a whole?" she asked Sybil. "Like, what's in store for all of us?"

"Oh sure. For a hundred and twenty dollars I do a comprehensive global forecast, but I can tell you right now, it won't be good. Carbon emissions over 445 ppm. Hundreds of species disappearing every day. Thousands. And of course the oceans are dying. But nobody cares because the ocean doesn't have a face, and big brown eyes."

"I know, I've done some research on coral reefs," Rose piped up.

"What's happening to the reefs is just a *trailer* for the devastation to come," said Sybil without losing her Delphic smile. "And don't get me going on human sexual reproduction! Count yourself lucky to have all that behind you."

Sybil turned back to Meryl, who was still sitting with her hands extended.

"Okay," said Sybil, "let's have a look-see."

She gazed at the palm of Meryl's left hand for a long minute, as if reading a page in a book.

"Huh," she said again. Her voice was slightly nasal. Afterward, Meryl would do a killer impression of it.

"What?" said Meryl avidly. "Is it bad?"

"You have a simian line, which I'll get to, but look here," she said, pointing to a crease inside the deeper line that curved around the base of Meryl's thumb. "Your line of Mars is very pronounced. It's almost an extra life line."

"But isn't that good? Two life lines?"

"It means that although you're easy to get along with, you can be fierce about standing up for things. A fighter."

"Well, my husband would not disagree," said Meryl, blushing again. Sybil tapped the plump bulge at the base of her thumb.

"And look at that Mount of Venus—so much energy." She peered at a chain of tiny islands that braided the lifeline.

"But you do have to watch your lungs."

"That's right! I caught some sort of bug when we shot *Osage County* and it took me *weeks* to get over it."

Sybil chuckled and put a finger on the fleshy pad under Meryl's third finger. "You also have quite the appetite for sensual excess." The actress gave Rose a sidelong tell-me-something-new look.

Sybil traced the single horizontal crease on Meryl's left palm.

"This simian line . . . textbook case."

"Simian, as in gorilla?"

"Yes. It's when the head line and the heart line run together. Only ten percent of the population have it, but it's fairly common among artists—and criminals. Nothing to worry about, though. It just means that you take a slightly maverick, intuitive approach to things."

"Okay," said Meryl tentatively.

"But sometimes it clouds your judgment. When you've got your sights on something, you can be opportunistic."

"Really?" said Meryl in a little-girl voice.

Rose sat forward.

"More tea?" said Sybil.

"Yes, please." Meryl held out her black cup. "What else?"

Now she took Meryl's right hand in her own. "You feel things deeply—sometimes too deeply."

At this Meryl looked as if she might cry.

"I hope you've cultivated a few ways to protect yourself."

Meryl snorted. "Well, I do hot yoga, if that counts," Meryl said. "Although I think it's wrecking my back."

"Just be careful about what you throw your heart into. Because once you commit, there is no turning back. And then the people closest to you can suffer too."

Meryl turned to Rose with one hand on her heart.

"I wish my daughters could hear this."

But Rose was thinking about Eric, his single-minded focus on work. How it had shaped their life.

"And don't confuse a commitment to acting with self-immolation."

"But how do you know this—have you been an actor?"

Sybil's sly smile returned, along with that flirtatious cock of her head.

"Not really. But I do write a little. And writers tend to be obsessive."

"Do you write poetry?"

Sybil now poured herself some tea.

"Yes. But these days it's mostly novels, or stories."

Rose could read the names on the spines of the books piled beside her. Valerie Martin, Edna O'Brien, Alice Munro. *Cat's Eye*, by Margaret Atwood. Several copies of *Cat's Eye*.

"How's your sleep?" Sybil asked Meryl.

"Not so good."

"That does not surprise me. Do you meditate?"

"I've tried it, but my schedule is so crazy . . ."

"You know what Flaubert said: If you want to be a revolutionary in your art, lead a boring bourgeois life. Or words to that effect. Let's have a look at those feet."

Meryl took off her Sorel boots and socks—Rose's socks, actually. She had the beginnings of a bunion on one foot and a recent pedicure. Nude polish with a pearly sheen. Sybil poked at her boot.

"These are great in the snow but they have zero support. You're going to pay for that eventually." She pushed down on the top of Meryl's foot.

"Ouch."

"Nerve supply seems okay. Have you tried toe-spreaders?

"Toe-spreaders?"

"The foamy things they put between your toes at the nail salon, only sturdier. When you walk with your toes separated, you distribute your weight properly, which means that you'll keep your balance much longer as you age. And get your husband to massage them when you watch the news. Look at mine," Sybil said, kicking off her slippers and flexing her slim feet. "I'm seventy-four, but I've got the balance of Nadia Comaneci."

Rose surreptitiously checked her phone. "Sorry, Meryl, but if we want to—"

"I think we're done here," said Sybil.

"Thank you *so* much!" said Meryl, standing up. "You've given me such a lot to think about. And I'd love to read something you've written. Could I persuade you to sell me one of your books? A novel, if you have one."

Sybil smiled her cat smile. "I have a few."

She retreated behind the curtain and returned wiping the cover of a book with her sleeve.

"You have daughters—yes?—so you might like this one."

"*Cat's Eye*," said Meryl, reading the cover.

And now it all fell into place for Rose: the voice, the knowing smile, the nimbus of curls.

"I'll sign it for you." Sybil took the book and opened to the title page.

"The thing is, once your balance goes, you're more likely to fall and break a hip, and then it's game over. Most people die within a year of fracturing a hip, did you know that? So we have to stay grounded. Especially given everything. Given the world right now."

She pointed to Rose's brogueish shoes. "Rose has the right idea."

Sybil scribbled some words across one corner and returned the book to Meryl. Then she put a hand on the actress's arm.

"And now I have to say something, something you might not want to hear."

Meryl looked at Rose. "No, what, say it."

"You've embarked on a new project recently . . ."

"That's right," said Meryl.

"It involves you playing a certain character, and you like to do a great deal of research for these roles. The way a person speaks, and moves."

"Yes."

"This new role of the woman, the failed writer who murders someone—I'm not sure this is going to work out well for you."

Rose felt the room recede, as if her hearing had shut down. She can't mean me, she thought. But it was done, the arrow had entered her. In the armchair beside her, Minky's claws flexed open and then dug into the fabric. Meryl's face reddened.

"But that's not how I see her, as a failed writer," said Meryl almost in a whisper. "To me she's a character I love."

Rose's thoughts ran backward, all the way to the spa, and to their first dinner. Meryl's penetrating questions. The talk about advances and broken contracts.

"It's not the role that's the problem so much as your approach to it," Sybil said. "You'll do what you do, which will serve the work well. But don't be surprised if certain relationships suffer in the process."

"It's always a little hard on my family," said Meryl quietly. She was gazing down at her hand and would not look at Rose.

"Besides them," said Sybil.

Rose's original plan had been to go to the movie, and then after for drinks at the star-worthy Shangri-la, where the fireplace ran the full length of the bar. They would talk about the movie, and how Darlene Love's amazing voice had been stolen without credit for the hit record "She's a Rebel." They'd marvel at how arbitrary it could be, success or failure. A writer and an actress, talking.

It's too late to just walk out, Rose thought.

A passerby on Ossington peered into the storefront window without seeing the three women. Sybil began to clear away the tea.

"Remember what happened when you played that Australian woman accused of killing her baby," she asked. "The dingo movie?"

Meryl put her face in her hands. "She said I made her look

coarse, and she hated the clothes they made me wear. But it's a movie, I kept telling her. It's fiction."

"Well, there's no such thing as pure invention," said Sybil mildly. "I'll be right back, I have a little something I want to give you."

They were left alone in bruised silence. Meryl came over to Rose and took her hand, made her meet her eyes.

"That's not how I see you, Rose. Please believe me. This has nothing to do with my work."

"How do you know? It's all fair game. I've done it too."

Rose remembered a newspaper story she had written in her twenties, about a woman who lived with thirty-six rescue cats, and was fighting an eviction. She had shared tea and homemade butter tarts with Rose, who then made ruthless fun of her (and her zodiac coffee mugs) in print. Months later they found themselves in the same lineup at No Frills. The woman glared at Rose, left her groceries behind, and stalked out of the store. Rose went home, reread her story, and saw what she had done. Felt deeply chastened, and never forgot the lesson.

"But I would never decapitate anyone," Rose said. "I think." Meryl laughed and then teared up with relief.

"I agree. I can just Google that part."

Outside, some snow had begun to fall, absentmindedly, like drifting thoughts. Sybil slipped back into the room and handed them two Ziploc bags. Rose opened hers: a pair of blue foam toe-spreaders. Meryl's were glittery. The actress thanked her effusively and Sybil went over to the chair with the sleeping cat.

"Minky, down you get, it's time for bed." She blew out the tea lights and turned to the two women with the cat in her arms.

"Don't forget what I said about the feet. And if you go right now, you'll still make your movie."

Mister Softee

Rose's mother was ninety-four, so it was expected—but still. Your only mother, poof, gone. Eric called from Philadelphia and sent flowers. Her stepson, Ryan, was on holiday in Thailand, and her daughter had just started a new job in Hong Kong. Ceri offered to fly home for the funeral, but Rose forbade her.

"It'll just be the caregivers and me anyway," she said, holding her phone flat on her hand like a canapé and talking into it, to avoid the keyboard. "Nobody else is left."

This came at the end of a year of dogged self-improvement for Rose—Spanish lessons, Zumba at the gym, the meditation app. She'd cut back on the wine, lost a little weight. And every day she did some research for her next novel, even though her publisher had declared bankruptcy. The Flo-Q copy-writing contracts she could do handily on the side and was grateful for. It felt good to finish something and get paid.

Her mother's death should have been another ending, and in certain ways it was, of course. But it also felt like the beginning of a new unmothered self, someone she didn't yet recognize.

It was September. The air felt cooler, like a silk lining, and the traffic had a new self-important urgency as everyone retreated indoors to school and jobs. Two days after her mother died she took her laptop to Starbucks, dropping into the safety of the screen. The pale guy with the thin head and his devices spread widely around him was there as usual. A number of her friends had sent condolences on Facebook. Should one "like" a death, though? In the afternoon, she drove down to Cherry Beach, a miraculously condo-free stretch of the waterfront that still resembled the shoreline of a lake. She felt a little truant doing this, but the funeral wasn't for another four days and all the arrangements had been made. The visitation room at Oak Ridges Manor, her mother's last home, was booked. The casket had been chosen.

The man at the funeral home who dealt with her was the owner's son. As he sat across from her in his ill-fitting suit, she had had an urge to shock him. To kiss him on the mouth. In the lee of her mother's death she kept being ambushed by strange impulses like this.

The parking lot at Cherry Beach was empty except for the usual chip truck, and something new, a Mr. Softee. On the side of the white van was a cartoon of a waffle-patterned man with a curl of soft ice cream on his head, like a plump white turd. And instead of the usual clown-calliope tunes, this Mr. Softee was broadcasting slow, lugubrious music. Something classical. Behind the counter was an older man with close-cropped silvery hair, wearing a black apron and a gray fedora. Familiar-looking.

As Rose walked past the truck on her way to the water's edge, Mr. Softee caught her eye, smiled, and gave a little ceremonial bow. She pretended not to have seen.

A few die-hard sunbathers lay on the beach. Cyclists rode along the already leaf-strewn bike path. Across the channel, where the sailboats slipped in and out of the harbor, were the islands, Toronto's peaceful archipelago. Cherry Beach reminded Rose of her childhood home, a brick house on a cul-de-sac with a view of the billowing and sometimes fiery smokestacks of the steel plants across the bay. Going down to the lake still made her curious about the world on the opposite shore, and whatever she was missing.

In the parking lot stood a Plexiglas-enclosed sign describing the city's plans for developing Cherry Beach. She wanted to vandalize the sign, because the place worked perfectly as it was. On weekends families came down to Cherry Beach with their coolers and lit fires in the rusted BBQ grills set back under the trees. This well-used place, tattooed with footpaths, would soon be ruined by streetlights, chain-link fences, and a glass Visitor Centre.

The sun had a low glare so Rose went back to the car to fetch her hat.

"Miss," a deep voice came as she crossed the lot. "Can I interest you in a complimentary cone? I'm trying something new."

It was Mr. Softee. Rose went up to the counter, where a ukulele with mother-of-pearl details hung beside the wooden menu board. The specialty of the day was something called the Cone of Perpetual Longing, made with "fresh Mission figs, coconut ice cream, spearmint leaves, and Okanagan black cherries." Kind of upscale for an ice cream truck, Rose thought. But she was hungry, she realized. She kept forgetting to eat lunch.

"Sure, thanks."

Mr. Softee bowed over the freezer, carving away at a well of ice cream with his comma-shaped scoop. He packed two balls into a waffle cone lined with thin white discs.

"What are those?"

"Communion wafers. If that's acceptable."

He piled the fruit on top, wrapped the cone in brown paper, and handed it down to Rose. He was old but handsome, with two deep furrows beside his nose.

She tasted it. Intense—more tart than sweet. And those quickly dissolving, tongue-friendly wafers. The ice cream began to melt and run down into the crevices of her fingers as she ate. "This is incredible."

"But I'm still not sure about the name," Mr. Softee said. His voice was a bass rumble. "Finding the right name can take years."

"What other flavors do you have?"

Mr. Softee tapped the board behind him.

"I'm partial to the Twist of Fate myself. Butterscotch ripple coated in bitter dark chocolate with a misting of Jack Daniel's, and a shard of broken glass on top, to keep you on your toes."

"Really? Broken glass?"

"Not for the young ones, obviously."

She saw that he wore a pendant around his neck made from two fused hearts, like overlapping Stars of David. A cool wind was coming off the lake now. Rose pulled a fleece jacket out of her pack.

"September," said Mr. Softee, casting an appreciative eye over the lingering sunbathers. "And a full moon tomorrow." Using a pair of tongs he adjusted a row of leathery-looking wieners as they revolved in their metal trenches.

"What brings you to Cherry Beach?" he asked. "Day off?"

"Sort of." She shaded her eyes to watch the lone windsurfer in a wet suit. He was fighting to stay upright on the choppy little waves close to shore.

"My mother died last week, so . . ." Rose hurried on. "I

mean, it's basically okay, she was old. Ninety-four. But there's still stuff to do."

Mr. Softee doffed his fedora and placed it over his aproned heart. "I'm so sorry to hear that. Please accept my condolences. I hope it was a peaceful passage for her."

"I think it was. I hope so." Rose zipped up her jacket and felt the tears beginning. "No one was there, actually."

"I'm going to make a little fennel tea," Mr. Softee said. "Please have some with me." He swung open the back door of the truck and invited Rose to perch on the top step as he plugged in the kettle.

"A month ago she had minor surgery for a skin thing, and never quite bounced back," Rose said. "Then she developed some fluid in the lungs." She wasn't sure how detailed she ought to get with Mr. Softee. "Which tends to happen with the elderly, especially when they're bed-ridden. So, some edema's normal." Why am I sounding like a paramedic? Rose thought. I'm talking about my mother. The brainy woman with a math degree and old-fashioned lavender sachets in her underwear drawer.

"Did you have a chance to speak with her before she left?" Mr. Softee asked gently. "Did you say what you wanted to say?"

"Yeah, pretty well. I visited her every day. We had a sort of code between us."

"But did you make your feelings clear?"

Rose thought about that for a moment. "I did, when she went in for her operation. I said 'I love you,' right into her ear so I knew she heard. But I waited until she was almost under."

"And was she able to express herself to you?"

"Well, sort of. But she was the farthest thing from senti-mental. A prairie woman."

"I still miss my mother," mused Mr. Softee. "When the light

changes like this in September, I always think about her. She died on the fourteenth."

"What was she like?"

He brandished a hand, as if conducting.

"Oh, very dramatic. Lots of weeping, lots of laughter. What they would probably call bipolar today."

"And your father?"

He sighed and adjusted the wieners in their troughs. "A dim figure. He died when I was nine. He had beautiful suits though. We're a family of tailors. Sitting in the darkness of a closet with his shoes all around and the drapery of his pants beside my ears was the closest I ever came to him, I think."

The windsurfer was now standing up on his board, leaning back, pulling and tugging on the transparent sail as it bellied in the breeze and sent him skimming across the waves, like a plane on a runway.

"Why don't we move further down the beach where it's still sunny?" said Mr. Softee. "Hold on."

He shut the door. There was an old-fashioned school desk in one corner, with a notebook open on it beside a chubby fountain pen.

Mr. Softee got into the cab of the truck and switched on the PA system. The almost-inaudible opening bars of something somber began. A few moments later Rose recognized it— Gorecki's Symphony No. 3. The saddest song in the world.

Through the back window she could see a woman under one of the big oak trees, bending over to lift a cooler out of her car trunk. As the volume of the music grew, the woman turned her head toward its turgid swell, put the cooler down, and buried her face in her hands, weeping.

"Occasionally I will play my own little Casio tunes over the PA," Mr. Softee said, "but I like the power of this Gorecki. It's so tidal, so inevitable. It feels like an infection moving up through the body, towards the heart." He smiled.

As they made their way across the wind-scribbled beach, she studied Mr. Softee's shelf of toppings: the classic multicolored sprinkles, a bowl of waxy-looking chocolate chips, some broken walnuts. There was also a jar of black tea leaves with curls of dried orange rind.

Tea and oranges.

Rose looked at Mr. Softee again. Yes, it was him. The man who sang "Suzanne," about the woman who gets you on her wavelength, and serves you tea and oranges. But Rose said nothing. If the famous and globally revered Leonard Cohen wanted to run a soft-ice-cream truck at Cherry Beach in Toronto, in the off-season, that was his business.

On a lower shelf were the sundae toppings. They included "The Phil Spector" (bourbon, gunpowder, and Manischewitz wine) and something called "Holy Smoke."

"That one costs extra, but it's worth it," said Leonard. "It's a shot of liquid nitrogen. When you pour a little on the ice cream it freezes the surface so hard you can't bite into it. So you just have to look at it and worship it without devouring it." He busied himself at the counter, then handed a dish to Rose. "Tell me what you think of this."

The cardboard boat held three scoops of peach ice cream inside two parentheses of sliced mango. At one end, where the mango slices met, was the pale glistening knob of a peeled lychee nut.

"It's called the Delta," murmured Leonard. "It's best if you simply bury your face in it without reservation."

The lychee nut was slippery as a pebble under water. Rose popped it in her mouth.

"I never tire of it myself," he said.

"It's delicious. Thank you, Leonard."

"Ah. Yes." He looked a bit saddened at this outing. "And you are?"

"Rose. Rose McEwan." They shook hands.

"You were performing until recently, right?" Rose said.

"Yes, yes I was." He changed the music to some more upbeat tunes. "Until this opportunity involving ice cream came up."

"I saw your last show, in Toronto. I loved it. And Sharon Robinson was so amazing."

"Yes, I've been blessed with the support of many wonderful musicians and technicians."

"That must feel so great," Rose said foolishly.

"It does," he said. "It's very humbling. But to offer an audience a performance that isn't false or indifferent, to do it again and again? That I haven't mastered. If I repeat my performance exactly, night after night, I find it works very well for the audiences. If not always for me. Whereas ice cream. . . ." He shrugged. "Ice cream never disappoints. The expression of people receiving their cones is still deeply gratifying to me."

In the distance Rose could see a young woman walking barefoot across the beach, almost marching, her one long braid flipping about like a slim fish. She wore black capris, a yolk-yellow sweatshirt with the words "Camp Sunshine" stenciled across the front, and carried a pair of blue Crocs in one hand.

"Shell's back." He watched her approach with a soft expression in his eyes.

The woman, perhaps twenty or twenty-two, eyed Rose warily as she climbed into the truck.

"Shell, this is Rose. She has just enjoyed the Delta."

"Yeah, it's a big seller," said Shell, a no-nonsense girl with sturdy calves and pale, evaluating blue eyes.

"Shell was a counselor at the same summer camp where I

once worked, long ago. I knew her grandmother as well. And now she works with me," said Mr. Softee, placing her Crocs on a rubber mat.

"Our whole family more or less ran the place," said Shell, warming just a shade now that Mr. Softee had alluded to their history. She pointed to her T-shirt. "Camp Sunshine."

Leonard took an oven-mitt tea cozy off a small iron teapot and poured cups of fennel tea for the two women.

"The fact is, my adult life was set in motion by Shell's grand-mother when she taught me three chords on the ukulele," he said. "And a finger-picking pattern for 'Blue Moon.' I still use it onstage."

"Did," Shell corrected him.

"Yes, thank you."

"Here, I'll show you," he said. He took down the ukulele and plucked the strings.

"A's flat," Shell said.

He twisted a peg and strummed a chord.

"Yes?"

"Good."

Mr. Softee bent over it and cocked his head. The instrument looked childlike against his body. His left hand found the chords as they sang "Blue Moon" together, sweetly.

"I used to play the ukulele at camp too," Rose piped up. "Songs like 'Deep Purple' and 'Sloop John B.'"

"My guitar playing is really an example of a ukulele player working on a slightly bigger scale," Mr. Softee said with a chuckle.

"I like instruments that sound like toys," said feisty Shell.

"We're all instruments," said Mr. Softee with a rabbinical hand to his chest. "But more kazoo than grand piano."

A thump came on the side of the truck.

"Hey, is anybody there?"

Leonard leaned out the window. He saw a boy, a lad about six or seven years old with a buzz cut.

"I want a cone," the boy said.

"Sure thing. What'll it be?"

"One Blood of Our Savior please."

Shell poured a stream of dark-red Ribena syrup over full-fat vanilla and handed it down to the boy.

"Good choice."

"It's not for me, it's for my dad. He's trying to make the barbecue go."

"Nothing for you?"

"I already had a whole tube of Pringles. Dad said that was enough."

Leonard put a curl of chocolate ice cream in a cup.

"Who's to say what's enough?" he said. "Take both."

"Hey, thanks Mr. Softee."

"That's why we can't afford snow tires for the truck," Shell said, with an eye-roll to Rose. "He's always giving it away."

"You sell ice cream in the winter too?"

"No, but he likes to drive around different neighborhoods with the PA on, playing music. It's how he works on new stuff."

"I find it's helpful to hear a song several thousand times or so—especially distorted through a bad system," said Mr. Softee.

"You should drive by the nursing homes," Rose said, thinking about her dead mother. "They could use some tunes."

"Not great for sales, though," Shell pointed out. "A lot of them can't leave their facilities."

"So, your mother's memorial service," Mr. Softee asked, wetting his index finger to pick up some sprinkles on the counter. "What are the plans?"

"Probably just me and a few of the staff at the nursing home.

And the casket. For some reason my mother wanted her body in the room."

"No other family?"

"No. All dead, or scattered around. My brother died three years ago, of colon cancer. My children are thousands of miles away. Their father lives in Philadelphia now."

Shell and Mr. Softee were quiet.

"It's good you're close by then," he said.

Oak Ridges Manor is a pink brick building, walled with windows and harsh with sunlight, on the suburban fringes north of Oakville where the roads still end in creeks. "So much natural light," visitors remark when they tour the place, hoping to install their frail parents in a place that is not technically depressing. Rose's mother lasted there for three years, most of that time in a wheelchair after surgery for a broken hip had failed. Her mother in her last years, well-medicated, became somewhat ribald and outspoken, bonding with one of the male nurses on the night staff named Edward.

"Edward's gentler than some of the women," she always said when Rose visited. She spoke in a low voice so as not to offend the other caregivers. "And we like to kid each other."

On the day of her mother's memorial, Rose arrived fifteen minutes early. The Bistro Room was empty, with folding chairs set up in four neat rows. Furtively she felt the petals of a flower arrangement on the piano. The lilies were real, from Rose's aged cousin in Ottawa. "We're thinking of you," the card said in the shaky handwriting of Margaret, who was ninety-two and had MS. Rose promised herself she would drive to Ottawa to see Margaret. Whatever tattered family remained, she now wanted to embrace. There was something cheering about laying eyes on your kin, some baseline DNA recognition, regardless of how different or unknown their lives.

The receptionist doubled as the pianist for functions like these. She was already seated at the piano paging through the American Songbook. Then Edward came in and solemnly shook Rose's hand. He was small, moist-eyed, and muscular.

"Your mother was a wonderful woman," Edward said. "I'm going to miss her, for sure."

"You took good care of her, Edward. She really enjoyed your company. And I appreciate you coming on your day off."

"Olive told me her own mother used to play piano for weddings and funerals. So this would please her." He tilted his head toward the receptionist.

The facility manager bustled in wearing a floaty print scarf.

"I think we can start then," she said to Rose with an unwarm smile. "Unless you're waiting for someone. Do you have family coming from out of town?"

"Not really," Rose said. There was a smaller arrangement on the piano beside the lilies. "The flowers are lovely, by the way."

"Yes, they're from Fresh and Fast. We use them all the time."

The manager pulled the curtains across glass patio doors that overlooked a space where the children at the daycare next door played in the afternoons, making happy noise. The staff believed that the proximity of the children was a good thing for their charges, but Rose had noticed that the residents were mostly indifferent to the patio with its view of the young and undiminished. The old were busy withdrawing to another place altogether.

The buzzer opening the front door sounded. In came Mr. Softee and Shell, carrying a large blue cooler and two ukuleles.

Leonard came over to Rose and took her hand.

"I've been playing the Gorecki since we left Mississauga," he said. "Someone honked and gave us a thumbs-up." Shell was carrying some yellow flowers in a funnel of paper.

"Freesia. Smell them," she ordered. Rose put her nose into the cone. In fact, her mother had loved freesias. "I brought a vase too, just in case."

Shell arranged the flowers on the piano and looked at the page of music the receptionist had turned to.

" 'Scarborough Fair'?" She snorted. "You must be kidding."

"You have any better ideas?" the receptionist said, eyeing Shell. She was wearing flip-flops and a halter top that showed off her tattoos.

"What about 'Hallelujah'?" said Shell, looking over at Mr. Softee.

He made a slicing gesture across his throat. "Overused."

"Well," Shell persisted, "I always think 'Let It Be' is a safe bet."

Leonard went over to the manager and introduced himself.

"You have a lovely building," he said. "So much light."

"Did you know Mrs. McEwan well?"

"No, I'm afraid not. I've come to support Rose." He flipped open the cooler. "Would you care for some ice cream?"

"Thank you, but I'll be speaking in a minute—"

"I find a little lemon sorbet clears the throat beautifully," said Mr. Softee. He turned to Rose. "What can I offer you?" She read the handwritten list on the lid of the cooler.

"I'll have the Sword of Damascus, with chocolate-almond bark."

"Good choice."

Edward rolled in a casket. Where had he been keeping it? There was a piece of fabric draped over it, a hideous magenta shawl. Rose yanked it off and handed it to Edward.

"Was it heavy to push?"

"Not too," he said. "She was pretty light towards the end."

"Edward, what did you talk about with my mother—do you mind saying?"

"We talked about her family, and her father. How he was away during the week and only came home on the weekends, and how her mother always had to bake a lot of pies for him. I think he traveled a lot."

"Yes, he sold farm equipment on the prairies." Rose had an image of a Model T negotiating rutted roads, a flat horizon spreading out on either side. "I don't think she was close to him."

"But mostly we'd joke with each other, gossip about the other staff. She had her opinions, as you know."

"Oh yes." They laughed. She felt her mother drifting through the room just then, eager to disagree with them.

"I think we can start now," said Rose, sitting down in the first row of chairs. Shell went over to the piano with her ukulele.

"Give me an A."

"I'm not sure the ukulele is suitable for this," the reception-ist said with a protective hand on the sheet music. Rose stood up and held her cone aloft, like a torch.

"This is my mother's memorial, who enjoyed ice cream, and loved music, all kinds of music," said Rose. "Let's have both ukuleles with the piano, and everyone singing. Also, I would like the patio doors open." Mr. Softee slid the doors apart and the children could be heard, but in a welcome way.

The receptionist started in on "Let It Be," not smoothly but with a determined bounce. Edward kept one hand on the cas-ket. He winked at Rose. Shell and Leonard stood beside the pi-ano, playing the ukuleles and singing. "*When I find myself in times of trouble . . ."* Leonard's voice rumbled along an octave below the others.

Then the security buzzer rang again. The manager frowned and bustled out of the room. Shell and Mr. Softee stalled for time, repeating the first verse as the receptionist got friskier on the keyboard, adding arpeggios. Rose was watching the children on the playground as they swarmed up and down a red plastic slide, so she didn't even see Ryan and Ceri enter the room. They came over to her and the three of them held on to one another.

"Did Dad call you?" Rose asked.

"No, it was someone else. A 'Mr. Softee,' " Ryan said with a laugh. He was growing a beard, like every other male his age, but he looked quite handsome with it.

Leonard came up to Rose. "I took the liberty of contacting your children," he said. "The Oak Ridges staff were helpful in that regard. I hope you'll forgive me."

Ceri's hand rubbed her back. "What were you *thinking*, Mom? Are you nuts? This is Nana!"

"But it's so far to come," she said.

"Mr. Softee let me fly on his points."

"I've accumulated quite a few," said Leonard, shrugging.

He turned back to Shell and the receptionist and counted them in. "Let It Be," now quite polished, began again. Ryan and Ceri sang along on either side of Rose. "*There will be an answer/Let it be.*"

Afterward, the director spoke about how Oak Ridges would miss this spirited and delightful member of their community. Her eyes flicked down to the paper she was holding to make sure she had the name right: Olive McEwan.

Then lemon sorbet was enjoyed.

Abra Cadaver

After my mother's death I found myself in a calm, unanticipated place. I no longer hated Eric for leaving me—that energy had finally been sprung. Our kids were off living their own faraway lives and I had stopped counting the exclamation marks in their texts in order to gauge their happiness. In the past year, two, three defining roles had slipped off me like loose garments.

But I felt a certain melancholy *glide* setting into my days—a willingness to simply mark time. At my age, if I chose to watch cat videos every day until felled by an aneurism, no one would begrudge me (or, possibly, notice). At the same time, certain desires still stirred: to drive the Dempster Highway, to fight for a cause, to flirt with someone inappropriate. In the twenty or so years left to me (*inshallah*) I wanted to become more of myself, not less.

So when Leonard and his assistant, Shell, gently broached the idea of moving in with me, I said yes right away. When I was young I had shared a house with several postgrad philosophers who liked to make dessert soufflés. Why not now? And this way I wouldn't end up lying stroke-ridden for days on the bathroom floor before someone discovered me. With the three of us sharing one bathroom, it would be more like a matter of hours.

I find it's a tonic just being around Shell's youth, the way she takes the stairs three at a time and talks to all the dogs in the laneway. Her relationship with Leonard is playful, tender, and (I think) platonic, although she chooses to sleep on a mat near his bed.

As for Leonard and me, our habits mesh nicely. We steer clear of each other in the mornings when we both prefer to work. I'll do a little Flo-Q copy, or maybe push on with my new thriller, *Abra Cadaver*. Around four in the afternoon we might have a cup of matcha and commiserate about our lower-back pain. I like Advil, he swears by Aleve. He prefers to stack the dishwasher, and I would rather empty it.

On warm days Leonard does Qi-Gong in the backyard, which amuses the neighbors. I caught the musician who lives across the lane taking a picture once, but mostly no one bothers him. Leonard has never cultivated fame and as a result he rarely suffers from its consequences.

Still, some of my friends remain skeptical about this new living arrangement.

"I've got an extra ticket for that Turkish film if you're interested," Sarah emailed me last week. "Unless you and the Tower of Song have other plans ;)."

"We're just housemates," I replied, "and anyway we're both too old."

"Right. How does that song of his go? 'She's a hundred but she's wearing something tight.'"

Couriers will occasionally come to the door with packages.

(My new boss at Flo-Q likes me to have what he calls a "hand-feel" of the new products.) If Leonard answers, often they recognize him, falling speechless or blurting out worshipful things. I can see how much gracefulness this requires, having to put strangers at ease. It makes me want to give Leonard a footbath, or some gesture that asks for nothing in return.

Whenever Leonard and I pass in the narrow corridors of my Victorian house, our bodies touch easily. We smile at the contact and move on. That's the extent of it, although he is closer to me than a lot of men I've slept with in the past. No doubt many of his fans feel the same way. Still, they haven't lived with him, or folded his laundry.

It's an innocent merging of the three of us that reminds me, strangely, of breastfeeding (which has its erotic quotient too). I know that sounds weird. But since they moved in I wake up every morning happy—a feeling I thought I had outlived.

Shell enjoys it when I show her how to do certain old-fashioned things, like making a pie crust with lard. She is no longer in touch with her mother and seems to want nothing more than to be around me, to sit near me. One afternoon Leonard painted my toes a tropical aqua while Shell did my fingernails a different shade and a Nina Simone record played.

All this is sweet and new.

L ately Leonard and Shell have gotten into the habit of watching an episode or two of *Call the Midwife*. Most nights I join them. But about ten minutes in, the picture will often freeze, then we have to reload Netflix, and a message will come up saying there is a problem with Apple TV and to call them. At this point my tendency is to give up, but Leonard is more persistent. He punched in the number and explained the situation.

"It's Leonard Cohen calling."

He rarely plays the name game, but it does come in handy.

The next thing we knew, a technician was at our door. It was Taylor Swift, holding an aluminum toolbox, her little cupid mouth a bright red.

"Hi, guys," she said. "I'm here to fix your connection." She didn't bat an eye when Leonard came into the hall.

"Thank you for your prompt attention," he said, shaking her hand with a small bow. "We're almost at the end of season four, so this is quite frustrating, as you can imagine."

"I hear you," said Taylor. "I had the same problem watching *Rectify*, until I had a little powwow with the Apple folks. Our relationship is pretty good—I'm, like, four percent of their iTunes revenue now, which is crazy. Anyway, they've promised to work on a whole new delivery system. Oh, nice high ceilings!" she said, stepping into my living room. She pulled out the mysterious black unit behind our screen and wiggled the cords.

"You'd be surprised how often it comes down to one box not being plugged into another."

Shell was gazing at Taylor in silent awe.

"We can take pictures of Pluto, but everything still needs a cable, right?" said Taylor with a wink at Shell to relax her. "Looks like you're okay here, though. It's a problem at the other end."

I took the tea towel off my shoulder and ducked back into the kitchen, where I had a rhubarb-strawberry crisp in the oven.

"Something in there smells *really* good," said Taylor loudly.

She wore pinstriped overalls with platform sneakers and

her hair was an interesting dark ashy blond. Not movie-star at all. She was on the skinny side, with the irresistible face of a small, alert animal.

"It's a crisp," I said, coming back into the living room. "You're welcome to have some with us."

"Really? Thank you!"

"The rhubarb's from our garden," Shell said. "Rose's garden."

"Oh, I love your faux tat," Taylor said, touching the Arabic-looking gold braidings on Shell's arm.

"It's supposed to last for thirty days." She twisted her arm around to show the underside. "I got my real ones removed. They were just initials anyway."

"Wrong guy?"

"Yeah. So wrong."

"Been there, shot the video." Taylor laughed.

She opened her toolbox, took out something that looked like a waiter's Visa machine, and held it against the Apple unit. Lights flashed along the edge. "Okay, good. Let's fire it up."

I handed her the tiny silver remote. "You have to hold it way up," I said, showing her how, like some new hip-hop move. The unit was tucked away on a top shelf. She raised her arm, clicked it on to Netflix, loaded *Call the Midwife*, and played a few minutes. We watched a wavy-haired woman on a bicycle speed down a cobbled road.

"I could totally get into this," said Taylor. "I love history."

"Shall we turn it off?" suggested Leonard. "I'm not there yet."

I put on my elbow-length oven mitts, which made me feel vaguely surgical, and slid the crisp out of the oven. Shell came into the kitchen with her hands crossed over her chest. "Can you believe this?" We could hear Taylor and Leonard chatting in the next room, until they came and found us.

"I hope you don't mind me asking," Taylor said, "but . . . why are you here? Are you guys all cousins or something?"

"No, we're just visiting the city," Leonard said, "and Rose has kindly opened her home to us."

Shell mouthed a silent *thank you* to me and turned to Taylor. "Are you, like, working for Apple full-time—or vice versa?"

Taylor laughed. "I try to do two days a week when I'm not performing. I like to get right into people's houses whenever I can, you know? It helps me actually connect with how they live."

I brought out a tray with the still-percolating crisp, bowls, spoons, and a carton of Kawartha Dairy vanilla. We sat around the dining-room table, where three laptops stood open and glowing like treasure chests. Leonard shut them down.

"This is excellent," said Taylor, taking tiny spoonfuls so as not to burn her lips. She had the prettiest mouth. "Thanks, guys. Normal is so rare for me."

"And it's good to have regular ice cream for a change," Leonard murmured. Through the window we could see the Mr. Softee truck parked in the laneway behind us.

"Is that your neighbor's?" Taylor asked.

"No, it's Leonard's."

"I use it as a studio of sorts."

She clapped her hands. "That is so cool! You record in there?"

"Yes, I have a little analog system set up. But mostly I use the PA to work on material. Shell and I like to drive around the city and broadcast the new tunes. I find it helpful to see how people in the street react. You know—do they clutch their ears and run away?" He chuckled.

"Right *on*! Getting out of the studio, man! Things can get so complicated when they don't need to be."

"Yes," said Leonard, giving her an appreciative gaze. "And people have very fixed ideas about how music ought to sound."

"A lot of people *still* can't stand his voice," Shell piped up, and then blushed.

"That's true," he said, smiling.

In the corner of the dining room were a couple canvas backpacks, some packages of dried soup, Ziploc bags of trail mix, and an ax. I had almost finished the tedious job of organizing the food and gear for our expedition.

Taylor went over to the pile of equipment.

"Whoa. Are you guys joining the military or something?"

"No, we're going on a canoe trip," said Shell, "with some Norwegian guy who's here to write a story about Canada. Look, we even have bear spray." She took a canister out of the top of a pack and held it up. It had a cartoon of a charging grizzly on the front.

"I am so jealous!" said Taylor. "I have never even *been* in a canoe, that's the one thing I haven't done!" Her face clouded over.

Leonard caught my eye and I gave a why-not shrug. She was young and strong, at least.

"Then you should definitely come with us," he said, touching Taylor's wrist.

"But we're leaving, like, tomorrow," said Shell. "For four days." Her brow furrowed. She had registered Leonard's enthusiasm.

"Done!" said Taylor. She pulled out her phone and made a call.

"Ed, please clear my schedule, I'm going to be out of touch for the next few days. And let Apple know I'm on pause for now."

Her eyes shone. "This makes me really happy. Will there be reception in the woods?"

"I doubt it," and "probably" Shell and I answered in unison.

I looked at Taylor's platform sneakers, which were roughly my size. She could wear my old Timberlands, I guessed. I hoped this wasn't all a big mistake. It was one thing to lead a bunch of newbies into the woods, but I did not want to deal with any twisted ankles on the portages. Part of our route was along the Madawaska, where the trails could be steep.

Also, I hadn't been in a canoe since the two college summers I'd spent working for a Temagami outfitter. But Shell had been a camp counselor, and Taylor was a quick study, obviously. We'd manage. As for Leonard, he was old for this sort of thing, but he knew how to husband his energy. A three-hour concert is a kind of expedition too.

It was mostly the group dynamics I was worried about. The wild card was Karl Ove Knausgaard, who was flying in that night. Not a barrel of laughs, to judge from his books. Leonard had an ardent following in Norway, but that didn't mean that Knausgaard was a fan. And when I told Leonard about *My Struggle*, the writer's hugely popular, 3,600-page, six-volume novel, he hadn't even heard of it.

"I'm afraid I don't have the patience for reading fiction anymore," he said.

But let me explain how Karl Ove came into the picture, because that was really strange.

Things with Flo-Q were going well. I had been promoted from writing copy for faucets and showerheads to their top spa features—the hydrotherapy tubs, infinity pools, and living-wall waterfalls. Leanna had been fired and my new boss liked to encourage my creativity, so I began to quote little water-related passages from literature (or "liquiture" as he liked to call it). *To the Lighthouse* has lots, obviously. I found some good stuff in *The*

Road by Cormac McCarthy too. After the world has been destroyed, water suddenly becomes a big deal.

"It's a bit dark, but that can be a good thing," my boss said when he read the quotes. "Just stay away from the shower scene in *Psycho*."

One morning, on the hunt for fresh inspiration, I sat down with Knausgaard's latest novel, a 740-page sequel to *My Struggle* called *The Truth*. Bathrooms and plumbing, I noticed, are a recurring motif, which is not a surprise. Our faces in the morning, our fears at four a.m., the sad mortal ring in the toilet bowl—they all confront us with the truth in the bathroom. Perhaps this is why I have no shame about my work for Flo-Q.

Knausgaard likes to take his readers into all the little shifts of consciousness that accompany us in the course of a normal day. So I was happily lodged inside his brain when I turned to page 243 and was shocked to find the scene below. The narrator has just returned to the house in Tromsø, Norway, that he had shared with his wife, Solvi, before their divorce and her sudden accidental death.

"I went round to the side of the house to the outdoor shower, a folly of ours given the climate in Tromsø. But we had just come back from Thailand that winter and felt nostalgic for bathing out of doors, so we had made a little stall out of birch, and *ordered a special showerhead on the internet,* [*my emphasis*]. Covered with tiny nozzles, it was *as broad and round as the face of a sunflower.* But it turned out we didn't have the water pressure to sustain the flow. After standing several times under an icy trickle, shivering, we abandoned our dream of the shower. And in a sense that meager trickle marked the beginning of the end of us."

It was an unmistakable reference to the Rainmaker, a wall-mounted twelve-inch-diameter nickel-plated showerhead that is a perennial Flo-Q bestseller. And the phrasing was exactly mine: "The Rainmaker, broad and round as the face of a sunflower, will transport you to a steamy Costa Rican forest . . ." Knausgaard had poached my simile.

I was pondering my next move when an email arrived from my boss, forwarding a message:

> *Dear Flo-Q*
>
> *In the course of doing some research, it has come to my attention that there are striking similarities between a passage in my current novel "The Truth" and phrases that occur in the Luxury Showerhead section of your website. I would be grateful if you could put me in touch with the writer so we can discuss this matter further.*
>
> *Sincerely,*
Karl Ove Knausgaard.

Was he accusing *me* of plagiarism?

I wrote back immediately. I began by saying that I was a great admirer of his work, and was rereading *Book Two: A Man in Love* for the second time. This was not strategic flattery, it was true. With its relentless self-scrutiny and searching earnestness *My Struggle* does invite parody. The way in which he exposes the people close to him raises moral questions too. But there is also something *necessary* about it that makes more conventional fiction seem hollow and contrived in comparison. You are trying to capture how it feels to be *alive*, I loftily wrote. And that includes paying attention to all the in-between moments in life: pushing a stroller, turning on a tap, standing under a shower.

But, I continued, it had shocked me to stumble on the sunflower simile, a phrase I thought I had invented. (I didn't add

that a large showerhead so closely resembles the face of a sunflower that it requires only the tiniest scrap of imagination to
make the analogy. It was neither my finest moment nor his.)

Instead I told him how honored I felt that our imaginations
had aligned like this, if only for one phrase. Then I signed off by
saying that Flo-Q products were "internationally revered in their
field, much as you are in yours." (I still shudder to recall this.)

Here is what Karl Ove wrote back to me:

Dear Rose,

*Thank you for your message and your kind words about
my work. I confess that I sometimes have a great fear that
I am boring my readers, so your belief in the value of the
mundane helps me to face another day of writing.*

*Of course, I accept your explanation about the "align-
ment of our imaginations"—a lovely thought. I was only
shocked, as you must have been, to come across a figure of
speech I assumed was mine alone.*

*I want also to say that I have now read much of your
work on the Flo-Q site, with growing admiration. I applaud
your attention to detail (the "tired" shimmer of brushed
aluminum). There are moments in your copy that succeed in
giving a difficult subject—plumbing—a human, even poetic
dimension.*

*Perhaps there is a favor I can ask of you? I have recently
agreed to write a travel story about your country for the
New York Times Magazine, a follow-up to a much-hated
piece of mine about a car trip through the United States.*

*However, I have no idea how to go about this. I dislike
interviewing people and have little feel for landscape. My
memory is bad, and whenever I take notes I can never read
them later. All this concerns me.*

My editor at the magazine has strongly urged me to take part in a canoe-camping trip or similar wilderness activity to reflect the abundance of this sort of thing in Canada. I understand that you are based in Toronto, where my journey begins, in September.

So I come to my point: any guidance you could offer me regarding canoe adventures in your area would be grate-fully received. And may your imagination continue to align with mine.

Sincerely,
Karl Ove Knausgaard.

I replied that September would be the ideal time for a canoe trip, given the fall colors. I offered to organize a four-day excursion for him through the northwest corner of Algonquin Park, an area made famous by the Group of Seven painters. My Flo-Q boss seemed keen on the idea. ("If you can get a picture of him under a waterfall, that would be great.") The *NYT* editor approved the plan, and as Leonard and Shell were running out of Netflix options, they were keen to join me. With Taylor, that would make five of us, in two canoes.

But I said nothing to Knausgaard about his celebrated trip mates. The wilderness treats everyone alike. I simply booked him a room at the Intercontinental and left a message the night he arrived, saying we'd pick him up at six thirty a.m., and be on the water by noon.

Don't hold it like a baseball bat. Put your right hand on the top of the paddle, and keep your left low on the shaft. Then reach forward and dig it in. You're shoveling water, basically."

"But if I lean out, won't we tip?"

Karl Ove was in the bow of my canoe. I had been under the impression that all Norwegians skied and spent time in the woods, but this was clearly not the case. It turns out that he had never slept in a tent and insisted on bringing along a large down pillow, which he said accompanied him everywhere.

"It is my stuffed animal," he said, shrugging. His thick pewter-colored hair was swept back in a leonine manner. He wore the sort of sunglasses with side bits that shut out all the light. Without them, his gaze was so direct as to be uncomfortable and his handsomeness was in a class of its own.

But he had a touching timidity as well. I noticed the way he treated each new environment, whether it was the hotel lobby or a doughnut shop, as an unmapped foreign country. He seemed at pains to preserve his lack of worldliness—not so easy, once the world discovers you.

"Whenever you see someone canoeing in a movie, the actors are *always* holding the paddles wrong," I said to make him feel better. He moved his left hand down the shaft and began to propel us forward with stabbing strokes. I had lent him an old flannel shirt of Eric's, which fit him perfectly.

"Good. That's the idea."

The blue canoe surged past us.

"Is this not gorgeous?" said Taylor. She was sitting up straight, kneeling properly, paddling in perfect sync with Leonard and Shell. At the end of each stroke she gave the paddle a little twist, like someone signing her name with a flourish.

We made our way across Round Lake, a route I had taken years before. Nothing had changed. After a broad and windy stretch, the lake narrowed into a meander that wound its way snakelike through a corridor of reeds. It went on and on; we had to follow it blindly, bumping into the banks as our canoes navigated the tight corners.

"Will there be moose?" asked Karl Ove.

"Quite possibly."

"Have you ever seen the males fighting, with their antlers?"

"No, but I was on a trip once where we were chased by a bull moose in rut."

"'In rut'?"

"In heat. During the fall mating season. They can be dangerous then."

"Oh." He paused. "But that's now."

"Don't worry, we'll be fine."

"And I hope to see the Northern Lights as well. For the story."

"Isn't Norway where people go to photograph them?"

"Yes, but I moved to Sweden some time ago."

I looked behind us for the others. Leonard was trailing his stern paddle in the water, doing a lazy J as Shell dug away in the bow and Taylor used her paddle to push them off the grassy banks.

"This is like a corn maze!" Taylor called. "How's my stroke, Rose, am I good?"

I gave her a thumbs-up.

We turned another corner and lost sight of them. The current flowed more strongly and all we had to do was steer as our canoe brushed through leathery green lily pads. A few yellow flowers sat on the surface like teacups.

"This is incredible," said Karl Ove softly. "It's like I'm traveling through the folds in my brain. I love it."

When we had picked him up that morning he had looked so tired, greeting me with an apprehensive, teeth-baring smile.

"Everything here is somewhat familiar but askew," he said. I had never been to Norway and pictured it as a large white LEGO railway station, with colorfully clad people moving about in trams and on skis, silently and efficiently. Like the vestibule of heaven.

"Where are you heading after this?" I asked him as we paddled on.

"Out west. A place called Jasper."

"Oh, you'll love the Rockies," I said. "Your sense of time completely shifts in the mountains. You can feel the great patience of the Earth."

Karl Ove absorbed this.

"And the west is interesting right now, geopolitically."

"To tell the truth, I have no interest in doing interesting things." He laughed. "Can we pause now to have a cigarette?"

We stopped paddling and he lit one.

"My wife and children beg me to quit, but I find it very hard," said Karl Ove. "Will you join me?"

I hadn't smoked since college, but sometimes even good habits should be broken. Cautiously he turned around in the bow and passed me a cigarette, some Swedish brand. I leaned forward to catch a light from his match, inhaled, and coughed.

"Cigarettes are like punctuation for me," he said. "I can't write without them."

"How's that going? Your new book." I could feel the shape of my lungs from the smoke.

"It is very problematic," he said. "Hideous, really." He drew hungrily on the cigarette until it sizzled and tossed the bottom half into the water.

"Why?"

"Originally I had set out to write about my life—not to invent a story, but to go more deeply into my own experience—

and then when the first two volumes came out and made a stir, my life changed. I had to do readings and publicity and go on television."

Far behind us, I could hear Taylor singing a Willie Nelson tune. The meander was now widening into a river.

"I felt I had to live up to this person I spoke about whenever I answered questions in an interview. I wanted to please my readers, of course, I wanted to be good at the business of impersonating a famous author. But it was also undermining my ability to write in an honest way."

"The same thing kind of happens on Facebook," I said. "The pressure to create a public identity—usually someone happier and more successful. It's like we're all authoring ourselves."

He stopped paddling and turned in profile so that I could hear him.

"Yes, I think you're right. So in the process I have become, what is the word, a *merkvare*, a brand . . . like Pepto-Bismol." He slapped a deerfly that was darting at his head. "Yet there is no reward in remaining unread and obscure."

I was getting used to Karl Ove's rhythms. He was either completely silent or else he would talk like this and wind on and on, like the meander. On the drive up he had spoken at length about his dead alcoholic father. He seemed a bit lost inside himself, so I changed the subject.

"I'm working on a book too. But just a thriller."

"Is that right? Will you kill me off in the woods for your story?" he said with his charmingly reluctant smile.

"Perhaps. It does need a body. It's about a dead Canadian painter, who may have been murdered."

"My friend Jo Nesbø has become very successful writing thrillers. I wish I had the knack."

"I can only write when I don't take it seriously. If I imagine a million readers, I freeze up."

"I'm afraid I'm exactly the opposite. I take everything too seriously. It's exhausting."

"You 'slip into the Masterpiece.'"

"What?"

"It's a line from one of Leonard's songs. About losing your grip."

Karl Ove looked at his big silver watch. "It's now midnight in Oslo. My body is longing to be horizontal. Will we stop soon?"

The river had developed some riffles and a faint roaring sound warned of a waterfall around the corner. I steered us over to the shore.

Behind us Taylor and Shell were singing "Ninety-Nine Bottles of Beer on the Wall." When they came into sight I saw that Leonard had put on his black-netted bug hat, like a Victorian lady at a picnic.

"That was such a mind fuck," said Taylor merrily. "Like, has time stopped? Will this meander ever end? I loved it. What's up now?"

"We portage here, around the falls," I said. "Then an easy lift-over into North Tea Lake, where we'll camp. Take the packs over first then come back for the rest. You might find that carrying the canoe solo is easier, especially if you wear a life preserver to pad your shoulders."

As I sprang out of our canoe I felt a twinge in my right knee. I better wrap it tonight, I thought. But the body memories were rushing back as I balanced on two slippery rocks, unbuckled the food pack from the thwarts, and swung it up on shore. I could still do this.

Leonard had blown up his air mattress and was lying on it in his tent, wearing headphones. Shell bent over the fire, squinting against the smoke as she stirred a pot of chicken curry that I had pre-cooked and vacuum-packed. I was planning to make chapatis from scratch too (showing off somewhat).

Taylor had changed into a red corduroy jumpsuit and was drinking an inch of tequila from a tin cup as she shot some video.

"Here we are on majestic North Tea Lake," she intoned, "land of the silver birch, home of the beaver." She zoomed in on me while I rummaged in the food pack for a baggie of fresh cilantro. "And this is our fearless leader, Rose McEwan, who is an awesome cook."

I was in a familiar canoe-trip state—irritable exhaustion combined with mild lower-back pain. I had collected the firewood, helped everyone put up their tents, and cleared a kitchen area beside the fire pit. Taylor was still bounding over the rocks, with a tiara of fireweed in her hair. Her energy was bottomless. Leonard had paced himself well but as soon as the tent was up, he had slipped into it. Karl Ove sat on a log smoking. It had been a long day for everyone.

Our campsite was on a finger of four-billion-year-old rock with tall white pines on the point. The sun was low and the air had a warning chill: Summer was over. On the opposite shore the trees blazed away, a mariachi band of orange and yellows. In July the same shore was a wall of green, almost monotonous. But now we could see the bright differences between pine and maple, poplar and birch. The leaves were becoming more of themselves before they died.

While the curry was heating up I boiled some water and made a cup of black tea. Shell and Taylor were down by the water's edge, talking in the low purling tones, with bursts of laughter, of women discussing discarded boyfriends. Karl Ove wrote in his notebook. I went over to Leonard's tent, where the light coming through the blue nylon cast a television pall on his lined, unshaven face. He was lying asleep on the open pages of a book.

"Leonard," I said gently, "have some tea."

"This is so kind of you," he said, brushing at the sides of his mouth. "I'm afraid I'm accustomed to my little pre-show nap."

"Dinner's ready when you are."

Shell was now shooting Taylor, who had changed into a crop top worn over silvery harem pants tucked into my Timberlands.

"Hey girl-squad," Taylor said to the camera, "you should all get your tushes out of L.A. and join me up here in Canada, in the woods! I am in bear country, see?" She held up the canister of bear spray with its drooling graphic. Shell panned around the campsite, where Leonard was now sitting by the fire, making an *I'm not here* gesture.

"I'm here with . . . a few new friends . . . in an untouched wilderness where you cannot buy things, at all." A loon let out a faintly ridiculing call, and Shell zoomed out to find it. Taylor continued. "I wish you could all be with me to experience the smell of the . . . pines, right?" Shell nodded. "And the excellent curry we are about to eat, around a fire made with branches and twigs that we gathered ourselves, actual wood from the woods . . ." Taylor raised her arm and flexed it. "Also paddling is very good for the triceps." She turned to Shell. "And, cut."

"I would *love* to get a team of synchronized swimmers up here, for a video," sighed Taylor. "With those crazy nose plugs?"

I dished the curry into our plastic bowls, and for a long moment we all devoured our meals in silence. The chapatis had turned out perfectly—a birch fire burns hot. But my back still hurt.

"Sit here instead," said Taylor, jumping up to give me her perch against a flat rock. I thanked her and took her spot. Then I reminded myself to slow down, look around, and take it in. The stillness.

Afterward, Karl Ove moved down to the edge of the water to smoke, and Leonard joined him.

"I quit some time ago and promised myself I would start again at the age of eighty," said Leonard. "I'm heading into year three now," he said, accepting a light from the Norwegian.

"Ever since I've had to travel more," said Karl Ove, "I find that drinking is no longer helpful. It turns dark too quickly. But the little rituals around smoking cigarettes help keep me sane on the road."

"I agree," said Leonard. "It's like a phone call home."

Their smoke mingled in the pinkish twilight.

"Will there be music at some point?" Karl Ove asked. "I have this image, of people sitting around a bonfire, playing guitar. . . ."

"No guitar. But there's this." Leonard produced a jaw harp from his pocket, which he began to play. After a few corkscrewing twangs, the loon gave out a long call as if in response. We applauded.

"Let's sing!" said Taylor. "What shall we sing?"

Silence. Whose material first? Then Leonard began.

Black girl, black girl
Oh don't lie to me
Tell me where did you sleep last night?

An old Lead Belly song. Taylor answered:

In the pines, in the pines
Where the sun never shines
And I shivered the whole night through.

"Kurt Cobain used to do that one too," said Karl Ove. He drummed on the bottom of a pot with his fingertips.

"Hey, that sounds good," said Taylor. "Don't stop."

"I used to play drums in high school, when I was in a band."

As Karl Ove kept time, Leonard and Taylor harmonized. They were like two people on separate islands, the sound of their voices were so different—Leonard's woolly, frayed, and ocean-deep, Taylor's like a thin, strong silver wire.

We stayed up for another hour, going through "All Along the Watchtower," "Red River Valley," and "Wake Up, Little Susie." The darkness surrounded us like a great cave as the temperature dropped. We kept moving closer together for warmth and then went shyly off to bed. Taylor and Shell shared a big dome tent—the Princess Pavilion, as it was dubbed—Leonard's blue one was nearby; and I had pitched Karl Ove's closer to the point, where the morning sun would strike first.

I led him there with my flashlight, looking back to make sure the red glow of his cigarette was still in sight.

"This is not what I expected at all," he said quietly, "which is good. Thank you."

"Sleep well, Karl Ove." On the way to my tent I switched

the flashlight off so I could feel the path under my feet and see the stars growing brighter above us.

I pushed the dial on my watch to illuminate the face. Almost four a.m. A sound had awakened me, the sound of something sizable bumbling through the trees. Damn. It had been so late when we went to bed that I didn't go through the rigmarole of hoisting the food pack high up into the trees, to keep it safe from bears. To keep *us* safe from bears. Instead we stowed the packs under the inverted canoes.

The thrashing continued. Small animals always sound enormous from inside a tent, I reminded myself. And we were in a national park, where raccoons were numerous and intrepid.

Who had the bear spray? Taylor, of course.

I quietly unzipped the door of my tent, trying to remember the strategies for bear encounters: For a black bear, you make yourself big and try to scare them off; for a grizzly, you curl up, protect your neck, and play dead. Or was it vice versa? Anyway, there are no grizzlies in Algonquin, and black bears are rare. Except for that one inexplicable attack a few years ago, where a couple were both mauled to death.

A branch snapped. I turned on my flashlight and shone it through the netting of my tent. I heard the hollow sound of a gunwale banging against the rocks and leaped out of the tent with my boot in one hand, ready to hurl it.

"I'm so sorry," said Karl Ove, raising his arms like a fugitive. "I was looking for the box of matches. I ran out."

He was wearing underwear, a T-shirt, and gray wool socks. Eric's socks.

"You scared me," I said softly. But nobody stirred in the other tents.

"I woke up and couldn't get back to sleep. Once the thoughts begin, the sentences, that's it and before long I have to have a cigarette."

"There are some waterproof matches in my tent, in the first-aid kit."

"You sleep with the first-aid kit?" He smiled.

"Yes, I do," I said. "In case a wounded bear comes by."

Karl Ove followed me to my tent, set apart from the others in a stand of jack pines.

"I'm finding the total silence here quite unnerving. We live in the country but there's always passing cars or dogs, or the sound of the refrigerator."

I crawled into the tent, felt around in the metal kit for the matches, and handed them out to Karl Ove.

"They coat them with something, so they're a pain to light."

He struck one hard on the side of the box. It flared blue and yellow, illuminating his face, its good bones. He lit his cigarette and drew on it deeply.

"You?" he said, tipping the package my way. I shook my head.

"It was a dream that woke me up," he said, "about my father. I had to write it down."

His father again. It's dreadful, how we continue to love our parents regardless of how they treat us. How we keep return-ing to them, to solve the mystery of who we are. I thought of all the fathers who have turned their sons into writers, com-pelled to re-create the family on the page. Slowly stacking up the sentences until they resemble a human figure, like a stone *inukshuk*.

Karl Ove sat at the entrance of my tent and used my flash-light to read from his notebook:

"I was sixteen, and had just come home from spending the

evening with a girl in my class whom I longed to kiss, but she was out of my league. I was in an agony of despair by the time I reached home, to find my father drunk, once again. He was either violent or sentimental when he drank, and sometimes sentimental was worse. That night he kept pouring me wine and saying how close we were. 'You and I are two peas in a pod, Karl Ove, don't try to deny it.' Then he asked, 'Did you have any luck tonight?' meaning with the girl I had failed to impress. 'Not so much,' I said, unsure of the answer he wanted to hear. His face darkened. 'You don't have what it takes to get the girls, Karl Ove,' he said, 'you're too soft and sensitive, you need to toughen up.' I watched him stagger to his feet and come towards me, with his big hand raised. And that's when I woke up."

He closed the notebook and put out his cigarette carefully, grinding it into the earth. I could hear someone in the other tents lightly snoring.

"It's cold out there, Karl Ove." I unzipped the top of my sleeping bag and he slid in beside me. His face was wet but he turned away, curving his back. I put my arms around him. He murmured something I had to ask him to repeat.

"I still want to please him, and he's dead."

The next afternoon, Karl Ove caught a pickerel, and Taylor made fish tacos. They were out of this world. Is there nothing that girl can't do? Leonard spent some time drawing little cartoons of us with his Sharpie. Instead of paddling farther down the lake, we had decided to stay at our campsite, where we puttered around most of the day, reading, snoozing. I gave Karl Ove my iPod with some of Leonard's music. He sat at the water's edge listening intently. Then he went over to Leonard, who was applying sunscreen to the tops of his ears.

"Leonard, this song of yours, 'A Thousand Kisses Deep'? It is perfect. It cannot be improved upon," Karl Ove said to him. "Can I ask how long it took to write it?"

"A thousand years, more or less." Leonard rasped. "I write very slowly. I write in geological time, where it can take several centuries for things to shift an inch."

"We are polar opposites then. My new book is already over five hundred pages and the main character is still *in utero*." Karl Ove laughed at himself. "My publisher begs me to shut up."

"Shorter is harder," I chimed in.

"You've been writing too much ad copy," said Karl Ove genially. "Brilliant as it is." Catching a fish had cheered him up.

"Short is a good discipline," I said.

"That's true," said Taylor, who was drying the insoles of her sneakers in the sun. "A chorus in a song might be, like, five dumb words that get repeated over and over. But coming up with the *right* five words can take forever."

"Can you work on the bus?" Leonard asked her.

"Sure. I like to have life going on around me. Sitting alone in a quiet room just makes me want a chocolate bar."

After dinner that evening (penne arrabiata with fresh cornbread) everyone had a smoke and we sat around the fire, reluctant to leave one another's company.

I held up a log. "Are we good for one more?"

"We should probably do the marshmallow thing," said Shell, yawning.

"Someone should tell a story," said Taylor. "A ghost story."

Karl poured some whiskey into his tea.

"Would a murder story do?" I said.

"What's it about?" Shell asked.

"A dead Canadian painter."

"But isn't that your novel?" said Karl Ove.

"It's not really a novel, it's just a mystery."

"Why do you keep doing that?" he said with genuine irritation. "Why do you patronize your own work?"

The others perked up.

"What do you mean?" I said.

"Can't a commercial, popular work of fiction be a masterpiece as well?"

"You mean, like yours?" I dared.

"I wouldn't use the word 'masterpiece.'"

"But you'd call your novels literature. Serious literature."

"Yes, I would."

"I agree," Taylor piped up. "I'm in the middle of Book One right now, and it is rocking my world."

"Maybe I don't believe in 'serious literature' anymore," I said, surprising myself. Was that what I thought?

"Or is that just your way of not writing about things that matter?" Karl Ove's eyes were very dark, almost black, reflecting the dance of the firelight.

"I do write about things that matter. There's a lot of environmental stuff in *The Bludgeoning*, for instance. My last book. About coral reefs."

"Good. But I mean things that matter to you, Rose, personally. The questions or regrets that won't let you sleep."

"Is that what you think it takes to write something worthwhile? Just being raw and autobiographical? Exposing the people closest to you to public scrutiny?"

"Of course not. Don't be so defensive."

I was stirred up. Why was he attacking me like this? The log I had put on the fire turned out to be too green—the moisture in it began to hiss and pop.

"You know," I said, "if a woman wrote one of your books, and went on and on about the horror of children's birthday parties, she would be called a self-indulgent lightweight. But when a man does it, the personal becomes elevated, significant."

"I agree. But I only have my life, and my experience as a man to write out of."

Leonard, Shell, and Taylor had all found quiet little activities to focus on while we argued.

"I'm not saying that I couldn't be a better writer," said Karl Ove. "I am painfully aware of my shortcomings in that regard. I'm only saying to you that a mystery novel can be as profound as the Bible—if you invest enough belief and meaning in it. If you open yourself up."

"Like the face of a sunflower."

He ignored this. I was beginning to feel like Peggy Olson confronting Don Draper in season five of *Mad Men*. Peggy was a copywriter too.

"A man who writes honestly about his intimate life is considered brave," I went on, "but when a woman does, it's called oversharing."

"Do we have to bring in gender?" said Leonard wearily. "It's like Israel and Palestine, we'll be up all night."

"Easy for *you* to say," I said with more bitterness than I intended.

"Tell us more about your novel," said diplomatic Shell. "You never talk about it."

"Well, I'm still working out the plot. Pedestrian as that sounds."

"You see?" said Karl Ove. "You fail to embrace your own material. Although I have little interest in plot myself. Obviously."

"All right then," I said, going over to the bottle of Jameson and pouring myself a good slug, "since you asked. It's called *Abra Cadaver*."

In the darkness it was hard to see anyone's expression. Leonard had on his bug hat, although the evening was too cool for mosquitos. I think he liked its veiled interior. I took a few drags off Karl Ove's cigarette and kicked the fire into brightness.

"The story begins not far from here," I began in classic campfire style, "on a lake near Nipissing, where the famous painter Tom Thomson died. Or was murdered. A young medical student, Julia, has convinced her boyfriend Martin to go on a canoe trip to the spot where Thomson was last seen, before his death in 1917. There are many theories about what happened to him. But Julia thinks she has the answer."

"An answer to the *mystery*," said Karl Ove.

"Can we skip to the cadaver part?" asked Shell.

"Yeah, hurry up and scare us," Taylor said.

"Hang on. You need the plot."

"Only the dead need a plot," said Karl Ove. This drew a laugh from Leonard, who was rummaging through the food pack for the bag of marshmallows. They were squashed under a can but he massaged them until they puffed out again.

"Julia wants to be a forensic investigator—someone who deals with dead bodies."

Taylor and Shell cheered and clapped.

"And Martin is studying to become an ophthalmologist, because he wants to make heaps of money while having the least possible contact with human beings. Just their eyeballs."

Taylor hugged her knees. "Uh-oh, trouble. Negative people are sooo toxic."

"Yes. But Julia is the very opposite of negative. She's Rachel McAdams in *Wedding Crashers*. And she persuades him to go on this canoe trip, in search of evidence to help solve the mystery of Tom Thomson."

"If I can interrupt," said Karl Ove, "would there be any physical evidence left, if he died almost a century ago?" He was looking at me warmly. He enjoyed a clash of antlers.

"Excellent question. The answer is that Julia has been doing research into some new tests that measure trace levels of cortisol and other stress hormones in human hair and nails—tests to help determine whether someone died in a heightened state of fear. And human hair and nails don't decompose, at least not quickly."

"Hello, Tutankhamun," said Shell.

"She thinks they might still find a strand of hair, or a sliver of a nail that could say something about how Thomson died."

"What do these say about me?" said Taylor, waving her nails with their greenish glow-in-the-dark polish, like ten tiny cell phones.

"That you like to shine," purred Leonard. He was handing around the marshmallows and five branches that he had whittled to a point.

"The coals are perfect now," he said.

"After two days of combing the shores, Julia does come across something—an inch of rotten canvas, perhaps from a canoe, with a tiny dark fragment embedded in it. She's convinced that it's a human fingernail, but Martin says it's a bit of shell, and she's just imagining things, being unscientific. So they begin to fight."

"Because he is a competitive nerd," said Shell.

"Correct. During the argument, he throws the fragment, the nail, into the lake."

"Way to sabotage her career," said Taylor. "El jerko."

"Plus, Martin is drinking," I said, and here I waved the Jameson bottle. Karl Ove held out his cup. "Some pushing and shoving goes on until Martin grabs a sleeping bag out of the tent and stomps off into the woods. Leaving Julia alone on Canoe Lake."

Taylor made a grunting noise and brandished the can of bear spray. *"Abra cadaver."*

Leonard held up his hand for a pause. "I just want to mention that if you completely blacken these, the inside turns to a delicious liquid."

"And Martin doesn't come back that night," I said.

"Okay. She got ghosted," said Taylor. "Been there!"

Everyone was now jockeying for position around the fire with their drooping wands.

"I know what you're all thinking," I said, "but Julia spends the night unmolested, either by bears or by Martin. She sleeps surprisingly well, wakes up to a fine fall morning, and makes a pot of coffee. Martin's tantrums are nothing new to her. But then she notices that their canoe and paddles are gone. Along with Martin's hunting rifle."

"He took off drunk, stood up in the canoe to pee, fell in, and drowned," says Taylor. "Case closed."

"Which is one theory about what happened to Tom Thomson."

"But why?" said Karl Ove. "Why do you care about this missing painter, whom many others have written about? What's left to say?"

I was irritated by how Karl Ove stood just outside the circle, smoking. I shone my flashlight on him, his face.

"Why do you keep coming back to your childhood," I asked, "still hoping for new evidence? Why keep writing about your father? I think he's your ghost story."

Karl Ove didn't reply. The last log in the fire collapsed with a *whump*, like an old dog settling down for the night.

"Anyway," I said, "that's the end of chapter one. To be continued tomorrow night."

Leonard propped his branch against a tree, like a pool cue. "I think I'll hit the sack now. Today was a great gift, everyone. Sleep tight."

"Good night, Leonard," we all said.

He swept the beam of his powerful flashlight across the path as he made his way to his tent.

"I'm not tired yet," said Shell. "Stay up with us, Rose."

Taylor pulled a pair of socks on her hands to keep them warm.

"Isn't there supposed to be a moon?"

Karl Ove was a dark shape outside the firelight, drawing on his cigarette until the tip glowed red. Over by his tent Leonard poked the silvery column of his light out across the surface of the lake.

"I have another story," Karl Ove said, moving in closer. But I put a hand on his sleeve.

"Shh! Look out there."

Leonard's light had found a low, dark object on the water, rocking. A canoe, it appeared, but with something in it that rose above the line of the gunwales.

"Yoo-hoo," called out brave Taylor. "We're over here!"

"It's just drifting, there's no one in it," said Karl Ove.

"It's Tom Thomson," Shell whispered.

Leonard came back to the fire, his sleeping bag draped around his shoulders.

"There appears to be a boat making its way towards us," he said softly, "with something, or someone, in it."

I went down to the water's edge with my light, pushing aside a superstitious thought that I had conjured up this floating coffin with my story.

Karl Ove came down and put his arm around me.

"Don't worry," he said. "It's probably just my dad again."

I punched his shoulder. Everyone giggled nervously.

The canoe was dark green, and appeared to be carrying a small tree in the bow; we could make out two raised arms, or forked branches. Our flashlights were all trained on the cargo like klieg lights at a movie premiere. Then I let out my breath.

"I think those are antlers," I said. "Deer antlers."

I went and dug out the coil of nylon rope we had packed, in case the canoes capsized. After a few throws the yellow rope snagged on the antlers. It took four of us to pull the boat up onto the lip of the shore.

Lying in it was half the carcass of a deer, skinned, butchered, and dressed. The deer's ribs had the same graceful curve as the ribs of the canoe. The antlers had been hacked off and stuffed into the V of the bow as a sort of grim hood ornament. A long rope trailed from the stern.

No one wanted to go closer.

"A hunter must have been getting ready to go home, then decided to wait till morning," I said. "Or maybe he was too drunk, and tied the canoe up carelessly."

"But all that blood," said Shell. "With the bears. Maybe he was . . . interrupted."

"I hope he was," said Karl Ove. His eyes glistened with tears.

"What a beauty he must have been," murmured Leonard. The antlers had eight points, although the left branch was smaller and oddly twisted.

"He's a buck, at least three years old, and one hind leg was injured," declared Karl Ove.

"How do you know that?"

"When I was driving through Maine to write about America, I stopped at a bar and had a few beers with a hunter. He told me everything about antlers. The velvet that covers them in spring also feeds them. They grow fast, up to a half inch a day. And if the deer injures a hind leg, that can cause the antlers on the opposite side of the body to grow in strange ways, like this one."

Amazing. The deer's body was telling its own story.

Leonard put his hands together over his heart and bowed to the animal. Taylor kept the cap on her camera. Small waves at the shore's edge lifted the stern of the green canoe and banged it against the rocks. The smell of salty blood was strong.

"Karl and I will take him across the lake," I said.

"We'll get the food pack up in a tree," said Shell.

I untangled the rope from the antlers so we could use it to tow the boat behind us. Karl Ove flipped our canoe upright, then tilted it gently into the water. The opposite shore was an inky, unseen horizon a half a kilometer away and we began paddling toward it. Whenever my hand touched the surface of the lake, the water felt surprisingly warm, almost swimmable. It was hard to keep the tow rope taut; the deer canoe kept lurching sideways, as if trying to escape. Karl Ove looked behind us to make sure the campfire was still burning. We needed a point of reference on this moonless night.

Shell's low murmur and Taylor's laughter carried clearly across the water, and then dropped away until there was nothing but the sound of our paddles, dipping in, lifting out. Behind us the canoe lunged forward, then tugged at us, like a dog not used to the leash. I was enjoying our companionable silence when Karl Ove spoke.

"Death is always ruining things," he said with a sort of laugh. "Don't you think?"

"I don't know, I feel strangely at home out here in the blackness, dragging a body towards a shore we can't see. Something about it seems familiar."

"Let's rest a moment."

Karl Ove lit two cigarettes and handed me one.

"You're bad for me," I said, inhaling. "This is my last."

We drifted as a current of air pushed us in the right direction. I lay back with my head on the V of the stern. Above us wheeled a skyful of stars, little corpses of ancient light.

"It was not my place to say those things about your work, Rose," he said. "I meant them as encouragement but I went about it stupidly."

"That's all right. I shouldn't have accused you of hurting people. "

"I have, though. It weighs on me."

"I only took you on because I feel I know you, from reading your books. And that you know me. Even though we're still strangers."

"I long to be known like that—not famous, but understood, with all my sins intact. When I am out in the world I feel obscured by a thousand small lies." He tossed his cigarette into the lake. "And that is why I torture myself with this business of writing."

"So will you put our poor slaughtered deer in your story?"

"Oh no, no one would believe it. Too novelistic." He did a figure eight with his paddle to correct the slow spin of our bow. He was perfectly at home on the water now.

"And you?" he asked. "What will you do next?"

"I'm free as a bird," I said, realizing with a jolt that this was true. "So I plan to act accordingly. I'll take some time to rethink my novel." I blew smoke his way. "Make it less mysterious."

"Will you write about this? About us?"

"I might. If that's all right."

"Some of your own blood has to be on the page or it's just an exercise."

"But there's no need for a bloodbath," I said, which made him laugh.

We resumed paddling. The other shore was close now, a silhouette blotting out the stars at the bottom of the sky. The two of us surged forward. I felt boundlessly capable in that moment, equipped to tackle the shapelessness of my future. Although I didn't know what lay in store, the important thing was to keep moving toward it, even in darkness.

With some effort we hauled the boat onto a point where it would be visible if the hunters came looking for it the next day. The metal keel made an awful sound as it scraped across the granite. I retrieved the tow rope, coiling it neatly, and we lost no time stepping back into the red canoe. And then we were on the water, weightless.

"Hello," came Leonard's voice from across the lake, "here we are."

ACKNOWLEDGMENTS

I enjoyed putting odd characters together in these stories. An admirer of the reclusive painter Agnes Martin as well as the legendary Jimi Hendrix, I saw no reason not to imagine them as a clandestine couple in love. I have also grown up steeped in the music of Neil Young, Leonard Cohen, Joni Mitchell, and Bob Dylan. Our son still plays their music. Why wouldn't I write about them as characters in my life, who accompanied all my changes?

So my first and deepest thanks are to the artists I've tried to invoke, for everything they've given us.

Stars began to creep into my writing long before this book took shape, and I think I know why. My husband, Brian Johnson, spent twenty-eight years as the film critic and senior entertainment writer for *Maclean's* magazine. During that time he interviewed every star in the firmament. He'd come home from work and we'd talk about Madonna or Mick Jagger or Al Pacino. Whether they were funny or shy or difficult. The famous became part of our household in a way. Certainly part of our relationship.

During the long incubation of this project, I received support and encouragement from many readers and editors: Layne Coleman, Anne Mackenzie, John Bemrose, Megan Williams,

Bernadette MacDonald, Beret Borsos, Susan Swan, Katherine Ashenburg, Andrew Wainwright, J. M. Kearns, Casey Johnson, Jill Frayne. I'm especially indebted to Ken Alexander for publishing an early version of "Bob Dylan Goes Tubing" in *The Walrus* magazine. "Don't I Know You?" appeared on hazlitt.com as "Bigger Than Money" and *Brick* magazine published an early attempt to capture Karl Ove Knausgaard's passionate and singular voice. Scott Young's wonderful book about his son, *Neil and Me*, inspired and informed the story "The Rehearsal."

I owe the book's existence to Samantha Haywood at Transatlantic Literary Agency. She saw where the book was headed well before I did, and gave editorial guidance at every stage. We were sunny partners in this enterprise. She also put the manuscript in the best possible hands, and I'm indebted to Amy Einhorn for her enthusiasm, collaborative spirit, and editorial vision. It's been nothing but a pleasure to work with Amy, her associate Caroline Bleeke, and the entire staff at Flatiron Books.

And finally—I live with a writer. Very handy. My love and gratitude to Brian Johnson for tactful feedback, unwavering optimism, and keen attention to *le mot juste*.